The New Teacher

A Sheridan County Mystery

Erin Lark Maples

LODESTAR
LITERARY

The New Teacher

Book One in The Sheridan County Mysteries series

by Erin Lark Maples

Copyright © 2022 by Erin Lark Maples.

Cover designed by MiblArt.

For my mother, who taught me to wield a pen.
For my father, who taught me to knock an arrow.

Prologue

"EVER CONSIDER THAT MAYBE you deserve to be alone?"

The words rankled his conscience like a wool undershirt, itchy across every inch of skin. He'd always played the nice guy, only to have his wants, his dreams, thrown out like last week's trash. Tonight would be the last time he let that happen. The last time he put everyone else first.

A rumble like an idle thundercloud broke the silence. He squinted into the black sky and hoped the sound was a dry threat. It was at least a ten minute walk back through the dark. The bright pinpricks of Scorpius, low on the horizon, served as a guide in the pitch black night. He stumbled over a rock, the toe of his boot upending a hunk of granite. Walking out here without a flashlight was foolish and he knew it.

The moon peeked over the ridge line, a sliver of champagne white that backlit the scenery. Cottonwoods loomed overhead, indicating the creekline. Scrub brush formed a sea of hiding places for nightlife. An owl swooped past in a swift flutter of wings and was gone.

A deepening shadow underscored the ravine ahead. In some places the creek flowed smooth and serene, flush with the banks. In others, it carved a deeper gash year after year, a scar across the prairie. He crawled down one bank, glad he'd had the sense to change into work boots.

Rivulets flowed alongside the stream in front of him. The water's reach expanded and contracted across the seasons.

He mapped out a stone pathway before venturing forward onto the rocks. The water wasn't deep, but one slip and he would be soaked. Wet jeans would make for a frigid walk home.

He hopped midway out across the creek and paused on an anchored boulder. From within one denim pocket he extracted a small, gray stone. A skipping rock, it would skim across the water surface if thrown by an expert arm with a neat flick of the wrist. When he was eight, his father had shown him the trick with the two of them perched on the yoke of their canoe on Lake DeSmet. When his first launch skidded, neat and agile across the water's surface, he beamed up at his father. The man, his mentor and hero, clapped him on the back and pulled him in for a hug.

From that day forward he carried a stone in his pocket for any chance to relive that moment. Over the years he'd collected and thrown thousands of rocks of various sizes, colors, and sources. It was a habit, a comfort he carried with him.

Nowadays, he'd reach into his pocket to extract the stone anytime he sought comfort. He'd rub a thumb across the smooth surface and think of the man who'd given him so much. Before he sent the stone across a body of water he would think of his father and ask for forgiveness. He'd give anything to have one more day with his fishing buddy.

Tonight he held a rock found in the corral that morning. Tiny flecks of mica reflected the light of thousands of stars smattering the western sky. He fitted the curved edge into the crook of his first finger and drew his arm back, wrist flexed. With one fluid motion, he launched the rock downstream. It sailed through the air before making a half dozen skips along the surface. Then it sank into watery depths with a muted plop. He nodded, satisfied.

The undercurrent of sound grew louder. No longer white noise, it was as though a dump truck aimed for every pothole in its path. The road ran parallel to the creek a few hundred feet to the north. This sound came from the east and echoed between the head-high walls of the ravine.

He eyed the opposite bank but overshot the jump and fell forward against the rocky wall. He braced himself as vibrations rained sand over his fingertips. Panic flooded his bloodstream. The innate rush of fight or flight chemicals arrested his senses. He reached up to grab the lip of the bank to hoist himself upward. The toe of his boots kicked pockmarks in the ravine walls. He would scramble out, get his bearings. Escape.

His hands slipped as the earth beneath crumbled under his grasp and he fell back to the creekbed. The earthen floor shook with sound. Terror propelled him to ignore the pain in his shoulder and try again. This time, he gripped the ledge with one hand and reached for a tree root with the other.

Dozens of dark shapes barreled toward him, writhing through the dark. Relentless and inescapable, their mass a heartbeat across the prairie.

There was the pounding of hoofprints.

Then, blackness.

1

ELIZABETH WOULD BUILD A time machine to go back and rewrite all her bad decisions, but such delicate calculations were impossible with a toddler flailing in his car seat for more nuggets. ***

The graveled edge of the road crunched under her tires as Elizabeth eased her vehicle to the side of the road. She dug in the lunch sack for the dino-shaped snack food her passenger preferred and slammed the trunk closed. With only a couple of duffels and a cooler inside, the car's storage space yawned, cavernous. A few yard sales back in Seattle had taken care of most of their belongings. Elizabeth could still picture the baggage of her old life: the branded suitcases, skis, stacks of paperbacks—the faithless ex-husband.

For this trip, she'd packed her determination, her favorite jeans, all her hope, and exactly one prayer.

Moving several states away to start over under the badge of a single mom was Plan A. She couldn't scrape funds together for a Plan B. At least, not until her first paycheck. Elizabeth couldn't afford big dreams at this point, let alone the next tank of gas.

Back in the car, the nearly two-year old placated in the back seat, Elizabeth slid tortoiseshell sunglasses-turned-headband back over the bridge of her nose, flicked her long, chestnut hair over her shoulder, and put the rickety hatchback in drive.

The job description for her new gig read like something out of the last century:

Seeking an experienced teacher for elementary school. Send resumes to Applications, Sheridan County School District, P.O. Box 17, Sheridan, Wyoming.

The clipping was tucked in a letter from her brother, the first surprise.

Casey. A faded brushstroke on her past, a shadow of a brother a decade older who'd survived and escaped the same family to which she'd felt chained. A wrestling scholarship to Laramie was an easy yes, picking up roping was icing on the cake of escaping the West Coast. She hadn't seen him outside of photographs since she was eight.

Elizabeth mailed Christmas cards. The last set was splashed with professional photos of her son playing in autumn leaves, wearing a sweater and tiny fedora while sitting on the lap of a ubiquitous Santa, sitting on her shoulders, eyes on the clouds. She'd heard nothing from Casey in return.

It would be easy to blame their absent and distracted parents, but she and Casey were grown adults now. Rhett deserved an uncle. Deserved a mom with her life together.

Elizabeth would think about this later. Get good and mad at Casey, her parents—later. She needed to crash at his place for a while first.

A highway sign proclaimed gas and snacks at the next exit. Time for a pit spot. Elizabeth flipped on her turn signal.

Once parked, she perched Rhett on one hip and pushed through a door that swished closed behind them. A fan rotated above the front counter but did little to stir the stifling air. Candy bars, beef jerky sticks, and motor oil lined the few shelves on the way to the coolers.

Icy air hit her face as Elizabeth opened a door to a tall, windowed case and freed a beverage from the racks. Pressing it first to her forehead and then to Rhett's, she smiled at the relief on his face. He reached for the bottle, his little fingers brushing streaks in the condensation. She opened a neighboring case to select a small carton of milk for him instead, a smiling cow on its side. He grasped it to his chest, teething on the capped end.

"Hang on there, we have to pay for that first."

The man at the counter in a Styx shirt watched her journey through the market, his gaze lingering on her curves. When she handed him a wad of bills, he asked the same question she'd heard two hundred miles ago. Yellowed fingernails tapped at the register to select her change, and matching teeth held an unlit cigarette in his mouth. "Passing through?"

Behind the man, a screen blared a regional news channel. The satellite timing was off as the woman in a gray suit and a smear of red lipstick mouthed words a hair after they sounded through the speaker, closed captioning lagging behind. *A cold front tomorrow. Keep your trash locked up from bears. A hunter hasn't returned—if you see anything, call 9-1-1. The Stallions routed the Panthers, 24 to 7.*

"Was it the Washington plates, the craft beer, or the fact that you know everyone around here and I'm not on that short list?" Elizabeth hadn't intended for her words to come out with so much bite, yet here they were. She was tired of offering her story to every stranger who questioned her journey.

To her surprise, he broke out in a wide grin as he handed over her change. "Too bad, then. We could use a fire like yours. Shake things up around here."

"Long-term exposure to gas fumes increases your cancer risk, you know. Have a nice day."

Fire. He made it sound like a compliment.

Rhett napped through most of Montana as fellow travelers dropped off the highway toward bigger towns. He jostled awake when she turned off the asphalt south of Sheridan. They hit a dirt road aimed straight at the horizon, ruts and rocks challenging the rickety suspension. She winced when the old tires hit one of the divots pock-marking the road. When they crested a hill, she braked to a stop, struck by the view.

The sun dipped an edge below the tallest mountain peak, piercing its crest. Official sunset was an hour or two away at least, yet the spread in front of her was paved in cobalt and shadow. Miles of grassy expanse, dotted with the occasional ranch and the salt and pepper markings of cattle herds, rolled out like carpet before them. No city, no traffic, and no ex-husband.

She rolled down the windows and bathed in sage-scented sweetness. Dust be damned, the freshness hit her with all she'd missed in the land of concrete. Barriers lowered, she could smell the air, clean and sunbaked.

As she rounded a bend in the road, a huge, black creature blocked their path. Elizabeth slammed on the brakes while gripping the steering wheel with both hands. Her purse went flying, strewing change and lipsticks over the passenger side floor mat.

If nothing else, her parents had taught her to wear a seatbelt.

2

DUST FILLED THE AIR from the tire skid and hung like a shroud, blanketing the mountain-sized bull. Its black eyes tracked on the interlopers, while its massive flanks heaved, glistening with sweat in the waning light. It snorted once and stamped a hoof. Elizabeth stared at the beast, paralyzed to do anything but note that one horn pointed forward and the other out to the side, giving it a half-cocked, wild look. Hours spent watching safari documentaries in the basement family room while her parents yelled at each other upstairs hadn't prepared her to face down a western cousin of the wildebeest.

Her brain slogged through the mud of frightened paralysis, helpless to prevent the inevitable payout, time a maddening lag. The enormous head swung their way as the body reoriented itself at an optimum angle, the whole of the creature aimed to charge the hand-me-down hatchback.

Sweat crossed Elizabeth's brow, and she smelled the tang of her body's response to danger. In a flash of decision, she did two things at once. With her left hand, she smashed the buttons to roll up the windows, alternating between the four in rapid succession. Her right hand threw the shifter in reverse so the car could follow suit.

The bull considered this development.

Her blockade snorted again, muscles twitching. She was sure he was ready to launch his two-ton self in her direction, preparing to body check the car.

Movement on the hillside flagged the attention of both woman and behemoth.

A cowboy on a big roan approached, rope swinging in a low loop, eyes locked on the bull. Elizabeth watched, heart thumping in her chest like kicks to a metal wash tub. Her brain registered this new variable, the introduction of a third party to the dance.

Rhett, silent in the back seat, had dropped his toy truck and empty milk bottle, eyes wide in fascination. He comforted himself by slobbering over a fist, clutching at the seatbelt and a matted, stuffed moose.

The man rode a repeated half circle behind the bull, herding him out of the road and back into the grasses. The trio headed over a hill, the bull leading, the horse and rider following a pace behind.

"We're okay, buddy," she said, turning to assure Rhett as well as herself. "We'll give the big bull his space. That was exciting."

A little too exciting.

Elizabeth eased onto the gas and continued their winding route. She willed her shoulders to relax, her breathing to slow, the adrenaline to vacate her system.

As she took the next corner, her foot again slammed on the brakes, lurching them forward against the seatbelts. The rider waited, astride his horse, half on the road, half in the grass.

Clouds of fine, pink shale dust swirled up from her tires. The man coughed, holding his sleeve over his mouth and nose while the horse turned its head away from the offending vehicle and gnawed at its bit, directing the rider to vacate their stance. A bright orange and blue blanket framed the saddle, silver tack glinted in the sunlight.

She rolled down her window, uncertain of protocol, and called out to him, "Sorry about that, and thanks for earlier. Your guard dog doesn't seem to like us, much."

A smile crinkled the corner of the man's lips in response to her joke. He lifted a gloved hand from its resting spot on his thigh and waved toward Rhett in the back seat. "Happens on open range land. Glad to help out. It's not every day that I get to play the knight to a princess."

"I hardly needed rescuing. I am in a car. It's twice the weight and faster than a bull."

"I wasn't talking about you. Big Joe found a busted part of the fence line and wandered out. He was about to miss his date with Princess, and she does love being a mama."

Elizabeth's eyes skimmed the workworn chambray shirt over well-muscled arms, jeans ending in laced boots resting in the stirrups. The man wore a ball cap that shaded his eyes and she debated, hazel or brown. A tan line at his collar betrayed a life outdoors in that saddle.

"Glad to hear it. They stay pregnant even longer than humans."

The corner of the cowboy's mouth turned up, and Elizabeth blushed. Ever since she was a kid, trivia had been her comfort. When her parents would fight, she'd retreat to her closet and reread the one book they owned, a science encyclopedia, to wait out the storm. In the upside-down world of a traumatic childhood, facts would reorient her, anchor her to truth and stability.

The horse swished a raven-colored tail and shifted weight among its hooves, impatient. Its rider leaned down to pat the long, sinewed neck and whisper assurances. Elizabeth wondered what it would be like to know an animal like that. To walk out in the morning, throw on a saddle, and spend the day doing whatever came your way.

These were foreign thoughts to someone who'd always existed in suburbia.

The object of her scrutiny cocked his chin to the left, a slight, unspoken question. Elizabeth realized she was staring. It was time to stop, resume full function as mother, protector, and suburban escapee.

"Would you know if I am on the right road to Cloud Nine Ranch?"

Recognition crossed his brow with something that flashed bitter. "Sure, just another mile or so up, you'll see it on the right. Gateway, iron work over the top."

"Thanks again," she said, adding, "and tell Princess good luck from me."

He laughed, touched the brim of his hat, and waved at Rhett in the back seat before turning his horse away from the road.

"Well, if all the locals are that cute, living here won't be too painful." She peeked at Rhett in the rearview mirror, her only partner and confidant, for now. "Your first real cowboy sighting. With any luck, far from our last."

In response, Rhett waved his fist in the air before returning it to his mouth.

"Me too, buddy. Me too. Let's get this started."

The mountain range drew closer as Elizabeth crawled toward it, wondering what else might pop over a fence line and startle her out of a daydream. Aside from a pair of deer with springs for legs, she hadn't seen anything—or anyone—else.

She hadn't minded the interaction with the cowboy. In fact, she'd tried to soak up the moment, relishing contact with a man. A good-looking man. It had been far too long since she'd allowed herself those thoughts.

Mileage in black and white numbers among the dials on her car's dashboard served as proof of just how far she'd come. Away from traffic, away from a cramped townhouse, away from a failed marriage. Away. A faint click from her odometer signaled the upcoming driveway.

Now, Elizabeth had a new direction for life. The pit in her stomach reminded her to be cautious, but the strength in her spine was proof she was going somewhere—and on her own terms.

Among the foothills ahead, a jumble of old buildings splayed over a hilltop. Their once white siding was streaked with black, a pair of chimneys and a crooked weathervane the only decoration. Solitary, the structures looked abandoned, a resting place for history.

Elizabeth shivered as a prairie breeze whispered through the window and across the back of her nec as she turned into her brother's driveway.

3

CLOUD NINE ARCHED OVER the gated entrance in bent metal letters, announcing their arrival. A solar panel sat atop a silver box with a red button on the side.

"Fancy," Elizabeth said and reached through her window to press the button. The gate inched open as she rolled her window up and drove through.

The stretch of driveway divided a field of tall grasses and ran up to a barn-shaped house trimmed in blue and gray. Elizabeth surmised the actual barn must be the low-slung, metal-roofed structure sided by a corral. A white pickup, its bed full of hay bales, waited by the barn. She eased into the circular driveway and parked near the front door.

After unbuckling Rhett from the car seat, Elizabeth held him close, slinging her purse over one shoulder. The car beeped when she locked it, the sound technical and invasive against the empty prairie around them. Unnecessary out here, she thought, but old habits die hard.

A doormat emblazoned with *Wipe Your Boots* greeted them. Elizabeth set Rhett on his feet next to her, taking his hand. She paused, her fist hovering an inch from the door.

The picket fence, her own brewery, a loyal husband—had all been washed away by an inability to register reality, even when a woman called at two a.m. and asked for "the cute guy from the bar." It took her a half dozen such calls to hear the message, loud and clear.

Now, out of options but away from Nick's lies, Elizabeth had a chance to rebuild. She could not mess this up, past be damned.

It had been years since Elizabeth had seen her brother. Casey, a decade older, treated college as his ticket to something else, something bigger. Something far from home.

Their father was an engineer who reminded Elizabeth's mother of the salary and prestige of a railroad job whenever he could work it into a conversation, which was always. He drank, they fought. Play this song on repeat, for decades, and by the time it was Elizabeth's turn to leave the nest, she was numb to their cycles of abuse. The same dance, played on repeat.

Casey became a weekend-only presence in her life his senior year, preferring the couches of friends to the crisp sheets and lies on tap at home. On Saturdays, he took her to the park, to get ice cream. On Sundays, the movies. He stayed in the house long enough to change clothes and spend time with his little sister. As an adult, she understood now what it took for him to come home to see her back then, to make himself vulnerable to the constant attacks, judgment, and threats.

Elizabeth remembered when he told her he was leaving the summer after he graduated. Her plans for them—the neighborhood pool, the fireworks show, and concerts at the zoo—disappeared from her schedule like bubbles popping in thin air. "I'll visit, and you'll hardly notice I'm gone," he'd said. But he didn't, and she did.

Her attention snapped back to the present moment, hand resting on the painted wood as if drawing strength from the surface. She bit her lip and knocked.

Silence. The prairie breeze loosened a few strands of hair that brushed across her forehead. She struck at the door again.

About to head back to the car, picturing the long drive of defeat ahead with no backup plans, she heard a voice getting louder as it approached from inside. The door opened.

Here was Casey.

Hair the color of coffee grounds, blue eyes, and freckled cheeks. Shorter, he seemed, as she'd grown taller. He had a phone pressed between his head and a shoulder, answering the door in a T-shirt, jeans, and socks. His face lit up when he saw his visitors.

"Roz, I'll call you back."

Elizabeth waited, unsure of what to say.

He pocketed the device and wrapped her in a bear hug before she could speak. The tension she'd carried in waves across her shoulders melted away as she allowed herself to relax into the dimly familiar arms.

"Is your gate using a standard 10-watt solar panel?"

"Same old Lizzy-beth. It's so good to see you." Casey released her and crouched to Rhett's level before waving at him. "And how's my favorite nephew? You are so much bigger in person."

Rhett, in his infinite shyness, hid his face between Elizabeth's knees, peeking out at his uncle.

"It's okay, buddy, we've got time to get to know each other. You let me know when you want to see the baby goats."

Rhett turned his face just far enough toward Casey to reassess this stranger.

"Would you like to see Uncle Casey's baby goats?" Rhett's face turned back into Elizabeth's shirt. "He's a bit shy, but he loves petting zoos."

"Well, now he'll practically live at one."

Elizabeth winced. "Casey, I...thank you. We were really out of options and I—"

"Liz, stay as long as you like. I want you here. Glad to be a landing spot."

His voice betrayed the shame of decisions made, of conse-quences born. Before the past could further divide them, he continued, "Come on in. Let's get you two settled, and then we can go see the animals. Got anything I can carry?"

She popped the hatch on her car and shouldered a duffel. Casey hoisted a second one over one arm and took the handle of a suitcase. He pushed the door all the way open with his foot and said, "Make yourselves at home. Mi casa es su casa."

4

E LIZABETH KICKED OFF HER flats onto the pile of shoes by the door as she crossed the threshold. Boots, sneakers, and flip flops crowded the little mat near a coat rack.

Her breath caught in her throat when she took in the great room of the house. The living room ceiling vaulted up to the roof, clearstory windows granting views of the first stars to pierce the growing twilight. A chandelier ringed with antlers hung above, the lights soft and warm. Below, a couch crowded with pillows faced a large, stone fireplace. Elizabeth spotted her Christmas card on the big beam of the mantle, tucked among a few other pictures. She recognized her family in one, a candid shot from a trip to Lake Chelan, decades ago. The others were of strangers, other gatherings, Casey's found family since he'd left.

Two wingback chairs completed the room's seating, a coffee table topped with design books and a laptop, centering the group.

"I'll set these in the guest room. Have a seat." He took her bag and headed down a hall. His retreating form called, "Can I get either of you something to drink? Wine? Lemonade? I'd offer you a beer but I'm sure it's all swill compared to what you're used to making yourself."

"Lemonade would be great, thanks. We'll share."

Elizabeth didn't feel much like sitting after hours on the road, so she sat Rhett on the carpet with his favorite book about a farm and wandered over to the squat, glass table to read the stacked titles. Photography, Roman statues, and an architectural magazine made the set, though a book on building a business sat open, face down, on the couch.

Casey returned, a glass in each hand. He held one out to her before moving the open book to the table, plopping down two coasters, and sliding one her way. He took a seat in one of the chairs, leaning forward, elbows on his thighs, rough, working hands circling his glass. The pose reminded her of their family's golden retriever, willing his owners to get up and play.

Better get this over with. She took a sip of the cool drink to steady her nerves. Icy tartness washed over her tongue, and she offered Rhett a sip before beginning the spiel she'd practiced for most of her drive. "Casey, I—"

"No, please, Liz. Let me start. I abandoned you, back then, and I'm sorry. At the time, I only thought of myself, only thought of getting the hell away from them. I didn't think of you. By the time I started to feel free, so much time had gone by that I...well, I was ashamed. I didn't think you'd want to hear from me, from a brother who just left. So, I stayed gone."

The words bit into her core, found a soft place she'd armored up, and exposed the hurt deep within. Rhett squirmed in her arms, so she sat him next to her and held the cool drink to his lips, using the moment to cushion her vulnerability.

"I don't think I'll ever forgive myself for doing that to you," he continued. "Mom would send me emails sometimes, letting me know how you were doing. I could read the pride in her words. She told me about graduation, your first job, Rhett...in college, she sent me care packages, socks and cookies and things."

He was careful not to mention Nick, she noticed. She wondered what their mother had told him about that mistake, the end of their marriage. They'd eloped. Elizabeth hadn't wanted a wedding, and Nick was happy to save the money.

Their divorce was just as private, again a handful of people and a piece of paper with signatures.

"Seems like she's always trying to make up for our childhood." The next sip of lemonade was sour with memories.

Rhett tugged one of the throw pillows into his lap and hugged it to his chest, small hands squeezing into the luxurious fabric.

"A friend of mine in Victoria makes those," Casey said, smiling at the little boy's glee. "She imports faux rabbit fur."

Rhett was wiping his face back and forth on the surface of the pillow, so Elizabeth snatched it away. "I'm so sorry! Rhett, we can't do that, it's not ours." She rubbed at the front of the pillow, checking its gray softness for sticky spots.

"It's fine, just fine. He can have it. I've got loads of pillows. It will be like a square stuffed animal friend. Kind of like a bison."

"Bison fur is finer than fox hair."

The toddler regarded his uncle in solemn appreciation as she returned the pillow.

"How...uh...is Rhett doing?"

"You mean, is he going to be silent forever?" Elizabeth was used to people dancing around asking her whether her child would be a permanent oddity. It always came up, somehow. Well-intended but always invasive. Direct information was the fastest way to interrupt the prying. "His pediatrician says we are watching to see how things go these next few months. So, we wait."

"Got it." Casey set his glass on the small cork mat. He stood up, a vertical signal of a change in topic. "How about I show you around?"

"Well, I recognize that," she said, nodding toward their grandfather's bird gun, mounted over the doorway.

"Yeah, that's pretty much all I took for my so-called inheritance," he said. "Still works, too. I keep it clean."

"Glad it's up high. I think it pales in use compared to those." On a rack at the back of the room, three compound bows hung at an angle, as if invisible archers held their weight.

"A guy has to have hobbies here. There's not too much in the way of external entertainment, otherwise."

The kitchen winged off the living room, industrial steel balanced with subway tile. Above the deep sink, microgreens sprouted in a tray on the window ledge, basking under a grow light.

"I tried to mesh farmhouse with function," he explained, waving toward the room. He'd majored in architecture in college, tucking in classes in CAD and Art History between rodeos. Not until she saw his house did she understand his passion and gift. He ran a hand along a countertop. "Made the cabinets myself. Couldn't find any that matched what I wanted."

A short hallway tunneled toward the back of the house and was sided by Casey's bedroom on the right, a bedroom and office on the left, with a bathroom in between.

"Move around whatever you want," he said in the guest room, opening a closet door to show her a bar dangling a dozen felted hangers below a shelf half full of knick-knacks. Oversized candles on pewter plates, holiday centerpieces, and glass vases of all shapes and sizes awaited selection. "I like to swap things out. Keeps the place fresh."

They hadn't brought much in the way of knick knacks to decorate. Between Elizabeth and Rhett, they'd only brought a few bags, the majority of which were already deposited on the crisp duvet. They would get more as they needed more, she'd told herself. She rationalized selling off the bulk of their belongings before they'd left in the name of traveling light. This was easier than admitting that she needed the cash. The hardest and most lucrative sale was her mash tun. Custom-welded by another brewer, there wasn't another one like it anywhere.

Elizabeth needed to stay focused on the present, not the past. She'd collect some paychecks, get their own place, and then rebuild her brewing business.

"Ready to see the goats?"

Casey waved a well-scarred hand at a selection of barn shoes and slipped into a bright orange set of clogs. Elizabeth approximated a pair that would fit before sliding her feet into their recesses. *His house is ten times more organized than my whole life.*

"We'll have to get some for Rhett," Casey said. "Guessing they'll have some at Sheridan Feed."

Approaching the barn, she smelled the earthy scent of hay and animals. As a teen, she'd been granted a week at summer camp. She learned to ride, falling in love with the horses. Every afternoon, she would brush them in turn, lingering in the assurances of the powerful animals, their soft noses nuzzling her palms for a carrot.

Near the end of the week, a close-lipped camp counselor had pulled her from a trail ride and brought her back to the acre of log structures. She'd offered to help put away the tack, but the camp counselor brushed her offer aside. A visitor was waiting.

Elizabeth's aunt, a boxy woman bedecked in acrylic clothing from a discount department store, filled a plastic chair on one side of a large desk. The camp manager, a man who looked everywhere but at Elizabeth, sat in the other. The woman pulled tissue after tissue out of a fabric tote bag, blubbering into its recesses. Elizabeth could only make out the words "terrible tragedy" and "utter selfishness" before the counselor surfaced and ushered her out to the cabins to pack her bags.

Uncle Dan waited behind the wheel of their minivan, two of her cousins in the back, eyeing her with somber looks as she buckled herself into a bucket seat. Dan's ever-present shadow of a beard shifted around thin lips as he explained the situation, his words punctured by the intermittent wails of her aunt. Her father had hit his head and gone to heaven. Like it was a trip one takes, Elizabeth had thought. Dan continued, forcing the words between his teeth as he watched the highway. Her mother, his sister, couldn't take care of her right now, as though she was inconvenienced. Elizabeth would have to move in with them for the time being.

After a week of eavesdropping on late-night kitchen conversations, Elizabeth learned the truth. Hushed whispers recapped recent events over the phone to other relatives, neighbors. Elizabeth's father had come after her mother, screamed in her face, threatened to kill her. The slight woman had grabbed for the closest thing she could. Golf club in hand, she walloped him in the face, spraying blood across a China cabinet. While the initial blow didn't kill him, the resulting crack to his skull when he stumbled and fell against the mantle, did.

The trial was brief. Her mother served six years in Walla Walla. These were map dots on Elizabeth's existence as life rolled forward. She switched schools, tried to focus, and put in just enough effort to pass her classes. Her teenage self was numb, empty except for the movie reel of her family's demise that played over and over in her mind.

Elizabeth's emotions were a twisted wreck at two o-clock on the first Sunday of each month when her uncle would drive her across the state to visit her mother. He would stand, aloof, as she described her science projects, mentioned the community college, and otherwise filled the limited time with the noise of uncomfortable conversation. Her mother's wan smile and thinning hair framed a physical presence, but that was all. When Elizabeth left the beige, brick buildings behind, she fought the urge to run for the safety of the car.

There hadn't been another chance to go to summer camp. The pension from her father's career went straight into the bank each month. "You'll want that for college," Dan said.

What she'd wanted, what she'd needed, was to be back with the horses.

"Maybe you'll learn to ride, one day," Elizabeth whispered to her almost two-year-old. He watched the new scenery for potential adventure from the safety of her hip.

5

I N THE DIM RECESSES of the barn, they trailed Casey down the row of stalls to a back corner. A window was propped open to let in the light, soft rays warming the straw-covered floor. As they approached the spot where Casey waited, she heard gentle bleating. Elizabeth leaned over the railing so she and Rhett could see in.

A nanny goat, udders pink and prominent, stood, head twisted, as if counting the kids nudging at her side. All three were black and white, the smallest was only white around his eyes and a little patch at his throat. The other two were evenly splotched, black on white, white on black. All jostled each other, negotiating for a prime spot.

Rhett reached for the boarded edge of the stall, willing himself down with the animals.

"I haven't named them yet. Maybe Rhett will help me think of some good names."

"Maybe he will," she said, doubt edging her reply. Rhett had ways of communicating, but they were not always what adults wanted from him.

"We'll figure it out, right, buddy?"

Casey didn't try to touch Rhett or push into his comfort zone. He talked to his nephew as though at any moment Rhett would reply, would say his first words. Today might be the day.

New people at the daycare would fail to understand resistance to their influence, and Rhett would go stiff with any invasion. More than once, the staff had called her at work to insist she collect him for the day. "He won't listen," they'd explain, and she knew what they really meant was that he wouldn't talk.

"A group of goats is called a tribe or a trip. How many do you have now?"

"Two dozen. Well, twenty-seven, now," he said, regarding the newest ranch inhabitants. "Only a half dozen cows, a few sheep. Goat milk is super popular, if you can believe that. Easier for the lactose-intolerant. Easier for me to flavor, too. I've got sun-dried tomato, tapenade, cracked pepper, and lavender so far."

"Fat molecules in goat milk are shorter than those in cow milk."

"Goat cheese is easier on the gut than stuff made from cows, that's all I know. Learned that myself the hard way. Anyway, I sell a ton."

"Oh, I thought that you, I mean, that most people with ranches, well...raise meat."

"Many, yes, but not me. I've actually been a vegetarian since high school."

"Oh." The awkward silences at the family dinner table made sense now. She remembered Casey refusing to touch the food on his plate, his father steaming red until he exploded in a tirade about her brother's ingratitude, her mother sobbing in the kitchen. The tension had been so thick she pictured reaching out to stab it with her salad fork, tines piercing opinions and resentment.

"My herd is for milk, only. When they age out of that stage of their life, I will literally send them out to a pasture to enjoy retirement in peace."

"Even the baby boy goats?"

"Them, too. We neuter them when it's time and they join the herd. When you raise them with love they can be super sweet. Lately I've been adopting a few out to people I trust.

People are super into goat yard guards and weed management in a cute, if sometimes cantankerous, form."

"That sounds like a pretty great life. Maybe I should sign up."

He laughed. "I think you have a few years left in you yet, sis. Speaking of which, tell me about this new job. Jo was over here the other day, going on and on about how lucky they are to have you. Said she is going to roll out the welcome wagon."

"Well, I—"

"Hey, Case—want me to unload the truck? Daylight's draining."

A voice interrupted their family unit a moment before its owner walked in from the gathering darkness. Elizabeth felt a dip in her stomach when she recognized the gorgeous cowboy from her almost-altercation with Big Joe.

His face split into a smile as he pulled the work glove off his right hand and held it out to her. "This must be your sister."

"Liz, meet Justin. Justin, my sister Liz. Justin takes pity on this old shepherd and helps me out. His family owns the ranch to the east."

"Shoot, Casey could run this place in his sleep. He doesn't need my help. He's just trying to get me to join the dark side."

"Dark side?" Elizabeth asked. She lost herself in Justin's steady gaze, registering the shadow of beard stubble that graced his jaw. *Get a hold of yourself.* How long had it been? She shoved her cravings aside and smiled at her new neighbor. "No such place."

"His family raises beef," Casey explained. "Quintessential cattle barons. Like since the 1800s or something."

"Meat, got it," Elizabeth confirmed.

"All grass fed, though. We're doing as much tree-hugging as we can, my friend. Get more money for it, too."

"I'll give you some credit, I guess. Let me know when you actually install that hydroelectric pump, and we'll talk."

"Your brother is such a funny guy," Justin said to Elizabeth. "Well, it was great meeting you. I'll leave you two to, uh...catch up. Call me if you need me later. Otherwise, I'll be by on Wednesday for processing."

As he walked out of the barn, Elizabeth watched, not minding the view.

"You're a grown woman, and you do what you want," Casey said, commenting on her attentions. "But I don't want to have to murder my favorite roping partner."

6

"STILL ROPING?"

"Can't seem to let it go. Body says I should, but I just don't want to, dammit. I'm getting old, Liz. I don't recommend it."

"Rodeo is one of the most dangerous sports in the world." She'd made a daisy chain for Rhett who sat in her lap, picking off the petals, one by one.

They lounged in the Adirondack chairs that faced west, the night air cool on Elizabeth's forehead. Casey handed her a beer from the fridge in the tack room, apologizing for his lack of selection, and they sipped, watching the moon trace an arc over the sky.

Elizabeth considered the domestic brew, mentally calculated the amount of hops used, the timing, and the pale yellow result. In college, she'd lucked into a job at a brewery, pulling taps. A year turned into two, and the owner taught her his recipes, let her brew alongside him. She loved the smell of mash, creating experimentals, and didn't mind access to free beer.

Maybe there was a brewing scene out here or in town. She could ask around, maybe convince Casey to give her some barn space, rustle up some equipment.

"It's a subpar lager at best, I know."

She clinked the neck of her bottle against his, took a sip, and said, "It's fine. Great, actually, to be sitting out here like this."

"Can I ask about Nick?"

"Nope."

"Got it."

She sighed. Better get it over with now rather than later. "He's fine. Or rather, I'm sure he's seeking whatever solace he's pretending to need in the arms of the flavor of the week. He didn't get upset when I told him about moving, if that's what you're asking."

"Are you sure about that?"

"That man was too busy trashing our credit, picking up STDs, and whining about how complicated his life got when he became a parent to care about me or Rhett. The waitresses were just icing on the worthless husband cake."

Casey put his bottle to his lips and then swallowed a sip. He looked at her. "Sorry. That must have been absolute hell."

"It was. It still is, in a way."

He tossed his now empty bottle into a barrel and reached for the second round waiting under his chair. "You two are welcome to stay as long as you like, little sister. I fell short on brotherly duties in the past, but that ends today."

"Thanks, Casey. We'll be out of your hair as soon as I get my first paycheck."

"Let me guess. Child support—"

"Is not something I can ever count on receiving. Nick does have your address in case he gets a generous streak."

"Hungry?" Casey offered.

Elizabeth stomach's growled in response. How long had it been since she'd snacked? Being a parent meant sometimes forgoing your own hunger pangs to focus on the needs of your child. "Fairly sure I could eat a horse," she said.

"Yeah, definitely don't serve horse at Cloud Nine, but I do have the set-up for nachos. Be ready in two shakes."

Elizabeth held her son's hands as she marionette-walked him inside the house. Rhett toddled into the bedroom and began to unpack his toys from a red duffle, somehow understanding the new arrangement.

"Might as well get comfy," she told him. "We'll be here for a bit, I think."

Elizabeth took her makeup bag from her suitcase and headed into the bathroom. After deploying eye drops under her lids, she tucked the bag in the cupboard below the sink and stepped out into the hallway.

She paused at the framed photographs lining the hallway, a handful of rectangles forming a timeline. They'd brushed past them on their way outside, and this time, she scrutinized these missed moments from her brother's past. Casey at a wrestling match, holding his opponent in a Cradle. Casey at graduation, his arms slung around people she didn't recognize. Casey at a rodeo, leaning against a railing, several other cowboys next to him in the same position. When she came across a picture of her brother, team roping at the Cheyenne Frontier Days, she looked closely at the other rider. The photographer had caught them mid-action; as the header, Casey's rope was anchored around the horns. His partner, mid-lasso, was about to catch the back hooves. She recognized the heeler's dark skin, bright blue shirt, and that smile, assuring victory.

"Those were the days."

His voice startled her, as though she'd been snooping in his personal life.

"I wish I'd seen some of your events. This picture makes it look easy—and fun."

"It was."

"You still rope out here?"

"Some. A lot of it ended when Justin got married. You know how that goes. You get used to a partner, and when they're gone, it just doesn't work the same. Even when they split, it was like she kept some kind of hold on him." He walked off, leaving her with the photograph, his memories, and lament.

⚶

Elizabeth joined him in the kitchen, taking a seat at one of the low-backed bar stools in front of the island. Casey wrestled a few glass storage containers from the fridge and lined them up on the counter. He selected one to set in the microwave and punched a few buttons before removing plates from the cupboard below. Open shelves displayed glassware and canisters of dried beans and rice behind him. A black and white photograph of his house and barn hung over a pantry door.

Elizabeth toyed with the ceramic salt and pepper shakers on the counter. The tacky souvenirs, one a bison, one an eagle, were the only items out of place in the magazine-worthy kitchen.

"Your house came out really good, big brother."

"Thank you. It's a work in progress, but it's coming along. Draws business, too. I was hired to design a law office in Sheridan when a buddy of mine who's an attorney saw my moldings—and no, that's not a euphemism."

Elizabeth smirked at the quip.

"I'm pretty sure Justin used his connections to a degree, but I am still calling it a win."

"He seems like a good friend," Elizabeth said.

When Nick took the job in Renton, she'd tried to find friends, even joining a local club for moms. The women were nice but distant, and the petty side of her struggled with watching their babies develop in typical ways. Her few coworkers were drowning in work, and even the guys at the brewery weren't sure how to incorporate a mother with a day job.

"Yeah. He hasn't always been." The timbre of Casey's voice wavered as he shared.

"Anything I should know?"

"Nah. Small town drama, is all." He shrugged as if to release the past from his dinner preparations and lined a pan with foil. He piled it with chips and shredded cheese.

"Well, he sure looks good on a horse, friend or foe."

"That he does, sister. Okay, what would my nephew like on his nachos?"

⚜

After dinner and tucking Rhett into bed, Casey had his feet propped on the coffee table, socks mismatched.

"Mr. Designer can't be bothered to find a pair of socks?"

"More like my mind is still half asleep at the ripe hour of five a.m. when the animals demand their breakfast. Don't worry, though. I get gussied up for dates."

"How is dating these days?"

"Slow," he replied, picking at a stray thread on his jeans. "It's better than it was, but folks around here aren't ...supportive. As long as they aren't reminded I'm gay, they can pretend it's not a thing. Online isn't much of an option out here. I've got a guy in Denver, though. We've exchanged a few pics."

"Pics?" Elizabeth cocked an eyebrow at her brother.

"What about yourself? Last I heard of you dating, there was no shortage of the willing, according to mom."

"Dry spell. Can't blame someone for passing by a woman with a kid, an ex, and questionable life strategies."

"It can't be all bad. There are guys out there who will take the complications for the honor of romancing my favorite sister."

She threw a pillow at him. "Those guys seem to have their own baggage. So, here I am."

"It's really over with Nick?"

"You've got to stop bringing him up. Yes, it's over, despite the average person needing eighteen months to move on from a divorce."

"Sorry, last time. It just seemed like you two got along, that's all."

"Let me guess, Mom told you that? Of course it seemed like we got along when Mom polished over the ugly parts."

"She was in the habit from her own marriage, I think." Casey rested his beer bottle on his thigh, condensation leaving a ring on the denim.

"What the hell happened to being honest and decent people?"

"Those values went out the door with the arrival of the internet, sis."

"You're right."

"Enough about our lackluster love lives. Tell me about the new job."

"You just want me to thank you for it." Elizabeth kicked off her shoes and put her feet up on the coffee table. She rested her beer on her hunched stomach.

"I was just helping a family member out, is all. Can't help if there are selfish benefits on the side."

"I know, and I super appreciate it. For all my talk, I don't know that I would have been able to leave without knowing I had something waiting."

"It's not often they can find someone with a lot of experience for this gig."

"I'm guessing they have a high turnaround?"

"A tiny school in the middle of nowhere? Nah."

"Yeah, I don't think the whole one-room-schoolhouse situation has the nostalgic appeal for teachers actually doing that work. There are fewer than 400 left in the country."

When he'd sent her the job description, she'd researched the tiny school and the town—or what was left of it—of Banner. She'd kept the tab open for a week, thinking. One room, a handful of students, and a tight-knit community. School would start in a matter of weeks.

One night when Nick was late coming home and she had a glass of wine and too much time to think, she opened his laptop to find a slew of messages from someone with the same name as a 19-year-old intern. She'd slammed the machine shut, decision made. An email to the school district with her resume, and plans were made.

Now, here she was. Broke, living with family, and about to step back into the past. The school building was over a hundred years old, having served some of the grandparents of folks still living in its vicinity.

"You have the Nelson family from just down the road and the Ramirez twins from a ranch to the east. Oh, and Polly's son. Next year, they'll likely add a few more."

"Wow. Definitely my smallest class ever." Elizabeth could only imagine the envy of her former coworkers. Bloated classrooms were the norm in Seattle. Budgets wouldn't support anything less.

"I'm guessing people are more than glad to have a teacher again. There's a school in Story, but that's still a drive, and in the winter, no one wants to go farther than they have to."

"I'm supposed to meet Mrs. Wolf at the school tomorrow in the morning."

"That'd be Jo. Sheriff Wolf's wife. Closest house to the school."

"Thanks. Figured I'd take Rhett into town for a few things from the store. Need anything?"

"Other than a deep tissue massage and a tall brunette? Nah, I'm good."

"I'll see what they carry."

7

THE SCHOOLHOUSE SAT ON top of a hill, stark and foreboding. No accident, Elizabeth thought. A single story with an old bell tower up top, the only external hints at modernity were solar panels on the roof and a woman leaning against a white SUV out front.

"You must be Ms. Blau. I'm Josephine Wolf, but call me Jo unless you want to be on my bad side. My mother was into France something fierce when she was pregnant, begged my father to take her to Paris."

"Did he?"

"On their 45th wedding anniversary. She said it rained every day and smelled like fish." The woman stooped to gather a few stems of sage, twisting at them with nimble fingers.

"So, she didn't like it after all?"

"Are you kidding? She loved every minute. Mom's way of showing love was saying everything that was wrong with everything. People, too. Now who's this little fellow?"

"This is Rhett."

"Hello there, young man. You seem a little young for kindergarten."

"He's just over eighteen months."

"Well then, you'll be needing someone to watch him while you teach."

"Oh, I...uh, yes. I do. I mean, of course I do. I was wondering what options exist for daycare around here." In truth, Elizabeth had avoided that consideration. Whether begging for her brother's help, taking Rhett with her in the mornings, or finding a center nearby, no options were reasonable. Avoiding the concern had been easier than acknowledging it.

"You're looking at it. Or rather, there's nothing for miles that would make it worth the drive. You can leave him with me. I'm happy to watch him."

"But I couldn't—"

"I know, I know. What business does someone with no kids of her own have in offering? But the thing is, I've helped raise just about everyone under twenty in a twenty-mile radius. Some years our house — that one over there — was crawling with toddlers."

Elizabeth looked where the woman pointed. A two-story, brick red house perched at the edge of a pond half full of cattails.

"Ten-minute walk is all it is. I don't charge much. We can work that out."

"That's very generous." Elizabeth had just met the woman, and she'd commandeered her firstborn child. "He isn't verbal...well, not yet. I mean, he doesn't talk. Yet. Boys can develop speech later. It's normal."

"I talk enough for two people. We'll get along fine, won't we, cowboy?"

Rhett, having observed the exchange, snuggled against Elizabeth's chest at the attention. When Jo held out the braided wand of greenery, he took the offering with a shy smile.

"Let me show you around."

Elizabeth followed the woman to the front door of the building. A sorting of keys was required before one was selected to fit the door. After Jo unlocked it, she passed the key to Elizabeth.

Instead of rows lined with linked wooden desks atop iron bases, a chalkboard, and a fireplace, this room held several tables, a bookcase, and a mammoth metal desk. Maps, posters, and a large clock ringed three walls, the fourth painted with whiteboard paint.

"It's not much, but we have a lot of materials in the storage closet. The school district will send us just about anything we ask for within a week or two, and I think you'll find the parents on the generous side."

"This is just fine. Good, really. I'd thought it would be more...rustic."

"Read some prairie novels, have you?" Jo tipped her chin toward Elizabeth who registered the slight. The woman continued. "Easy. I don't mean much by it, only that we have trouble keeping folks in this job because they have one idea of what a schoolhouse like this is supposed to be, and it rarely matches reality. I just like to operate in honesty, that's all."

"You're right, I was expecting more dust and the 19th Century inside."

"We do have some pictures from back then, if you like. They're in the teacherage, out this way."

They set off across the grass to a building with a slanted roof and flower boxes under the windows. A small porch held an ancient chair facing the mountains.

Inside was a suite of rooms, long vacated. They made quick work touring the miniscule kitchen and living room area, single bedroom, and bathroom.

"It's not much, but it's insulated, and this wood stove will do it justice in the winter. Clint could haul over our spare cot for the little one, push the small dresser against it. It's yours to use, part of the benefits."

"Thank you. It is a...bonus. I think I'm staying with Casey for now, but I'll keep it in mind." She'd let Rhett claim an old calendar featuring horses for each month, and he flipped through the pictures, enamored.

"No one has lived out here in well over a year," Jo said, running her finger through the dust on the windowsill. "The last teacher we had left midyear, and the kids had to be bussed.

If you do move in, be sure to lock the doors at night. We've had to chase a bear or two out before. They can smell food a mile away. Especially in the spring when they come off that mountain, half starved. Don't want the kids served up like bait."

Jo exited the tiny cottage, and Elizabeth followed behind. The abandoned building smelled of loneliness and a hint of decay.

"I'm just down the hill if you need anything during the day. I always have a glass of wine around five, and you're welcome to join me any day you like. Just give a holler. We want to keep you, just so that's clear."

"I appreciate it and I don't plan to bail. This may be a stupid question, but you know so much about the school and everyone, why aren't you the teacher?"

"That was the plan, once upon a time. Much too busy, anyway. School starts next Monday, but we have a tradition of an Open House the Friday before, after most parents get off work. You good with that?"

"Sounds like I better be."

"I like you. I'll sound the alarm, then. School is in session. Bye now." Jo climbed into her car and drove off, leaving Elizabeth and Rhett in the driveway.

"What do you say we lock up and go brush your uncle's horses?"

‹‹‹

In the front yard of her brother's house, a palomino was tethered to a hitching post with a hot pink lead. Elizabeth pushed on the door to find a blonde woman addressing a countertop full of parts.

Without looking up from her work, the woman asked, "Hey, Casey, do you have any spare strings? Justin's cams are out of sync."

"I wouldn't know," Elizabeth said, waiting on the doormat. "But I do know an arrow flies two and a half times as fast as a cheetah runs."

The woman turned to reveal tight jeans, a cropped top, and a half smile. "Oh. Hey there. I didn't know Casey had company."

"I'm Elizabeth. His sister." Something about the woman's familiar demeanor was irksome, like a mosquito buzzing in her ear.

"Well, I knew you weren't his date, honey." The woman laughed.

Strike two, thought Elizabeth. "And you are?"

"I'm Rosalyn. Call me Roz. I'm his neighbor."

"Great," Elizabeth said, voice edged with animosity. She shifted her keys from one hand to the next, a standoff move.

"I think I'll go," Roz said, placing what looked like a jagged wheel on the counter. "I'm going to leave this here for Casey. That man can work wonders. Nice to meet you."

"Likewise."

As the woman brushed past her and through the door, Elizabeth caught a whiff of her perfume. Roses and desperation.

8

RHETT ANGLED HIS BODY toward his toys on the living room floor, straining to reach the bright plastic shapes sprinkled over the rug.

Elizabeth set him down to stack the blocks and picked up her phone. The line rang twice before a groggy voice picked up.

"Hello, Liz."

"Nick. You said you'd have money here before I arrived, but the mailbox was as empty as my wallet after months of this."

"I forgot, okay? It's sitting right here. I'll put it in the mail today."

"I don't get paid until the end of the month, Nick. I need you to follow through." Elizabeth hated hearing those words come out of her mouth, true as they might be.

"I told you, I forgot. Today, Liz. Promise."

She hung up and regarded her son, wishing in vain she could be the mother she'd planned to be. He'd taken the opportunity of Elizabeth's diversion to toddle into the kitchen. He reached for the colorful boxes lining the counter, one hand on the stainless steel dishwasher.

"I see Uncle Casey likes the same crackers you do, and I know he has goat cheese. How about a little indoor picnic and then we get you some boots?"

"How about pizza?" Casey asked when they returned. "Or a salad? Both?"

"That's fine. A woman came by for you, a neighbor."

"Oh, yeah, that was Roz. I called her."

"Do people just make themselves at home wherever out here?"

"Kind of. Also, technically she's been over here more than you have." He'd collected the parts Roz had left on the counter and reassembled them into a functional compound bow.

"Sorry," Elizabeth mumbled. "I think I'm just sensitive to random blondes showing up where I live. It's your house. You're right."

"As you know, she wouldn't be my type, even on the loneliest of nights."

"Fair enough."

"On a non-confrontational note, I've been thinking. What if we took one of my old milk tanks and modified it for brewing? I think I've got a 100-gallon free, at least."

"Ooh. Keep talking." A kernel of hope dug into her side.

"We'd need to remove the cooling compressor, rig it back up for steaming."

"Get some kegs. Order some hops—can you grow those here?"

"Not this time of year."

"Right. Hops require at least 120 days. And for it to be summer."

Elizabeth pressed at her temples, calculations running through her brain. Depending on equipment, she could have a batch in a couple months, start a second. An IPA was a solid start, but a barley wine couldn't hurt things in this part of the country. People liked big beers when it was cold out. Putting in the time wouldn't be too tough in the evenings. When she got things going, they'd need a license. Bottles. Labels. A name. She needed cash. Damn.

Inhaling through her nose and exhaling through her mouth just like the hyper-bendy yoga teacher had instructed, she concluded, "I'll write it out, see what's possible. Now tell me about this goat cheese we tried. Was that lavender?"

"That's not how this works."

When she clicked the bedroom door shut behind her, having kissed Rhett goodnight, she heard her brother on the phone, a quiet anger in his voice. The low and steady tone reminded her of the nights he'd fought with her parents. He preferred to sear with curt and subversive commentary, prey far too intelligent for the predator.

"You cannot leave me high and dry...those are not liquid assets. Even if I thought I could swing it, that can't happen overnight."

She hesitated in the hallway, wrapping her fingers around the edge of the wall.

"Dammit you will not do this to me. I could lose everything."

Elizabeth turned on her heel and headed for the back door. The blanket of darkness rolled out, thousands of sparkling pinpricks scattered to its edges.

Wrapping her cardigan tighter around her middle, she sat in one of the chairs Casey had fashioned out of wine barrels. Each was tipped at the exact angle one needed to spot the Milky Way, a belt around the heavens.

"Thought I might find you out here."

She jumped at the combination of Casey's voice and a cold bottle tapping the skin of one arm.

"I came out for some fresh air. The night is gorgeous."

"That it is. No one around for miles. Peace and quiet." He collapsed in the other chair and tipped his chin toward the sky.

Elizabeth drank from the bottle Casey offered. Amber, she knew without looking. Not bad, she thought, though a little too much caramel.

"Sounds like things weren't exactly peaceful back in there."

"Work stuff," Casey said, and she didn't press.

"Speaking of work stuff, Jo offered to watch Rhett while I'm at work. Thanks for offering to cover until I found someone."

"She's a treasure. I figured she would."

"I get the feeling she knows me better than I know myself somehow, and I've only known the woman for a day. She suggested we try leaving Rhett with her for a trial run before school starts to see how it goes."

"Makes sense."

"I was hoping you could suggest a place where a single gal with a babysitter could get a drink around here."

"I know just the bar. Family outing?"

9

A CARAMEL-COLORED DONKEY HUNG her head over the corral, accepting all manner of pats from Rhett. At Elizabeth's hip, a goat reached for the buttons on her jacket, and she side-stepped him just in time.

Jo had all but begged Elizabeth to drop Rhett off so they could grab a beer. Called it a trial run.

The two pets were only part of the draw for Rhett. Elizabeth saw the giant bucket of toys in the living room, just waiting to be tipped over and explored.

JRhett successfully installed at the Wolfs' house, they drove south.

The Crow Bar served the sleepy town of Story, a stop sign on the map, complete with a post office, tiny market, and summer camp. Just off the highway, the neon lights blazed along the front of the bar, and a wraparound deck framed the back.

Casey held the poster-covered door for her. While a record player didn't screech to a halt, all eyes tracked the newcomer.

Before they'd left the house, Casey made a show of looking her up and down when she emerged from the bedroom, squeezed and tucked into her favorite jeans.

Elizabeth had applied a swipe of lipstick which she pocketed in her coat before lifting the puffy garment from the hook. "What?"

"Not a damn thing," Casey said. "Just getting used to having you here. In adult form."

Now, inside the bar, curious glances flitted her way like moths bumping against a porch light.

I guess I still look good. Not ready to be touched, held. Not yet. However, she was ready to be noticed. Tonight.

She followed Casey up to the long, walnut-topped bar where he greeted the woman pulling taps. Her face was familiar to Elizabeth, somehow. Long lashes over a small nose and rounded chin reminded Elizabeth of a pony, shaggy blonde hair wrangled into a ponytail, not to be underestimated.

"Liz, this is Polly Michaels. She makes a killer old-fashioned."

"You flatter me, Casey. I couldn't tell you the last time someone ordered a proper cocktail." She turned to Elizabeth. "You're the new teacher, right? We've been waiting for you. What are you drinking?"

"The old fashioned was invented in the 1800s in Kentucky. Sign me up."

"On the house. For our new teacher."

When the bartender set the drink in front of Elizabeth and turned to the next customer, Casey raised an eyebrow at his sister. "Since when do you drink out of a glass with a stem?"

"You've fed me enough domestic beer for the week. Need to cleanse my palate. Besides, I think I'll be judged by this crowd no matter what I order."

"Go easy on folks, Liz. These are my people."

"Well, your people are sizing me up like a piece of meat."

"They are mostly cattle ranchers."

"Hah. Hah."

Polly handed over a rocks glass to Elizabeth, a glass to Casey.

"Darts?" Casey grabbed both their drinks and headed off.

"Winner buys the next round," she called, trailing after him.

When Casey nailed his second bullseye, Elizabeth headed back to the bar. Polly was slammed with customers but waved Elizabeth up for her order, handing a bottle and a low ball glass, complete with a twist and cherry, across the counter. Drinks in hand, Elizabeth almost collided with Justin.

"Easy there," he said, steadying her, his hands warm on her shoulders. "You almost ran me over."

"You know my family, all brawn."

"That I do. Are you here with Casey?"

Elizabeth gestured with one of the bottles to her brother. Casey waved from his spot near the dart board. He leaned against the tobacco-stained wall, glass in hand, watching a football game that played on all six of the screens. A man next to him said something to Casey, and they laughed. Each held a glass, a half empty pitcher on the table next to them.

"Looks like this beer is for you," she said, handing it to Justin.

She'd never seen Casey flirt before. Was this that? He watched the man, whose eyes were trained on the screen, as if assessing the next time to insert witty commentary.

"Cheers," Justin said, taking both the drink and stool near where she stood. "What do you think of our local watering hole?"

"I like it, I think. I guess I still feel like an outsider, though, and that's strange for me. In the city, you don't even think about it. Everyone is no one you know, if that makes sense. Starting over here is...different. You know, adult things."

"I hear that. I remember being a kid, when all I had to do was ride my horse around the ranch for hours at a time, catching frogs and watching sunsets. Adult responsibilities suck the joy out of far too much of life."

"It's not like I planned for this life. I did everything right. Married the guy, had the kid...only neither of those turned out to be as advertised." Elizabeth's lips rested on the edge of her bottle before she tipped it upward for a drink. "Could be a lot harder, I suppose."

"That's what I tell myself."

"Do you have any kids?"

Elizabeth didn't want to outright ask if he was single. If she got desperate, she could ask Casey, but this might be the ticket. He took a long sip of his own beer, and she watched him swallow, eyes following the shape of his jawline. Get a hold of yourself, she thought. He's not a prize bull.

Justin set the bottle down and peeled at the label. "Naw, my ex kept putting that off. Endless talk about whether we were ready. Well, we weren't ever ready, turns out."

"You still have time," Elizabeth said, realizing the insensitivity of the comment the moment it left her mouth. "If you want, that is. Over half of couples don't have kids." *Pathetic attempt at a save.*

"It's tougher in a small town to meet someone, you know. Let alone someone who gets you." He rested one elbow on the bar, watching the sea of faces in front of them undulate, like jellyfish in a tank.

Casey appeared over her shoulder, his breath reeking of cheap lager. "Hey, sis, want to join us for shots?"

"Thank you, but no thank you. I have to be functional when I pick up Rhett from your sheriff's house, you know."

"Suit yourself. How about you, Justin?"

"I'm keeping it mild tonight, brother. Have one for me."

"About to," Casey said, a wild grin pasted on his face. "Don't wait up." He winked and raised his bottle at the two of them before heading back to the tables.

"I should close out," Elizabeth said to Justin. "Don't want to push the babysitter my first night out."

"Same. I've been at this way too long for one night." He leaned his forearms on the bar as they waited for Polly, sliding his near empty bottle from one hand to the other. "You're lucky, you know."

"Lucky?" Elizabeth had been digging through her purse for enough bills to cover her tab, thinking exactly the opposite. A grown adult who had to move in with her brother and who could barely scrape together the cash for a minimalistic night on the town wasn't her idea of luck.

"Your brother. Lots of people don't have families like that."

Elizabeth spotted her sibling, in an animated discussion with the group in the corner. She loved when he got like this, all gestures and eyebrows, remnants from her childhood memories.

"Yeah, he's pretty great. We had to band together as kids for some pretty not great family reasons, though."

"Want a ride home? It doesn't look like Casey's interested in leaving any time soon."

"I do, but only if I can drive. I hardly know you, and I've got a son I plan on watching grow up."

"Sound thinking. Pit stop first. I'll be right back." He tossed her the keys before excusing himself, trusting she'd be around when he returned.

Elizabeth watched him saunter to the restrooms, the casual walk of a carefree person, or so it seemed.

Casey sidled up to her, the sheen of sweat on his forehead. "Justin behaving himself?"

"That he is. Even offered to escort me home. I took him up on it, by the way. I've seen the way you've been hanging all over that man with the curls and spectacular calves."

"I've been trying to get Otis into me for years, but nothing works. It's a habit at this point, fruitless but automatic. He sure is nice to look at, though. Speaking of hot..."

Justin exited the bathrooms and headed their way.

"Stop. He's nice."

"He comes with some baggage, sis, just saying."

"I can handle myself."

"That's what I'm afraid of," Casey said as Justin returned. Each second-guessed the intended recipient of his mile-wide smile.

"I'm ready when you are," Justin said. "See you later, Case."

"You better not drive home, Casey Blau. Every drink raises your blood alcohol .02 percent, and I lost count of your current ratio."

"I'll get a ride or crash at the Patels' place. Don't worry about me, Lizzy-beth."

On their way out the door, another group pressed in. The taller man leading the way caught Justin's shoulder with his own. He reached out to grab Justin's arm and spin him around. "Leaving so soon, Hart? I think you're forgetting something."

"A pleasure as always, Kade. You know we're meeting up next week."

"Don't be late," the man growled. A bulge in his lower lip belied a wad of chewing tobacco, a trimmed beard framing his cheekbones. He wore a navy, button-up shirt and black boots tipped in silver.

Kade gave Elizabeth a once-over, as she did the same. A slow smile ran across his face. "Hart. You didn't introduce me to your new friend."

"And he's not going to," Elizabeth retorted. One hand on the strap of her purse, the other clutching her keys, she assumed a position of defense. "We're leaving."

"The lady's wish is my command," Justin said. Tipping his hat, he followed her out.

"What an ass," Elizabeth said. "What did he mean by you forgetting something?"

"Oh, Kade Michaels and I go way back. Just some old business. He isn't exactly part of the Sheridan County welcome committee."

Elizabeth pushed the button on Justin's fob to unlock both doors and then climbed into the driver's seat. After adjusting the seat and the mirrors, she caught Justin watching her.

"What? I've got to see. You can put them back."

"It's not that. Been a long time since I've been alone in a truck with a woman, that's all."

"Don't get too excited, cowboy. Our first stop is to pick up my kid."

10

"GIFT ME WITH YOUR child again anytime," Jo said. "We loved having him."

"Is the sheriff still here?" They stood in the living room, looking on as Jo stooped to gather scattered toys and tuck them back into a wicker basket stationed in the corner.

"He was for a bit, but then he got a call to head out. Someone reported a campsite in the forest, tossed, abandoned car with Idaho plates. When there are only two of you in the whole county, you're on call night and day. I'm used to it after 28 years, though. Don't worry, he'll be by the school at some point to meet you."

Rhett pressed on the glass of a large fish tank in the living room, his eyes tracking the mollies and their fan tails.

"Thank you for this, again."

"Happy to have a little one to hang out with again. It's going to work out just fine. Let me know if there's anything he shouldn't eat or things like that so I can stock up."

"You don't have to go out of your way. I can send him with a lunch."

"Going out of her way is Jo's style. Hard to find someone kinder."

"Justin, you old flirt, you wait until Sheriff hears that."

"He knows it as well as I do."

Elizabeth said, "I better get this little cowboy to bed. Wait. I'm such an idiot."

"What?"

"The car seat. It's in Casey's truck."

"There's a spare in the garage," Jo said. "Just a sec."

In Jo's absence, Elizabeth watched Justin with Rhett. He'd crouched down to whisper with the little boy about the fish, pointing to each and naming them. She wondered about his ex, their decision, and hoped kids were in the cards for this man. A family.

"Got it!" Jo sang, returning to hand the seat to Justin.

"Jo, you are a lifesaver!"

"I've been called worse."

Down the road, she dropped Justin off at the gate to his ranch. In the moonlight, she could make out a long driveway angled north, a small shed about fifty feet from the road. A brief flicker from the shadows sparked like a lit cigarette then was gone. He waved off her offer to drive him up to the house, preferring the walk.

"How will you get your truck back?"

"If I can't get away, one of the hands will pick it up in the morning."

He's planning to be hung over, got it.

Justin stepped down out of the cab before leaning in to wave at Rhett. "See you soon, cowboy."

In her old habit, she reassured the audience. "He likes you."

"He's a cool dude. We'll have to hang again. I'd also like to see his mom, too, if that's all right. Just you and me. Thursday night?"

"I had fun. You have yourself a date."

Under the guise of safety, she watched him walk along his driveway until she could no longer tell him apart from the shadows.

When Elizabeth eased the truck into Casey's driveway a few minutes later, she saw a lamp click off in the house. *Odd*. Maybe Casey had one of those automatic lighting systems, the kind where you can set the mood with your phone.

With Rhett in tow, she made for the door. The latch made a kachunk sound when she inserted the key, the door already unlocked, and she stumbled forward into the dark house.

11

ICE RAN DOWN HER spine. Could someone have been there? Still be there?

Who to call? Casey was far from in a reliable state, but she sent him a text demanding he call as she debated what to do. Emergency services could be miles away. Jo? Maybe. Moving through the house, she turned on every light switch, making her way to the back of the place, clutching her son.

As she approached the hallway, she heard the faint snick of a door closing. Elizabeth froze. Whomever it was had been inside. Someone had been inside—and they were now outside. She strode to the back door, cranked hard on the deadbolt, and flipped on the porch light.

"It could be just a neighbor," she said to Rhett. "Someone borrowing sugar. Toilet paper. Totally innocent things."

After double-checking the rest of the doors and windows, all while humming a lullaby to calm herself as much as Rhett, they camped on the couch, waiting for Casey.

He stumbled in a half hour later. His clumsy attempt at matching the key to the lock followed by extensive swearing would have been a comical alert on any other night.

"Welcome home."

"Jesus, Liz!" He dropped his keys in surprise and stooped to fish them from the floor, hand sweeping the painted concrete.

"Someone was here. I know it. I heard them. *Inside.* What would they be doing in your house and just then running off like that? Who dropped you off? That would narrow our suspects."

"You are going to have to slow the hell down so I can process."

"Casey. Someone. Was. In. Your. House."

"I got that much, thanks. They here now?"

"They went out the back."

"You didn't see who?"

"No."

"Then how do you know?"

"I *heard* them. And saw the light go off."

Casey rubbed at his face with his right hand as if wiping the fog of beer and a night out from his brain. He fished a flashlight from a kitchen drawer. "I'll make sure the barn is buttoned up. You stay here, lock the back door behind me, and wait for me to get back, okay? It will only take a few minutes. If I don't come back, call the sheriff, and the ranch is yours."

Elizabeth waited by the window, vigilant. Each minute that passed chipped away at her sense of security.

Outside, moonlight seeped between the structures, high-lighting shapes. The few trees on her brother's property loomed over the landscape, their undersides a black, cavernous space. Elizabeth wondered how much property extended beyond the corrals, how far someone would have to run.

Casey's face loomed in front of the window, and she yelped. After closing the door and latching it behind him, she demanded, "Well?"

"The animals are fine, the gates are closed. There's a billion footprints out there. Might have been someone dropping something off." He took off his hat with one hand and scratched at his head, considering. "I'll take a better look in the morning. I need to sleep, Liz. I have a date with some aspirin."

Elizabeth turned back to the window as her brother shuffled down the hall. A shadow flickered behind his truck. She peered into the darkness but saw nothing beyond the light cast by the hallway light over her shoulder. Moths fluttered against the window, obscuring her view.

12

CASEY HAD FOUND NOTHING amiss in the morning light, told Elizabeth that people come by all the time to borrow tools, animal feed, or just see if anyone is around for a porch chat. More than likely, they'd realized it was Elizabeth and not Casey and left so as not to disturb her.

Elizabeth was too distracted by the long day ahead and her abhorrent lack of solid sleep to spend time dwelling, and after dropping Rhett off at the Wolfs', she'd committed to her workday.

Jo assured her the lights and heat in the schoolhouse were ready for occupation though a chill raised the goosebumps along Elizabeth's arms when she removed the giant parka. She hung it on the wooden peg rack and carried her bag to the large wooden relic of a desk. Hand-carved drawers opened to reveal paperclips, some broken pencils, and a vintage bell. The lower right drawer housed a bottle of wine with "For after. —Jo" on a card taped to the front. Elizabeth tucked her purse next to the bottle and unpacked the rest of her items on the desk.

Binder. Laptop. Was there wireless internet out here? Lunch, water bottle, and lip balm sat near a small vase of sunflowers—must have been Jo, Elizabeth mused—and a file folder decorated the rest of the scuffed and scarred surface.

Elizabeth cracked the file to find her class list, profiles, contact information, and assessment data on her students. The

Wi-Fi password, with a note that it was slow so not to hope for too much, was written on a sticky note affixed to the folder.

Flipping open the laptop and tapping in her password, Elizabeth connected with the outside world. A notification alerted her to an email from her mother-in-law. Elizabeth clicked a split second before her conscious self could stop her.

"You don't need to move halfway across the country to avoid your motherly duty. We are willing to pay for Rhett's care under the best doctors here in Portland, but we need you to bring him back so he can be with his family..."

Elizabeth closed the computer. "So you can take my son? No thank you."

Nick had been furious when she told him they were moving. Rather, that's what the process server told her after he delivered the paperwork. Started throwing things, yelling at the guy. A few court appointments later and she was given permission to move. To be with family, to escape Nick's influence—in this case they were one and the same.

She hadn't told the pediatrician about the fights but wondered if she should. Some internet searching paired with a bottle of pinot noir had convinced her that Nick's constant screaming at her absolutely could have been what kept their son silent long past the age when most babies are babbling, cooing, and crying, beyond when the first words tumble out of the gibberish. Guilt ate her up from the inside out, parasitical. It was too late to travel back in time and be the mother she should have been, stand up for herself, and leave earlier.

Elizabeth was lost in a self-shame spiral when scuffling footsteps on the welcome mat shook her back into the present. A familiar woman escorted a small, dark-haired boy in front of her. He peered up at Elizabeth under thick, dark lashes.

"Hello. Sorry we're early," the woman said. "Polly, Polly Michaels, from the Crow Bar?"

"Yes, hi, I remember you. Welcome! This is...?" Elizabeth smoothed her pants as she stood, brushing away thoughts of the past she'd left behind.

"Go ahead, hun, remember what we talked about."

"Benny," the child said, holding out his hand.

"Nice to meet you, Benny. Would you like to hang up your coat and backpack on the pegs and then choose a book to read? We've got a little bit longer until the other students show up."

Benny nodded at her, hugged his mom's legs, and followed the directives.

"He's really great," Polly started. "I'm not just saying that because I'm his mom. We've had a hard time with things, but he's always loved reading. I have Jo to thank for getting that big grant for all the books. She's really done so much for these kids. Shame she never got to be a mom. Natural-born, you know?"

Elizabeth nodded. Everyone around knowing your reproductive business didn't seem to be an issue, and she was beginning to understand how much Jo Wolf was the heartbeat of the area.

"Again, sorry we were early. Wasn't sure the car would make it. I wanted to be ahead in case we needed to get a ride. Taking it into town today before my shift."

"Where do you go? Mine picked up a rattle on the drive over the passes, and I've been avoiding the inevitable."

"Kade's shop, on Coffeen. Big sign. You won't miss it."

"I met him at the Crow Bar. Well, sort of." She remembered the man who'd shoulder-checked Justin, the icy glare, the threat in his words.

"He's not that bad when you get to know him. A good mechanic, fair, and mostly quick about it."

"Well, thanks for the recommendation," Elizabeth said, unsure if she meant it.

"If I am not back to pick Benny up at the end of the day, he can always go home with the Ramirez twins. Mirabel watches him the nights I have to work."

"Got it."

"Willing to hear me out on one more piece of advice?"

"Sure." Elizabeth liked Polly. Beneath her worn appearance was a hunger, a countenance that didn't miss a beat. She tried to picture her in a city like Seattle: slim, black pants with flats, an electric car, a job in a skyscraper.

"Think twice about Justin. He's a heartbreaker."

13

BEFORE ELIZABETH COULD SPLUTTER out a reply, Polly slipped out the exit and was replaced with a bustling arrival of her other students. A short tour followed introductions, then the kids were back in their seats, staring at her. Expectant.

Three girls, two boys. The Ramirez twins were five, fraternal, and very into horses. In contrast, Rachel Nelson, a precocious seven-year-old, dreamed of being a fashion designer in New York. Ashton, also five, wanted nothing more than to be on the farm with his dad. Natasha Nelson confided he was not the most motivated in school. Elizabeth sat Ashton near Benny, curious if the pair were destined to become friends.

Five kids, one her, all subjects. Elizabeth taught high school back home, biology. In Washington, she corrected herself, this was home now. Here, she was an elementary teacher.

"How about we start with science?" The students cheered and filed out into the waning autumnal sunshine. Elizabeth handed each of her charges a circle of string, a clipboard, and a pencil. She watched Rachel carefully set out her circlet before sketching the contents of its enclosure. Benny and Ashton followed her lead, circles in the grass. The twins took a different route. One hung her string on a bush to sketch an abandoned spider web within while the other used her loop for a game of cat's cradle.

The students settled in, sketching their shapes of leaves, stones, and other bits they found in the grass. At Elizabeth's prompting, they added labels or first letter sounds to objects in their drawings. A cloud of dust signaled a car approaching the motley crew.

Justin. An internal flutter in Elizabeth's chest, anticipation running hot through her veins.

The last year of dealing with the end of Nick wore her out. Constantly anticipating the smell of another woman on his skin when he rolled into bed hours after she gave up on him coming home. Her doctor's face when she gave Elizabeth the prescription for an antibiotic, apologetic and pitying. The last months before she left, fighting alternating with silence, a relationship distilled to paperwork. Elizabeth had been with one man those eight years. Would she be willing to risk that mess again?

The way her insides turned to jelly when Justin stepped out of his truck was a clear sign that her body wanted in, even if her mind was still catching up.

Justin waved before turning to grab something in the backseat. She traced the lines of his body, the muscles under tight jeans and his work shirt used to stacking hay bales and pounding fence posts. Work for which a body is designed.

He turned around, holding something behind his back, a shy smile on his face. Crows' feet betrayed the years squinting at sunsets and a nick from the morning's shave left a tiny rent on an otherwise perfect jawline. *Hold on now*, she warned herself, *it's not like you know anything about him.*

"Hello," he said, on approach to her. "Hey, Benny. Ashton."

The boys smiled hellos, then went back to poking at the dirt.

"Hi," Elizabeth said. "I don't think we have a desk your size, but I can check with Jo."

"Could you? I meant to have these out before you got here, but I got hung up at the ranch. I hope the thought still counts."

From behind his back, he revealed a small bouquet in a green glass vase. A half dozen wild roses grouped together in a burst of summer pink.

"Thank you, these are beautiful."

"I thought they would be a cheerful welcome for your desk."

"They will, thank you. They're perfect. Normally, I'd invite a fella inside to meet my daddy, but..."

"I gotcha," Justin said, shifting his weight from one foot to the other. "I'm not here to disrupt the learning. We've got goats who need milking, and you have a great day ahead of you. I just wanted to wish you luck and make sure Thursday still works."

"It does. And thank you, again. This was really sweet."

"I am nothing if not sweet." He tipped his hat to the kids and climbed back into his pickup.

Breathe, Elizabeth thought. She watched as his truck disappeared down the road. "Rosa woodsii," she whispered.

Rachel Nelson sidled up to her as she stared after Justin. "What did you say, Ms. Blau?"

"Just the scientific name for these flowers."

"We always call them prairie roses."

"Did you know all living things have a scientific name? Let's all go inside. You can tell me what you call the things you found, and I can tell you the scientific names."

As she rounded up the children, Elizabeth looked out toward the prairie. The vast hills glowed a faded gold, the slide of summer into fall long since gone, winter not far off. Thinking back to her urban school, the fire alarms, the lock down drills, the day the water main burst...these students would never experience that kind of drama. She made a note to ask Jo about a landline phone as she ushered the last student inside. Wind whipped at her hair as she admitted to herself that the school's isolation was both beautiful and spooky.

The rest of the day was a flurry of talking and papers, snack time and books. Elizabeth read to the students from *Treasure Island* as they waited for parent pick-up. She realized she was smiling, big time. Not only had they made it through the day, but she liked them and thought they might like her. This could work out.

Mrs. Ramirez was the first to collect her children, talking into an earbud tucked in one ear about deliveries while tugging coats onto the twins before coaxing them out the door. She mouthed *thank you* to Elizabeth, pointing to the device in her ear.

The Nelsons left on the back of a quad, their father nestling them amongst his hunting gear. Elizabeth sat on the squat front porch with Benny to wait.

"She's always late," the boy lamented while Elizabeth worried she should have sent him home with the twins.

"It's not a problem. I don't mind waiting."

"Do you have kids?"

"I do. Jo Wolf is watching my son while I'm at work."

The boy nodded, understanding the role of babysitter. "How old is he?"

"Almost two. He loves animals."

"Me, too. We would get along."

"I bet you would. What's your favorite animal?"

The boy considered her question, solemn expression furrowing his brow. "I used to like horses, but now I am into koalas."

Polly rolled into the driveway in a faded maroon sedan, leaving the car idling as she hopped out. "So sorry, little man. Mirabel told me you stayed behind."

"It's okay, we were just talking about our favorite animals. Ms. Blau has a son, too."

"I super appreciate your watching him," Polly said to Elizabeth. "We lost a server to the new brewery in Casper, and I picked up the day shift to cover."

"We had a good chat, got to know each other a bit. I should get to my own son, though. Thanks for the chat, Benny."

"You're welcome."

Mother and son walked toward their car, hand in hand. Elizabeth was curious about their story but knew it was too soon to ask. Boundaries, she reminded herself.

She'd stacked Polly's warning about Justin atop the one from Casey. They were looking out for her, people who knew the area and its inhabitants. Yet, there was something jagged in their cautionary missives, something hinted at but unspoken.

14

O N WEDNESDAY EVENING, ELIZABETH headed north along the highway. Dwight Yoakam on the radio, her hands tapped out the rhythm on the steering wheel as she sang along to the album.

With Polly's directions, the shop wasn't hard to find. Sheridan in autumn was quiet, wind kicking up dried leaves as people greeted each other at the bank, the feed store, and the grocers, starting each conversation by predicting their first blizzard.

Hydraulics accosted her ears as Elizabeth parked in front of the triple bays and made her way to the office door. She'd donned an oversized, burnt orange sweater over leggings, heeled boots that gave her a few more inches. Faded leather satchel in hand, a set of beaded bracelets circled her wrist. While she hadn't dressed up for the encounter, she'd taken care to look polished, flinty. Taller.

Kade surfaced from the depths of the garage, wiping at his hands with a rag, while sounds of tinkering continued behind him.

"Can I help you?" He squinted into the sunlight, the flicker of recognition evident in his smirk.

"I hope so. With my car. Polly Michaels referred you. The mother of one of my students. She must be your..."

"Cousin."

"You're Benny's uncle."

"That's usually how those things work. What's going on with your car?"

"I need my brake pads changed, and there's a rattle in the steering column. I'm a thousand miles away from my usual shop, so I'm hoping you can help."

"Haven't met one I couldn't fix yet." An accompanying wink caused her upper lip to twitch.

"Glad the sign isn't a ruse."

Initial impressions had been less than stellar, and this exchange wasn't helping. His animosity the other night had put her on edge. Animals with something to prove don't react well to being cornered, but she needed a mechanic.

"Funny. Look, I'm not sure what else you've heard, but I'm the best in the county. The state, likely. I'll give it a look, but I won't be able to work on it until tomorrow, Friday at the latest. Can you come back, or do you want to leave it?"

"I'll leave it. Clint is going to give me a ride back to Banner."

Kade pulled a fresh form from a rack by the door and began filling out the boxes.

Elizabeth withdrew the card from her bag on which Jo had scribbled a phone number and tapped at her phone. Casey had offered to pick her up, but Jo had insisted she try the sheriff first as it would get him home for dinner on time.

After two rings, a gruff voice picked up. "You the teacher?"

"I...I, uh. Hello. Yes. This is Elizabeth Blau. I'm at Kade's garage. I'd love a pick-up if it still works with your schedule."

"Be there in five," he said, and hung up without waiting for a reply.

Kade slid paperwork her way along with a pen emblazoned with the name of his shop. His brows lifted when the recognizable voice came through the speaker of her phone. Better to be associated with the good guys when dealing with the questionable, she reckoned.

As she filled out her details with Casey's address, Elizabeth did some mental math. Calculating when his bill would come due relative to the receipt of her first paycheck made her head spin. When she handed back the pen, their hands touched in a spark, his warm and dry, hers clammy.

"I'll call you after we take a look, give you an estimate. You can give me the go ahead then."

"Thanks." Elizabeth had one hand on the glass window of the door, watching for the cruiser to pull into the lot.

"Maybe I'll see you at the bar again," he said. Kade tapped the paperwork on the table to align the edges and ducked into the office before she could reply. "Pay off my tab."

Kade had recognized her.

⟞⟝

A long, low patrol car lumbered over the curb outside, and the driver climbed out. The county emblem on the door paired with the lights on top pointed toward this being her ride. Sheriff Wolf himself had walked off the pages of a western magazine—bushy mustache, iron-creased slacks, badge, giant belt buckle, and a hitch in his stride to match.

Must have been a bull rider.

"Elizabeth," she said. "Thanks for coming to get me."

Wolf took the hand she extended and shook it once, with precision. "Clint." He lifted his chin in Kade's direction, a silent hello, before wedging himself back into the vehicle.

Elizabeth guessed the front seat was fine in a non-official context and popped the door open. She tried to ignore the humming and static of the machinery around her, a laptop mounted to the dash.

"Buckle up," he said, turning the thin leather-wrapped steering wheel between his hands. Elizabeth saw a thick gold band over rough knuckles, a half dozen tiny scars on his right hand. He straightened his sunglasses before flicking the turn signal, and they were off.

The first mile extended ahead, an asphalt carpet of relative silence. A herd of antelope nibbled in a field by the college as a hawk scanned for rodents from its perch on a telephone pole.

Elizabeth wondered how the landscape would change under the ever-present thick blanket of winter. Bleak and white, covering and exposing the landscape for what it was: vast.

"Jo tells me you've been the sheriff for decades now. You must know this place like the back of your hand. All twenty-five-hundred square miles of it."

"That's the truth."

"I'm guessing that's either boring because not much happens out here or interesting because whatever does happen, you're the one they call."

"You've got the long and short of it."

Tough nut to crack, but Elizabeth wouldn't stop fishing. "Bet you know everyone's secrets, too."

Sunglasses masked Wolf's expression as he shifted a wad in his mouth to the other side and spat in a bottle freed from the cupholder.

"If you're talking about your brother, there's nothing to worry about."

"Why would there be?"

"Casey's different. That's just fine with us, with you, but not everyone. Don't worry, though. Nothing gets past me in this county."

"I gotcha."

They'd reached the part of the drive that was all hills and ranches, harvested fields now dormant until next season. She stared out the window, counting the horses as they drove by.

"Before we get home, I need to thank you," he began.

"It's me who needs to thank you for this ride."

"I'm thanking you for bringing your boy to the house. Rhett. For Jo. We tried a long time, you see. Kids have always brought her joy. It's hard to find an adult she hasn't mothered in these parts, but it's not the same. She would have loved grandkids, you know? Our own. Would have been the best at it, but we play the hands we're dealt." His eyes watched the road while his mind time-walked through the past.

"Rhett likes her, I can tell. He's a good judge of character."

Clint nodded, satisfied at their mutual understanding as the miles clicked by on the dash.

The Wolf house came into view. Two stories, brick-colored siding, and a steeply slanted roof. The red shale driveway looked as though it had been raked. Twice.

Jo opened the door, Rhett in her arms. He reached for Elizabeth, and the older woman handed him over.

"He's been such a peach today. We looked at every hunting guide around the house—but don't worry, only the before pictures." The woman handed one of the brochures to Elizabeth, a majestic elk on the cover.

"He loves the animals at the farm, especially Casey's baby goats," Elizabeth said. "Not sure how much he'll get into hunting."

"Some do, some don't. With grocery stores at every corner now, folks have a choice."

Clint headed inside, pausing to set his hat on the end table, brim up. The smell of something savory and homemade filled Elizabeth's nostrils, and her stomach rumbled.

"Would you two like to stay for supper?"

"That's very nice of you, but I think Casey would smell it on me, and I'd never be forgiven. He's attempting some kind of ragout tonight."

"A raincheck, then. Bring Casey with you. Oh, and Elizabeth—"

The woman handed her Rhett's diaper bag.

"Hmm?"

She stepped outside onto the welcome mat and pulled the door nearly closed behind her. "Thank you for this. I mean, for letting us keep an eye on Rhett. Clint always wanted a full house and, well..."

Elizabeth looked into the face of her neighbor and saw the same look she'd seen earlier on the sheriff. Love and longing, stress and acceptance.

"Jo, I don't know what I would do without you, truly. Rhett gets bored with just me to deal with all day long, right bud?"

"Okay, partner," Jo said to Rhett, brushing at this cheek. "Tomorrow, we move on to the ungulates."

The toddler returned the woman's smile and then leaned into Elizabeth's shoulder as they walked down the driveway.

"Tired from a big day? You, sir," she said to Rhett, "are pretty popular in that household."

As she walked the half mile home, Elizabeth considered the progress of her first week. She'd reconnected with her brother, Rhett was at the safest daycare situation in the county, and she was able to breathe in the distance she'd created from the drama back home. Could this life, this space on the plains, become a new normal?

15

AN AUTUMNAL WIND SWIRLED around her shoulders, and she hugged Rhett closer, wrapping the wings of her coat around him. Elizabeth would need more layers for the promised heavy snows.

Jo had offered to drive Elizabeth home, but she'd looked forward to the walk. Ten minutes of fresh air was good for the soul. A walk was another way of prolonging the space between now and when she would have to sit down and talk with her son's father. A barrage of texts had come through while she was at the shop, and she could only get away with ignoring them for so long.

Rhett reached up to grab at the ends of her braids. She watched his faraway look, as though soothing himself through the gesture. What did he think of their new arrangement? She wished she could ask, sometimes, wished he could answer her.

The scene from Nick's apartment the day before they'd left replayed in her mind, a confirmation she reminded herself of whenever second-guessing her upheaval. A pizza box, open on the dining table, beer bottles on every surface, Elvis Costello blaring through the speakers. Her son sat by himself in the middle of the couch, babysat by cartoons on the screen of his father's phone while its owner showered, oblivious to the scene.

She hadn't yelled that time, hadn't bothered. She'd picked up Rhett, sent Nick a text, and locked the door behind her as she left, the water still running in the bathroom. And now here she was, walking a dusty road in an all-but-empty state, a blessed thousand miles away.

Her toe caught a rock lodged in the dirt, and Elizabeth stumbled, managing to right herself but not without scaring Rhett. The fright on his face crumpled her resolve.

Hugging him closely, tears flowed. Leaving Nick was hard, and she still wasn't sure it was the right thing, however much of a lying cheater he'd proved to be. When they'd married, she'd believed all the promises, believed all the storybooks. She made a habit of believing him for years, even when his lies were blatant, and it's hard to stop doing a thing once you've made it a part of you. Bad things wouldn't happen to good people—until they did.

Caught up in her self-pity, she almost missed the flash of movement in her periphery. This stretch of road had a few dips where gullies ran with stormwater but were dry now, lined with browned sedges. Pink—or purple?—was an unusual color to spot in their depths.

"Hello?"

Elizabeth felt foolish as soon as the words left her mouth. There was no one out here.

Nick had tried to throw that exact fact at her when he called twenty minutes after she'd left his apartment that spring day, heated and vengeful.

"There's nothing out there. You tell me I am the one not doing anything to help our son, but you are the one taking him far away from any kind of specialist that could help him. Taking him away from his father."

"His father who leaves a baby alone while he washes the stink of his latest conquest off his body."

"Don't make this about your jealousy."

She spluttered, "You're dreaming. Been there, had that. I am doing what's best for Rhett and me, and if that no longer includes you, maybe that's for the better."

Only later that same night, after the anger had dissipated, heartache flooded in behind. Elizabeth admitted to herself that she didn't know what was best for her son, couldn't know. What if taking him away from Nick, no matter how much of a piece of work the man could be, would mess him up somehow, make things worse?

Another flicker in the grasses, this time a glint of metal. Elizabeth was certain something was out there. Had to be a cow, she thought, left behind from its herd, or a deer. Still, she quickened her pace.

Her brother's truck waited in the driveway, another familiar vehicle parked next to it.

She rounded the house to find Casey and Justin in the deep, wooden chairs. Sleeves rolled up and beers in hand, they were silent and contemplative, facing west. A beat after Casey registered their arrival, his face rearranged itself into a wide smile.

"There's my favorite nephew! How are things? Give me some skin." He'd taken to giving Rhett a modified fist bump, a cute gesture she was desperate to catch on video.

"Hey, Elizabeth," Justin said, putting a bottle to his lips. "Glad to catch you."

"Happy to be caught." Too obvious, Elizabeth chided herself. "We walked from the Wolfs'."

Casey spat on the ground, put fisted hands on his hips. "You didn't fly, that's for sure. How are they?"

"Good. I hadn't met the sheriff—Clint—before. Seems decent, quiet."

"He's all right," Casey replied.

"I'm just glad they're close by," Elizabeth said.

"A little too close, sometimes," Justin murmured.

"It's too bad they didn't have kids of their own," Casey mused. "Jo's family is down in Denver. Her sister, I think. Anyway, they have a whole collection of nieces and nephews."

"Sounds like it wasn't in the cards for them."

"Shame."

"Hey, you aren't missing any goats, are you?"

"Nope, Justin and I were just doing the deworming, and all were accounted for. Had you been here a half hour ago, it would have been a different scene with the goats all kicking at each other and us, eager to be done with it and get to bed. Why?"

"I just thought I saw something, an animal, in the brush on the walk back."

"Probably a deer."

"Or maybe a hunter," Justin added. "They should be wearing orange, though."

"Not pink? Or purple?"

"You can wear whatever colors you want, stripes and polka dots if you like, as long as blaze orange is part of the outfit."

"That a fact?"

"Not everyone follows the law, though," Casey interjected, interrupting their flirtation.

"True enough."

"I guess as long as it isn't a bear, I won't worry."

"It's a good idea to keep an eye out, regardless." Her brother removed a hiker's backpack from a hook on the wall and rummaged through its contents. He handed a canister to Elizabeth. "Bear spray for your next walk, in case. I'll get another canister."

"Those only shoot thirty feet. Am I supposed to wait for a bear to get that close? You two are making me question my illusion of safety, living way out here."

"Just keeping you prepared. When will Kade have old Betsy fixed up?"

"He'll call tomorrow after he takes a look. It has to be the brakes again."

"I'm headed to Bozeman to meet with a restaurant owner this weekend, but I bet Justin here would be happy to run you over to pick up your car if it's ready before I get back."

Justin didn't look as ready as promised. His jaw was tight as he swallowed the dregs of his bottle before wiping at this mouth with the back of his hand.

"Thank you, both of you," Elizabeth said, sure she'd missed a nuance of backstory. For a small town, where everything was out in the great wide open, there sure were a lot of secret undercurrents. "Clint can take me back, too. He offered."

"Clint?" Casey snickered. "On a first name basis with the sheriff, I see."

"What do you call the man?"

"Sheriff Wolf, of course."

"Seeing as how I don't intend to need his official services, Clint works for me." She went from new resident to an outsider again in a span of ten minutes.

"Aw, Liz, don't mind us, we're just teasing. I'm going out to test the new motion light. Back in a couple." Casey gave her a knowing look that slid over to Justin before he ducked into the barn.

"I ought to be headed back to my own place. Been here just about all day, it seems like." The evidence was all over Justin's clothes in the form of dust and mulch in every crease and a few pieces of hay sticking out of his hair. He got up from the deep recesses of the chair and reached for his hat, upended by his feet.

Without looking at her, he ran the hat brim through his hands and said, "I'm happy to take you to get your car. It's not a problem. Me and Kade just don't get on well. Been that way since high school, really."

Elizabeth remembered the scene from the Crow Bar. Saw the tension in Justin's shoulders.

"I'll figure it out. Really, it's fine. I appreciate the offer, though."

"Thursday is still good?"

"Sure is."

16

CASEY RETURNED AT THE sound of Justin's truck engine starting up, having taken his time inspecting his new external lighting.

"So," he teased, "made it to first base yet?"

"Funny. I didn't think you thought Justin and I together was a good idea."

"Does any brother think their sister plus a rich cowboy with a killer smile is a good idea?"

"Point. Wait, rich?"

"In cattle baron terms, yes, as far as that kind of thing goes. Justin Hart inherited the bulk of the operations from his dad. They also stud horses out there. When his mother shuffles off this mortal coil, he will own the whole place, lock, stock, and barrel."

"I had no idea. He seems so..."

"Idle? Without a care in the world? I've known him a while now and can vouch that some of that is the pleasure of not having to work too hard for your supper, but most of it is just who he is. He never struck me as the eager, ambitious type. In fact, I think he worked to hide most of that from me when we were at school. Better not let on that I told you. It will come out, just not likely on your first date."

"Don't worry. I'll just give him the usual line about my curfew and Granddaddy's loaded rifle waiting. Not to mention the single mother thing."

"Painting an accurate picture never hurts. While you two are out on the town, me and my little deputy will get out the brushes and give the nannies a spa night. They deserve one."

"Then again, maybe I'll stay here. This nanny could use a spa night. Speaking of night, do the barn lights work?"

"They do. Everything seems fine. I'm not too worried about it, but I am considering the purchase of a couple of alpacas. They act kind of like guard dogs for the herd. Might be a good idea to have them around, deterring predators. I also think I'll install a camera out there, see what wildlife action we get."

"I bet Rhett would like that. The llamas and the video."

"Speaking of Rhett, Jo offered to feed us boys supper tomorrow night while you're out on your hot date."

"She adores him, that much is clear."

"What am I, too past the little and cute stage to be appreciated for my own merits?"

"Each of the Wolfs told me the other was disappointed they didn't have kids, that's all."

"If you want to bring out the latent fierceness in Jo, just threaten one of the dozens of her surrogate kids around here. She took me right in when I followed Justin out here after college, unsure what a gay man in rural Wyoming was going to do with a double major in business and architecture. She listened, more than anyone else would, and she never asked me to be anyone else."

"Must make for huge Thanksgiving tables."

"Absolutely. Sheriff has to work most holidays, so she takes turns visiting all of us. Make no mistake, though, the sheriff is just as fierce a protector, especially when it comes to kids."

"Then I'll rest easier knowing I'm likely family by proxy," she teased.

Outside, the new motion light snapped on.

17

The contents of Elizabeth's two suitcases-worth of clothes lay strewn about the room. Rhett sat in a pile of tops, lifting the fabric and draping the silkier ones over his face. He tumbled back onto the blankets, and she floated a large silk scarf overhead. As it fluttered, he reached for it, eyes pinched in glee when she snatched it away last minute only to float it above him again.

The typical baby babbling hadn't come and certainly hadn't transformed into the dozens of words he should know by now. He made faint gurgles, sighs, but they didn't register much. Nick was right, it was time to start hunting for a specialist, especially if she planned to stay. Maybe Billings would have one, it was the closest big city.

She replaced the scarf he clutched with a black lace poncho, his eyes visible between the stitching. Rhett looked like a miniature mourner, she thought, as he stroked the dark fabric, shifting the holes.

After rejecting her jeans as inauthentic and boots as cliché, she moved on to her dresses. Casey vetoed a sleeveless floral for a navy stripe. "It's September, you'd freeze in a strapless."

Tires crunching rocks in the driveway forced Elizabeth to snag some flats before kissing Rhett on her way out the door. "Thanks for babysitting!"

"Don't do anything I wouldn't do," Casey called behind her, waving to Justin inside the pickup.

The inside of the truck cab was warm, amplifying the coziness of proximity to Justin. He turned down the volume of the radio and said, "Thanks for coming. You look great."

Elizabeth didn't know if it was the heady scent of his cologne or the crease in his jeans, but she would kiss this man tonight.

On the drive to Buffalo, Justin told her about his father, his love of riding over open range, and a heart attack that came too early. "He was Mom's rock. I still don't think she knows what to do with him gone. Puts most of that energy into hounding me, seems like."

"Her way of dealing with grief?"

"I think they'd given up on kids, figured it would just be the two of them when I came along. My mom had a whole troop of Scottish terriers, and my dad raised horses, so they had plenty of hobbies. I think I remind her of a time when she had everything, which only makes her think of how much she's lost with him gone."

"I know a little bit about having a son, and I can tell you that your heart is given away the moment you meet, no matter what. How did the Scotties take being shoved down the line?"

Justin laughed. "They made me a somewhat hairless member of their pack, from what I remember. Like a runt. They'd always bring me their toys to play with, share their treats."

"I think that sounds...a little like the *Jungle Book*. But in a sweet way."

"They were older parents. I didn't have any siblings, and around here, we don't exactly have neighbors in the traditional sense. The dogs were better than nothing, easy. I loved them, actually. Broke my heart whenever we'd sell the litters."

"Some people would trade their brother or sister for a golden retriever. Heck, I'd consider it."

"Trade Casey? You can't mean that."

"Nah, you're right. He was a good brother, better than most, especially knowing what we had to work with at home. What he had to put up with."

"He never said much about them. About you. I always wondered. Said it was complicated when I asked."

"He wasn't wrong. My father was an angry man who drank his feelings, and my mom coped with painkillers she claimed were for fibromyalgia. Vacant most nights, volatile on the worst. Not the most horrible humans but far from great. Casey got out of there as soon as he could, and I did the same."

"Both of you have done well, despite not getting much support."

"Good enough, I suppose. I'm impressed with Casey's whole set-up. The design work and the goats. Teaching isn't nearly as glamorous, but it has rewards."

"I heard you have a second means of employment. Casey said you were talking about starting up with brewing again?"

"We've talked about it," she replied. About all she could afford was talking about it.

18

J USTIN NAVIGATED THE THRIVING, quaint Main Street on which the Occidental Hotel had held court for nearly a century and a half.

The building loomed over the western side of the street, a two-story brick expanse fronted with striped awning and wrapped with cornices. Elizabeth could hear the music seeping through the doors before they stepped into the snug front parlor, bluegrass calling her name like an old friend.

As they wound their way through the crowd in the bar, people tucked into every nook and cranny, Justin was hailed by every other person they passed. Older folks clasped his hand, asked after his horses. Elizabeth watched the older women blush at his attention as Justin switched from soft and welcoming to serious and rigid depending on the conversation. He knew how to work a crowd: flexible, attentive, ready. He ruffled the hair of a few kids who danced and wove their way among the adults, righting a chair they toppled in their game. She was on a date with a popular man. The warnings of Kade, Polly, and her brother didn't track with what was his very public persona.

Justin nabbed a tiny table in the back of the long room under a collage of former diners shaking hands with the owner, rodeo posters, and the head of an antelope mounted above their heads on the wall. Moments after they'd wedged themselves into the seats, a sweaty waitress with a pen behind each ear sidled up to them.

"Justin! It's been way too long. How are ya? Are you playing tonight?"

"Not tonight. You know how things get," he replied. Elizabeth was only just starting to understand what he meant.

"That I do. If it's not one thing on a ranch, it's another. Who do we have here?"

"This is Elizabeth, Casey's sister."

"Blau?"

"That's the one," Elizabeth said, extending a hand. "Nice to meet you."

"Likewise. I'm Tessa," the woman replied. "Your brother helped us figure out what to do with all the junk we found in the basement. Refurbished some, sold the rest. Now we get to call them antiques.

Elizabeth laughed as Tessa waggled her eyebrows. "My brother's good like that."

"That he is. What'll it be tonight? The soup is corn chowder, and we have chicken fried steak on special."

"Two specials, please."

Twenty minutes later, they had two hot plates in front of them, steaming with a heavenly aroma. Elizabeth and Justin watched the crowd as they chewed, a natural pause in their conversation. Musicians, returning from a break, surrounded the stage with chairs, with a few choosing to stand near the back, tuning up together. The twang and hum of plucked strings tuning up filled the room. Diners caught on, nudging each other to focus up front. An announcer took the mic to welcome the crowd.

Elizabeth took in the room. An ancient, mirror-backed bar banked one wall, with countless bottles lining its shelves and people parked on every available stool. A jumble of chairs crowded around and between the tables. Finding a seat was a fight for prime real estate with proximity to the sound. The place was elbow-to-elbow people, willing sardines, leaning in as the concert began.

An opening reel kicked off the night, followed by a blue-grass tune. Toes tapped, heads nodded, and a collection jar was passed among the table, church-like. The emcee explained its role in funding music scholarships, and Elizabeth added a few dollars as it came by. She saw Justin tuck in a hundred-dollar bill.

Justin lost himself in the music. He eased back into his chair, one arm over the side, jaw relaxed, eyes closing as he drummed the beat onto the tabletop with a finger. He loved this corner of the world, it was clear, and that glow drew Elizabeth to his flame.

As she watched him, he opened his eyes to meet hers. He reached his drumming hand over to where hers lay on the tabletop and drew it to his lips. The quick brush of softness across the back of her hand sent her insides smoking.

Musicians rotated in and out of the group in some pre-arranged order, players taking breaks, swapping roles, or otherwise serving a part in the revolution of sound. When the current band iteration started in on *Cripple Creek*, Justin stood, his chair teetering between their table and the next. He held out his hand and bent toward her. "Care to dance?"

Elizabeth summoned the bravery of the two merlots downed earlier and followed him to the thin strip of floor saved for dancers and the waitstaff. The latter took the service complications in stride, deft at dodging people while carrying trays of plates, precarious in their hands.

His touch at the small of her back was light but warm. Elizabeth stepped close, willed the floorboards to keep her upright, steady. Two other couples joined them, touring the lane of space through focused maneuvers.

The song ended with the draw of a bow. Breathing labored, Elizabeth made for her abandoned water glass.

"You all right?"

"I am. Just winded. I haven't danced like that in, well, ever. It was great."

"Good." His cheer was genuine, reaching the corner of his eyes. "Again?"

A waltz took shape through the string work of fiddles, a mandolin, and a gigantic bass, wielded by a man in a vest and bolo tie. Elizabeth considered Justin's offer for the space of a heartbeat before putting her hand in his and following him back onto the floor. This time, he pulled her into his chest, her left hand on his shoulder, her right hand cradled in his left. He smelled like fresh hay, leather, and soap. Elizabeth, inhaling the scent of him, willed the memory to lodge in her conscious mind to unpack and revel in later.

At some point, she closed her eyes, allowing the music to guide their movement, trusting Justin to support them, and gave in to the moment. For a few minutes, she wasn't a broke schoolteacher, couch-surfing at her brother's house while fighting her ex-husband over what was best for their silent toddler. She was in the arms of a cowboy, a romance novel come to life.

Elizabeth opened her eyes to meet the menacing stare of a blonde woman at the outskirts of the crowd. A hot pink tank top, tanning bed glow, and a glare that would freeze the sun were all Elizabeth registered before the face was gone. Where had she seen her before?

19

WHEN THE SONG ENDED, Justin offered a tour of the old hotel, and she took the hand he offered. The highlight was the creekfront lawn out the back door, no pink tank top in sight.

Clear Creek bisected Main Street, and a long expanse of grass ran up to its edge. Other couples, stray groups of smokers, and the kids, warm from the stuffy interior, spread out along the lawn, enjoying the night. Elizabeth and Justin walked to the lip of the rock wall to peer at the water running below them.

"Any fish in here?"

"Some," Justin said.

"When I was a kid, I always wished I was a salmon, swimming all day, few worries, shiny scales."

"You make it sound like a good life. I'd have to wave from the banks, though. I'm afraid of the water."

"Afraid?"

"Can't swim. One year, we took innertubes into the creek. I got caught in a current and my tube flipped. The current pinned me underwater. I flailed around and Mom pulled me up and out—I think I was three. Haven't been in it since."

As if in reflex, Elizabeth took a step backward, away from the rushing water. "That must have been frightening."

"Shook me up something fierce. Mom, too. I'm better with both feet on land, thank you very much."

"You're a good dancer."

"Wouldn't be, without a good partner," Justin teased with two piercing, caramel-colored eyes. "Should we get out of here?"

"Do we need to say goodbye to all your adoring fans?" Elizabeth hoped her tone was playful, but she didn't want a run-in with Pink Tank Top to ruin their night.

"Nah. I know a back way out. Come on."

He took her hand again, a soft tug steering her through the crowd.

When was the last time she held hands with someone? Hell, been flirted with? Nick had stopped long before she left. She'd forgotten what touch meant. Could mean.

Elizabeth's mind ran away with her focus, wanting to both lose herself to the dizzy feeling and rein it in at the same time.

Eight years she'd devoted to Nick. They'd been in the same dorm; she remembered him as part of the group that would take over the rec room for tailgating, making any other activity impossible. Her sophomore year, they'd been in a British Literature class together. Feminist, she'd thought, when he complained that all they read were dead, old, white men. Now she knew he didn't understand the material, it was just a line he'd picked up.

It was easy to dip into her trusty well of contempt now, she knew. Now, they had history, a son, and a lot of anger between them. Back then, they were young, she was trusting, and he was cute.

A light squeeze of her hand brought her back to the present.

"Where'd you go just now?"

"Uh, I uh...was just thinking about the moon. It's waning."

At the truck, he held open the passenger door. The silver crescent rose over his right shoulder, dwarfing the streetlights. For a heartbeat, she locked this man, this moment, in her memory. One could restart, she confirmed. It was never too late.

"They say the galaxy is a big place."

"Big enough for all our memories, and then some."

"I'm a good listener," he said before closing her door and walking around the truck to his own.

"I guess I was thinking how it's funny how the past catches up to you, reminds you that you left parts of it behind. Like an unpaid debt."

"You're on to something there. When we try to outrun our history, I think all we do is open ourselves up to a surprise visit when a reminder comes knocking."

Justin was right. Elizabeth had moved several states away from her baggage and still worked to shake off Nick and his mother.

"Right about now, the Oregon Trail is sounding pretty appealing. Two thousand miles with no technology, all open roads with minimal traffic..."

"...no grocery stores, raiders, and don't forget dying of dysentery."

Laughter was the medicine she needed to shake the guilt of old decisions. "How well do you think you would have done a hundred years ago?"

"Are we talking about the video game or the cross-country trek?" Justin watched the road as he drove, though it was late for deer. Most would have found a spot in tall grasses, rolling out circles with their soft bodies, tucking in for the night. Coyotes, mountain lions, and even bears were about, though, often hunting in the night.

"The actual gig. Oxen, rations, and everything."

"I think I'd be all right. I'm decent with animals, and I can handle being in a saddle for days. Not too keen on rattlesnakes, though. You?"

"Pretty sure I'd love it. Hours of time to read, plenty of quiet, and nothing better to do but enjoy wide, open spaces. Sounds heavenly."

Justin turned his truck down the long, dirt road. He paused as they approached Hart ranch. Elizabeth bit her lower lip, disappointed the night was about to end and wishing for an extension, to dally in this dreamland.

"Can I walk you home?"

"If you can find the place in the dark. All the houses out here look the same."

He had the kind of deep belly laugh she wanted to hear everyday. *Easy, Liz. Don't go throwing your heart away on the first cowboy you meet.*

Justin parked his truck alongside a small, windowless building with barn doors and a stove pipe sticking out of the top. Elizabeth angled back into her jacket and reached for her purse before sliding down from the high bucket seat onto the soft, packed earth. Flats weren't the best choice for the trek, but she'd trade a blister or two for time with Justin.

"Home sweet home?" She gestured to the gray-shingled shed, yard tools leaning against an outer wall. He hadn't shared much about his daily existence thus far, and she was nudging.

"Naw, just a thinking spot. I use this place as a warming shed sometimes, so I don't have to go all the way back to the house when I'm working. Some storage, too, and I come out here when I want to be on my own for a bit. Or I need to ditch my wheels, so I can walk a woman to her door."

A slow fire burned in Elizabeth's insides. It had been far too long since she'd had anything close to this. Courted was a word she would now allow herself to use as a new resident of the Old West on a date with a real cowboy with plans to escort her home.

"It's quaint. I like it."

"Just a sec," Justin said, ducking into the building.

Solar panels on the roof shone jet-black in the moonlight. A wheelbarrow tipped up against the side of the building, and a boot jack waited on the doormat. A getaway spot for Justin. She was all the more curious from what, or from whom, he needed space.

Justin returned with a thick, woolen blanket. He draped this around her shoulders along with what looked like a heavy-duty pair of binoculars.

"Night-vision," he said, answering her unasked question. "My new toy. Well, we do use them to look for coyotes, but it's also fun just to see what's out and about in the dark. Hunters use them, too."

"Sounds very...stealthy. You could just grow a tapetum lucidum." The case was heavy, the weight pressed against her chest.

"Buying a pair of these is easier. Not that I know what a—"

"Tapetum lucidum."

"Yeah, that. These are military-grade. I thought I'd lend them to Casey for a bit. He said you've heard some noises around the place."

"I did, but he didn't seem too worried. Put up some motion lights in the barn. Threatened to get a llama. You know."

Justin laughed. "Your brother may act like he doesn't care, but that's all it is, an act. He loves those goats and is crazy proud of the creamery business. Did he tell you about the distribution contract he's trying to land?"

A twinge of jealousy nipped at her side. This man knew her brother better than she did, could read through his bravado. She tamped down on her insecurity, reminding herself that she had a new chance to get to know Casey again. They'd rebuild that closeness. She was happy her brother had found Justin.

"I am all but certain that if we stay here, Rhett is going to follow in his uncle's footsteps. He spends all the time he can in the barn with him."

They'd begun a stroll along the road. Elizabeth was grateful for the blanket as a night breeze raised the hair on her exposed forearms. She drew the wrap tighter around herself. While the days still eked out sunshine and a smidgen of afternoon warmth, the nights made no secret of the approaching season.

"I learned to ride when I was three. Pretty sure they strapped me down to the slowest, most trustworthy horse on the ranch and sent me off onto the prairie for a day. Think Rhett will want to ride?"

"Some days, it's hard to know what he wants, but yeah, I think if we are still here, he'll want to ride every day if he can."

"Casey told me about Rhett's...speech. Is it okay to talk about it?"

Elizabeth pressed her lips in a line and squeezed her eyes shut for a moment. She had practice in holding back tears, explaining in a calm way what ate at her heart, her identity as a good mother, every day.

"Yeah, though there isn't much to tell at the moment. He hasn't started talking. We know he can hear us, and while the doctors told us that boy babies take longer and say we shouldn't panic until he's two, they've also been talking about therapy, learning delays..."

She paused to take a deep breath, letting the mountain air fill her lungs. Every time she thought of the endless stream of doctor visits, debates with Nick, and repercussions that could chase and limit Rhett far into life, her lungs seized up, and she had to force them full again.

"I'm sorry. I'm an idiot for bringing it up."

"No, no, it's me. Talking about it is helpful, however scary sometimes. My ex and I don't agree about the what and the when of treatment. I also have to wonder if our fighting, some of those nights...there was a lot of yelling. He would come home late, lie, I would confront him, and he would yell, I would cry..." Elizabeth could see the tears streaming down her son's face as he stared at her, eyes wide with fear when she ran to pick him up. She didn't know if she could ever shake those images.

"You think you two are to blame. That's a big burden to bear."

"Yeah, I do." This was the first time she'd said it aloud. It was both freeing and stifling to do so.

"I'm not going to give you some clueless comment to try to fix your guilt or tell you everything will work out. But as a son, I can tell you love Rhett more than anything. You will make the right decisions."

Elizabeth swiped at the tear streaks on her cheeks with one hand, clutching the blanket with the other. "Thanks. For listening. For letting me be."

"Anytime," he said, putting an arm around her as they walked the last of the steps to Casey's porch. The floodlight in the driveway beamed a weak yellow above their heads, a couple of moths circling beneath its bulb.

"This was great. I loved it. Not just the confessional part. I can't tell you the last time I danced."

"Are you busy Saturday?"

"I'll have to check my dance card, but I just might be able to clear it."

"Then pencil me in. For all of them. I'll make dinner. I can only eat chicken fried steak so many times."

"I thought it was decent."

"Excellent, then my cooking has a chance."

When he leaned in to kiss her, soft lips and electricity, she tasted mint. When he drew back to assess her, she smiled and brought her face back to his. This time, he lingered in his contact, stepping forward to press his hips against hers, his hands low on her back. The promise of more.

When he pulled back, she was breathless, heady, her knees unreliable structures.

"I sure hope your brother isn't waiting for me with a shotgun on the other side of this door," he teased.

She wanted to taste him again, to bite those perfect lips. Her body craved the warmth that had just left it, wanting. "Actually, he told me he keeps the .45 out for such occasions."

"Then I better give you these," he said, holding out the night-vision binoculars. Justin draped the strap over her neck, over the blanket. "Goodnight."

Elizabeth watched him head off in the direction of the road and only when the cold threatened to settle further into her bones did she commit to the night's end with a sigh.

20

A SINGLE BULB BURNING over the sink and the blue light of the television were all that illuminated Elizabeth's entry. Casey sat on the couch, watching rodeo footage. Beer in one hand, remote in the other.

"Did you have a good time?" he asked the big screen. Elizabeth swore there was a sharpness to his question, a new wall between them, somehow.

"I did. Thanks for watching Rhett for me."

"Not a problem. Jo made pasta. There's some leftovers in the fridge and cookies in the container on the counter if you didn't have a chance to eat."

Casey's words outlined kindness, but his tone betrayed a hint of bitterness, like metal to the tongue.

"Everything okay?"

"Yeah. Just tired. I should shut this off and get to bed."

"What were you watching?"

"Old clips of my roping days."

And of Justin, she thought. "Oh, hey, Justin wanted me to bring you these."

When Elizabeth crossed to hand the case to her brother, she smelled the alcohol, noticed a rocks glass and a bottle of amber colored liquid among the detritus on the coffee table.

"I see," he said, taking the binoculars out of the case and steadying their bulk against his brow.

"Night vision. He thought they might be useful with what we've been hearing and seeing at night. They seem pretty industrial."

Casey turned them in his hands, thoughtful for a moment, then rose from the couch recesses. "I think I'll go give them a try."

"It is nighttime." She watched her brother stumble, then right himself, setting the bottle on the counter and tucking his feet into his tennis shoes. "You sure you should be wandering around in the dark?"

"I'm fine," he growled, and headed out into the night.

Casey still slept when Elizabeth and Rhett rose early the next morning. The door to his room was closed as she tiptoed her way to the kitchen. She fought back an urge to clang pans together, a passive aggressive move, yet his words last night had irked her. She couldn't shake their sting.

She flicked on the coffee pot and dug in a drawer for a cast iron skillet. Their grandma made a killer German apple pancake, and Elizabeth was confident she could manage a reasonable facsimile. Maybe the way to soothe the situation was through a family breakfast. Rhett busied himself with the plastic measuring cups on a rug as Elizabeth located a mixing bowl.

As she collected ingredients, Casey's phone, abandoned on the countertop, began to vibrate, a number she didn't recognize flashing on the screen.

"Whoever you are, you'll have to wait. Mama always said never poke a sleeping bear," she confided to Rhett. He'd abandoned the cups in favor of a new toy car Casey had brought home. Rhett raced it around the legs of the tall stools fronting the kitchen counter. When she spoke, he looked at her, chubby fingers grasping the miniature hot rod, a round-headed, faceless driver suspended in the air.

That he could hear was good, doctors said. That fact helped them eliminate some of the possibilities that were scarier, more limiting. Still, she wanted a close relationship with her son throughout his life, one in which he talked with her, confided in her. What would that look like if speech was not a big part of the equation?

The phone buzzed again, migrating across the granite in earnest alert. Elizabeth wondered if it might be someone calling about the distribution deal Justin had mentioned and glanced at the wall clock. After seven there meant nine a.m. on the east coast.

Deciding it was worth the risk, she padded down the tiled hallway in her slippers to Casey's bedroom door. She paused, fist raised, to listen.

Nothing.

She knocked twice, then called through the door. "Breakfast will be ready in twenty, and your phone is ringing off the hook."

A muffled "mmph" was audible in the depths of his room. Elizabeth counted her roommate duties complete and returned to the kitchen. Casey surfaced just as she rotated the piping hot pan in the oven, waiting for the top of the pancake to brown.

"Smells good," this morning's version of her brother conceded. He wore an old Pendleton Round Up T-shirt, sleeves cut off, over basketball shorts. As he scratched at his chest and yawned, Elizabeth could see a little of the teenage boy she remembered in this independent, adult version in front of her.

"I made coffee. And I used the last of your butter, so I'll get more today or tomorrow when my car is finished. Need anything else?"

Casey picked up his phone to scroll through the messages before putting the device to his ear, bypassing her question. A few seconds into a voicemail, his face turned ashen as shock erased his hangover.

"Casey?"

He dropped the phone on the counter as though it had burned him and moved away from the tiny silver device in horror. Grief wracked his face as he doubled forward, clutching his head in his hands.

"Casey. What's wrong?"

Rhett stopped his play to watch his uncle. As Casey's body shook with silent sobs, the little boy toddled over, holding out the car. Elizabeth picked him up and held him close to her, wanting the comfort of his closeness for whatever the impending news may be.

"Casey? Talk to me." The scent of roasting apples filled her nostrils as fear inched into her bloodstream.

"It's Justin," he said, raising his head from his hands to look at her. His skin was blotched and red, tear-stained. "He's dead."

Elizabeth stood in shock, frozen by the words that couldn't be unheard, no matter how she willed them away, all while questioning whether she'd heard them at all. Justin couldn't be dead. He'd just been there. She'd been with him.

They'd had a date. He'd kissed her. She could feel his lips on hers.

The smell of burning batter wrested Elizabeth back to her senses. Shoving her hands into pot holders, she removed the steaming pan from the oven and set it on the range top to cool.

Casey was broken.

Justin was gone.

21

AFTER SHE WATCHED RHETT shovel pancakes into his mouth, Elizabeth took him outside, more for her own sake than his. The rest of the breakfast went into storage containers in the fridge. Elizabeth and Casey hadn't eaten. Her stomach turning in knots, her brain rode a rollercoaster of denial spun through disbelief.

Outside, the chilly morning air smelled of pine and regret. Rhett struggled in her arms, willing freedom and adventure, sensing confusion and loss among the adults.

Her brother was in the barn, leaning against the stall that held the baby goats, watching them jump and play around their ambivalent mother. Elizabeth joined him, holding Rhett so he could stretch his small hands out to touch the soft hides. The animals nuzzling him for crumbs. Her little boy smiled as the noses brushed his overalls, accepting him as a new member of their little herd.

Each nestled in the quiet warmth of the animals, the silence interrupted only with an occasional bleat. They stood that way for a while, comforted by the menagerie.

Casey rested his chin on his arms, muffling his voice when he said, "You know, the goats were Justin's idea."

"They were?"

"Yeah. He came back from Maui where he'd been to some fancy creamery there. He thought I could do the same thing. Raise goats, turn their milk into fantastic cheese, sell it everywhere. Justin said my design clients are the exact people who will pay serious money for some fancy chèvre. He was right."

"Sounds like he knew business."

"He did, which is hilarious because he hated everything to do with just about all of it. Said it brought out the worst in people, including his entire family. I think the only reason he stayed at the ranch was out of duty."

"That's a hard way to spend a life."

"There's a lot you didn't know. Will never know." He lifted his chin from his arms and pushed back from the railing.

"Casey," she started, then paused, unsure if she wanted answers. "How did he die?"

"Trampled."

"Trampled? By animals?"

"That's what they think. The cattle. Killed by the very industry he tried to escape. If that's not ironic, I don't know what is." Casey wiped both his eyes with his hands and said, "Guess I'd better get everyone fed."

She watched him walk to the shed, head hung low, wondering if she should offer to help. Better not, she decided. His mood had darkened her own, and she had to bring sunshine to the schoolhouse.

After dropping Rhett off with a solemn Jo, Elizabeth made it to the small, squat buildings on the hill just as the Nelson siblings got out of their car.

"We were waiting for you," Rachel said. "Mom said we couldn't wait alone in case you didn't come at all like the last lady."

"I see," Elizabeth said, questioning why she came to work, why she hadn't called in, called off this day that couldn't—wouldn't—make sense. Mrs. Nelson was talking on her phone inside the car, engine running, and lifted a hand in greeting to Elizabeth.

"Why were you late?"

"I couldn't get a head start like I usually do. I got some sad news this morning," she explained to Ashton, willing her lip not to tremble, willing her resolve to steel itself for a day. "Why don't you pick out a book for some reading time while we wait for the others."

Elizabeth unlocked the school building and walked over the threshold. She shrugged out of her coat only to replace it over her shoulders and check the thermostat. The room was frigid that morning. Elizabeth dropped her bag on her desk and walked to the back window. The sash was a few inches from the sill, cold air seeping in. She shut the double-paned glass, a firm thunk confirming the barrier. A long strand of blue thread was caught on an errant splinter on the windowsill. As if in reflex, she flipped the window lock and loosed the thread from its snag.

The Ramirez twins followed on the heels of the Nelsons. Elizabeth watched their mothers lean against each other's cars, talking in the parking area. Natasha in a cowled sweater, Mirabel pulling her hands into the sleeves of her jacket for extra warmth in the brisk morning. One of them would glance at the school and then back to the other, as if to verify all other ears were still indoors.

A beat-up sedan crawled up next to the other vehicles in the parking area, and Polly extracted herself from the front seat, her face contorted as though every muscle ached with the movement. Benny's lunch perched on the top of the car before she leaned into the vehicle to help her son hop out, grabbed the bag again, and ushered him toward the door. As she passed by the other women, they stopped talking to gape. When she entered the school building, Elizabeth understood their scrutiny.

Polly's hair was a fuzzy halo where pieces had fallen out of her ponytail to hang loose around her face. There were dark circles under her eyes, and she still wore barn clothes, the dusty boots and rumpled clothing adding to her disheveled appearance. She handed Benny his lunch box and gave him a quick kiss on the cheek after she brought him indoors.

Before she could leave, Elizabeth called, "Hey there, everything okay?"

"Yeah, sorry he's late. It's all my fault. I forgot to set the alarm again. We had to rush. You know how that goes."

"I was worried, that's all."

"You're right. I could have called. I will next time."

"How about I give you my number for the meantime, just in case."

"Thanks," Polly said, taking down the information. "I've got to get home and change so I can get to my shift. This is going to be a long day. Justin...I..." Tears flooded her eyes and she looked away.

Elizabeth reached out to hug the woman, and Polly welcomed the hold.

After a moment, Polly sniffed and gave Elizabeth a weak smile before leaving. When Elizabeth heard about Justin, she'd been thinking of him as hers, somehow, even though they'd just met. Just began to get to know each other. The truth was that he'd belonged to this community long before that.

After a deep breath, Elizabeth returned to her students. She would make it through the last day of the first week of school, and then she could think about what all this meant.

⋆

Jo, contrary to her usual fountain of discourse, was tight-lipped when Elizabeth collected Rhett. The woman handed her a finger-painting and sniffed into a wad of tissue clutched into her hand, closing the door.

"We all handle grief differently," Elizabeth said to Rhett. He watched the golden retrievers play tug-of-war behind the fence. The two warm brown bodies tumbled over each other in their quest for playful dominance. He pointed at them as if to highlight their struggle. "Maybe we can get a puppy or a dog. Can't have two beings in diapers. Let's see how things go, okay?"

At Cloud Nine, they came home to an empty house. Casey's horse was absent from his usual afternoon range in the paddock. In the tack shed, there'd be an empty saddle stand and Elizabeth couldn't think of a better way to get some air. Settling Rhett with some graham crackers, she began heating water for pasta.

While she wouldn't consider her brother's home her own, not by a long shot, she was starting to pick up the pieces of its knowledge that led to comfort. The location of soap refills, the creaky floorboard in the living room that announced every trespasser, and the extra thirty seconds it took the guest room shower to heat up. These facts were familiar to her now. These added up into a settling. Not into full familiarity, but to coexistence, breathing space.

Casey walked in the door just as she grated parmesan on bowls for her and Rhett. She slid her bowl toward Casey across the countertop and started a new one for herself. After assembling a third bowl, she strapped Rhett into his highchair and then took a seat. They ate in silence, each with their own thoughts.

Rhett loved spaghetti, every last noodle of it, and he was fun to watch—until clean-up time. The boy would paste himself up to the eyebrows in red sauce by the end of the ordeal, joy in every nook of his smile. Elizabeth went a little lighter on sauce for him as she knew the bulk would wind up on the tray, his face, and his bib, and she had to hose down the kitchen afterward. Still, she loved the clarity of his adoration of the eating process of this slick and tasty food. Her favorite moments with her son were when she had a window to his world, when she knew what made him happy.

Casey watched his nephew's glee. Rhett abandoned the short fork to take a fistful of noodles and cram them at his mouth where some met the target and some slid to the floor. A slow grin inched across Casey's face in response to the sight.

A brisk knock startled each of them. Casey dropped his fork with a clatter and checked the peephole before swinging the door open. "Sheriff. Come on in."

"Sorry to disturb your supper."

The sheriff filled the doorway, his frame thick and bolstered by a heavy-duty jacket and equipment belted around his middle. He didn't change expression, only waited, blinking, like a goldfish.

"Hello," Elizabeth said. "Spaghetti?" Rhett turned to see who'd interrupted his pasta party.

"Evening. Thank you, but no thank you. Ms. Blau, I need you to come down to the station tomorrow, so you can tell me about the last hours you spent with Justin Hart. Nine o'clock. Mr. Blau, I'm hoping you'll drive her as I don't see the Subaru back in the drive."

Wolf wasn't asking, he was informing her of his expectations.

Casey had planned to drop her off to collect the car on Saturday morning, several hundred dollars and new brake rotors later. Now they had a detour.

"Is this an investigation now?" Something in her brother's voice cracked at the end, fragile and telling.

"I can't tell you more than I'm at liberty to. I can tell you we are looking into some things to get a clear picture of what happened to Mr. Hart last night. We're asking anyone who saw him yesterday about the circumstances of his day and appreciate your cooperation."

"Wow. Okay."

"Thank you. I'll let you all get back to your supper." He touched a finger to his hat brim and closed the door behind himself.

Casey sat, in his seat, unmoving, staring at a spot on the wall. Steam dissipated from his meal.

"Case?"

"I'm going to make a phone call." Her brother abandoned his food and took his phone outside.

"That interruption sure killed the mood," she said to Rhett. He looked up from his forkful, errant curl extending onto his forehead. "Glad you're still enjoying the meal."

Minutes later, Casey stormed back in, slamming his phone down on the countertop. Elizabeth winced at the sound. "They think it might be murder."

"What? Who? And how? Who did you call?"

"Margery Hart, Justin's mom."

Elizabeth thought about the woman now handling the death of her only son. "What did she say?"

"There's a busted lock on one of the stockyard gates. No one remembers the combination, and they've bent it up trying to cut it off. As a solution, they just pull the pin out of the other side to open the gate. They found the gate, pin out, this morning. The cattle that trampled Justin were Hart stock."

"Someone forgot to shut a gate? That's hardly murder."

"That's the thing. They know it was shut last night. The vet had been by to give vaccinations yesterday afternoon, so the cattle had been penned up ahead of time. The stock hands left them in the corral to keep an eye on them and planned to turn them out with the rest of the herd this morning. At first light, they found the gate open and the animals gone."

"Which is why they noticed Justin's truck."

"Yep, they were looking for their stock."

Elizabeth thought back to when Justin had dropped her off. Ten? Eleven? "Justin could have let them out himself, couldn't he? But that doesn't make any sense. Why let them out in the middle of the night?"

"I don't know. He didn't have anything to do with the cattle when he could help it."

"I guess he could have been drunk? He'd only had a couple when we were out, though."

Rhett squirmed in his seat, meal complete. Elizabeth swiped at his hands and face with a dish towel and freed him from the confines of his chair.

"There's something else," Casey said, tone reluctant, as though his brain were still turning a fact over in its recesses.

"What's that?"

"They didn't find him on the ranch. He was in the creek ravine."

"Across the road?"

He nodded. "A quarter mile from the corral."

22

ELIZABETH CHEWED AT HER nails while they sat in front of the squat Sheriff's Department entrance, a corner of the building at the end of 13th Street which held the city police department and a small jail. She watched the clock on Casey's dash flip to 8:50 and figured early was better than late. With a quick kiss on the cheek for each of her guys, she entered the building.

This couldn't take long. There hadn't been much to her date night, at least not much that could be of help. Zero intimate details and her knowledge of his evening ended when he'd dropped her off, very much alive.

The front desk person, a woman in a sage green blouse and too long, manicured nails, waved Elizabeth over to a faux leather couch to wait. Moments later, the sheriff entered from the back hallway.

"Ms. Blau, thank you for coming in as requested."

Not like I had a choice. "I'm not sure what help I'll be."

"That's my job to worry about. You just tell your story. Come on back."

He led her past a break room and into an office crammed full of a desk, bookshelves, and several filing cabinets. A window looked out to the parking lot, blinds twisted open, splicing the light. Casey's truck was already gone. He'd taken Rhett to see the elk near Kendrick Park.

"Take a seat." Wolf picked up a stack of files from the vinyl-wrapped chair cushion. "I'd like to record this, if that's alright with you."

"Sure. The first recording of the human voice was over a hundred and fifty years ago. Not sure how my story will add much."

"Mmhmm." He tapped at a small recording device between them and took a seat in his desk chair. Fishing out a yellow notepad from the piles on the desk and taking a pen from his pocket, he stated the details of the meeting for the record and began. "Tell me about the last time you saw Justin Hart, Ms. Blau."

Elizabeth cooperated, down to the kiss.

"My brother was home when I walked in the door. He was watching Rhett, my son," she said for the recording.

"So, your brother was home all night?"

"Yes. Well, no. Sort of. When I brought him the binoculars, he went outside to try them out, and then I went to bed."

Wolf scratched a few notes onto the paper. "He went out?"

"Yeah, he walked outside to test them out. Optoelectronic image enhancement is very cool technology."

"I see. When did you next see your brother?" Wolf looked up at Elizabeth, as if to ascertain the level of truth written on her features.

"The next morning when I knocked on his bedroom door to tell him his phone was ringing." A sinking feeling pitted Elizabeth's stomach. She interlaced her fingers and squeezed her hands together to keep them from shaking. *When had Casey come back inside?*

"Did Casey say anything about having seen Justin Hart?"

"No. He was really upset when he heard Justin died. He didn't say much at all."

"I see. Thank you for your cooperation, Ms. Blau." Wolf pressed the stop button and set his pen on the pad of paper. "Mr. Blau coming back to get you?"

"He is."

"I need to chat with him when he gets here. I'll walk you back to the waiting area."

Replanted on the olive-green couch, Elizabeth called her brother, whispering into the phone when he picked up. "Casey, where are you?"

"We're on our way. How'd it go?"

"Fine. He wants to talk to you now," she said.

"Who?"

"Santa Claus. Who do you think?"

Casey swore on the other end of the line. He was silent for a moment. "I'll be there in less than ten."

Elizabeth cupped her hand over the mouthpiece and rotated her body away from the woman at the desk. "Casey, is there something you aren't telling me?"

"It's nothing, I—"

Elizabeth glanced behind her. The desk clerk made no pretense of hiding her interest in the phone call. One hand rested on the receiver of the phone in front of her, poised to dial. *It's not like I'm taking off*, Elizabeth thought. "Just get here soon. Please."

She hung up the phone and crossed her legs, bobbing her foot up and down in anticipation. Within five minutes, Casey's truck was in a parking spot, her brother plucking Rhett from the back seat.

⋆⋆

"Mine wasn't too long," Elizabeth said to Casey, accepting her son and his pack of snacks off Casey's arm.

"Roger that."

"Mr. Blau, thank you for coming." Sheriff Wolf's voice boomed into the lobby, and Elizabeth shot the desk clerk a look. The woman's shrug admitted her role in alerting her boss to the arrival.

"Oh, and Ms. Blau, I've asked Deputy Ryland to take you to the auto shop, so the little one needn't get impatient waiting for his uncle."

She nodded a thank you. Casey didn't acknowledge her before following the sheriff back to the same office Elizabeth had vacated.

The deputy chatted her ear off about the turning weather, football season, and somehow at least a dozen other topics in the three minutes it took to drive Elizabeth and Rhett to the mechanic's.

Kade slid out from under a vehicle as she entered the garage.

With Elizabeth's wallet several hundred dollars lighter by way of her credit card, Kade slid the keys across the counter. "I was sorry to hear about Justin."

Their fingertips touched when she took the keys, a braided leather keychain and roadside assistance card on the loop. Elizabeth looked down at his hand, yanked hers away and then returned her gaze up to his face. "Oh?"

"I know what he meant to your brother, and it looks like the two of you were getting friendly, is all. Besides, I've yet to wish a man dead."

His words wrenched at her heart. Justin was dead.

"I'm touched."

"Listen," he said. "Justin was one of us. There's been a lot that's happened before you ever got here and a lot that will happen long after you leave."

Elizabeth stared hard at the man. Jeans layered with grease, his long-sleeved shirt advertised a fishing company out of Alaska. Red-gold hair curled tightly to his head, and his beard was trimmed. Crows' feet framed a piercing stare that dared her to argue. The tone in his voice was accusatory, defensive, and human.

"I hope so," she replied, and left.

23

I N THE LIVING ROOM, she wore a path in the rug. She tried calling Casey's number, but he didn't pick up.

As Elizabeth put Rhett down for a nap, she heard Casey's truck. She paused before the closed bedroom door to allow Casey time to come in, get settled. She heard the rattle of his keys hit the counter.

"Well?"

He pressed his hands onto either side of his face and inhaled, as if deciding how to start the conversation. Elizabeth crossed her arms, tucking her hands in opposite armpits, waiting.

"This is hard," he started.

"Casey, what exactly is going on?"

"Okay. Yes. So. You know how Justin has an ex?"

"As do I, it happens."

"Roz left Justin because he cheated on her."

"Oh," Elizabeth said. Memories assaulted her, of the first night she'd heard the messages on Nick's phone. Saw the emails. Smelled the evidence of a partnering. "Yeah. They say forty percent of marriages end when someone cheats. That can be one heck of a deal breaker."

Would she have been interested in Justin had she known this information? Elizabeth wondered why Casey had kept it a secret. No wonder his mood had been dark when she returned from the date. He'd tried to warn her. Sort of.

"Liz. He cheated on her with me."

Reality slammed, solid, into her chest. "What?"

"Look, it's complicated. Roz doesn't know it was me."

"Cheating is never complicated. You either mess around or you don't. You break a promise or you don't. There's no middle ground."

"I meant the relationship part."

"You had a relationship with him?"

Casey nodded.

"When?" She knew the answer as she asked the question. They'd traveled together, wrestled together, roped together for years.

"A bit when we were in college. I followed him back here. I was next door. It would be perfect. Then, when his father died, something changed. He said he needed to get serious about his family obligations, that we were never going to work, not here. He started dating Roz, and..."

"They got married."

"They did."

"But you got back together."

"Off and on, we did." Her brother, who knew everything she went through with Nick, was no better than her conniving, lying ex.

"Roz found out."

"One night, she got drunk, confronted him. He told her."

"The whole truth?"

"He admitted to cheating but not the details."

"She thinks it was with a woman. That you are a woman." Elizabeth sat back to enlarge the space between herself and this person who was again disconnected from the brother she loved. The brother she respected.

"Yes."

Elizabeth frowned. "Does anyone know it was you?"

"Jo. She caught us one day, here. She wouldn't tell, though."

"So, then, why did the sheriff want to talk to you?"

"Because I was one of the last people to see Justin. After you came home that night, I went out to meet him."

24

"YOU WHAT?"

"It's horrible, I know. Nothing happened, though I wanted it to. I took the night vision binoculars out with me and spotted him, out by the barn. He said he hoped I'd come out so we could talk. He said he liked you and wanted to make sure it was okay if he kept taking you out. I said yes, even though I didn't mean it. We hugged, he left, and I had some more drinks about my feelings. Alone."

"This is what you told the sheriff?"

"I had to. Jo told him about Justin and me after Justin died, so Wolf did his job and asked me about it. I get it."

"Casey, I...this is a lot." Elizabeth rubbed at her cuticles, noting one hangnail and then another.

Elizabeth and Casey hadn't had those hands-off-my-boyfriend conversations. She was furious he hadn't told her. She felt sorry for him, too. Watching your best friend, your lover, walk away would crush anyone.

✦

A bottle of whisky and two glasses awaited Elizabeth after she put Rhett to bed. Casey poured two fingers into her glass, added a splash from a water bottle, and slid it to her.

Elizabeth took a careful sip. "This is good," she said. "Smooth. Burn-y"

"Fifteen-year," he replied, sipping from his own glass before eyeing the amber liquid inside. "It was a gift to myself when I started shipping the cheese."

"I haven't asked you much about your business before. What's your most popular flavor?"

"After our double cream, I would say either the cracked pepper with garlic or the honey lavender. The better the girls are doing, the better production, and the more I get to experiment."

"You love those goats."

"I do. I also don't know what I'm going to do without Justin. Whether out of guilt for dragging me here or because it got him out of the house, he was a huge help. I can't afford to hire someone."

"I can help."

"Thanks. I'll have to see what happens."

"Are you still going out tonight?"

"I'm not quite in the mood for it." From the flush of his cheeks to the twitch in his right eyelid, guilt crawled across his flesh. The man wouldn't be able to maintain himself in public. Thus, the whisky.

"What did you learn from the chat with our sheriff?"

"Wolf asked if I could think of any reason Justin would have let the cattle out, but I came up with nothing."

"No one else knew anything?"

"If they did, I wouldn't be drinking."

25

"**H**EY, BUDDY. LET'S GET you breakfast and get Mama some coffee."

Elizabeth had settled into the morning with some scrambled eggs and a steaming cup, when her phone rang.

"Hello?"

"It's Nick."

"I know. Caller ID was invented in 1987. What do you want?"

"Liz. Mom hired a lawyer."

"You've got to be kidding me."

"She wants to support my relationship with Rhett. Help me get to see him again."

"What do you mean?"

"It's not good for him, Liz, to be away from his father like this."

"On the contrary, I think space away from someone who neglects you is a good plan, an important step for healing, even."

"Come on now. You know this isn't right. Just because you can't handle me being in other relationships—"

"Oh, please, that's all I did for years, handle you being in other relationships."

"Liz, she's going to say you're avoiding getting him medical treatment. That you are unfit to be his primary parent."

Elizabeth's blood boiled at his words, a thousand pinpricks on her heart. "How dare you. How dare she. This is outrageous. I have done everything those doctors asked. He's not due for an evaluation for another few months. He's not even two!"

"Liz, I love Rhett. I deserve to see him. He deserves the best care. Come home and let's put this back together, make decisions as a family."

"You want to see your son? Well, come see him here because I will not be coming back to you, Nick. Not now, not ever." She disconnected the call before the tears could spill out onto the screen.

Casey shuffled into the kitchen, then, scratching at his chest with one hand and yawning. "I heard some of that," he said.

"The part where Nick's mother is trying to take Rhett from me? She hired a lawyer."

"Oh, dang, Liz. I'm sorry."

Elizabeth's hands shook with rage, her jaw clenched. She scooped up a mouthful of room temperature eggs with her fork and shoved them in her mouth.

A knock on the door shook them from their current focus.

Casey again welcomed the sherriff into his house.

"Good morning," Wolf opened.

Elizabeth noticed he hadn't left the welcome mat. "Would you like some eggs?"

"No, thank you." Wolf exhaled through his nose and continued, "Mr. Blau, I'm arresting you for the murder of Justin Hart. You have the right to remain silent. Anything you say..."

"Wait, what?" Elizabeth's exclamation was part terror, part fury. Her spoon hit the floor, scattering egg bits on the tile.

"You've got to be kidding me," Casey said. "I told you, we talked and then he left. Nothing happened. I didn't kill him."

"Mr. Blau, we can do this the easy way or the hard way. I think you know me well enough to know which is my preference."

"Casey, go with him. I'm sure it's just a misunderstanding, and you'll be back in no time."

"Call my lawyer. His information is in my desk drawer. He'll know what to do."

Rhett toddled into the scene, his face regarding first his uncle and then his friend, the sheriff. She watched him stare, confused, then go wide-eyed when he realized his uncle was leaving.

"Mr. Blau."

"Fine. I'm coming willingly and all that." Then, to Rhett, Casey said, "Hey there, cowboy. I'm going to go with the sheriff here for a little bit, and then I will be back. No need to worry about your Uncle Casey."

⋅≪≫⋅

After a phone call to the office on the card found in Casey's desk, she sat on the couch, numb and staring while Rhett played on the rug. He toddled over to Casey's boot rack to try on the giant shoes.

The lawyer, a man who sounded like a soccer coach calling plays, promised he was on it—whatever that meant. Elizabeth was curious as to why Casey had a lawyer he consulted often enough to necessitate a card and a relationship, but she couldn't ask that question now.

People liked Casey. Casey was the teammate you could count on in high school. The one who would have your back, spot you, and otherwise make sure you knew he was in your corner. At least, the Casey she knew.

This Casey, current Casey, had a little edge. A tender space that surfaced with regard to Justin. This Casey welcomed her and her son to live with him, no questions asked, for as long as she needed. This Casey wanted her and Rhett in his life. He cared about this community, his businesses. No matter the hurt feelings between old flames, he wouldn't risk it all for a man who was now just a memory, would he?

Light streaked through the clearstory windows, painting lines down the walls. *Time to be helpful. Sisterly.*

Rhett attempted to plod around in Casey's boots, triumphant at the feat of standing up-right in the clunkers. Elizabeth wrestled him into his own shoes and sweatshirt before donning hers and heading outside. However long Casey would be held downtown, animals needed feeding. After a couple mornings of helping, she was confident she could at least keep the quadrupeds alive.

Late morning sun licked at the corral railings with a hint of warmth but falling short on effect. Elizabeth's breath was visible in the morning chill, and frost across the railings sparkled in the sun.

Elizabeth peeled off several layers of alfalfa, rummaged around in a grain bin, and checked the autofill mechanism on a couple troughs. She felt accomplished, practiced in the routine, a helper. The four-legged residents had been fed, patted, brushed, and watered. Anything to distract her from the dread pitting in her stomach.

When they emerged from the barn, dusty and smelling of goats, Jo's car waited in the driveway, its owner inside. She stepped out in the cold as they approached, crossing her arms to rub her hands briskly over her sleeves.

"It's freezing. Hey, I thought I'd apologize for my lout of a husband. The job has to be heartless, sometimes. How are you two taking things? Need any help with the animals? I've got a goat and a donkey of my own, so I know my way around a barn."

"Just finished up, actually. I'm not sure how long he'll be gone so I..." Elizabeth trailed off, the unspoken words sinking between the two women.

"Shame about Casey. Can't picture it."

"Are you allowed to say that?"

"I wouldn't have been married this long to the sheriff if I worried too much about being allowed to. He has his duty, his boundaries, and I have mine."

"I know he's just doing his job. I can't be mad at that. I'm scared."

"Regardless of responsibility, sometimes the law is just dumb. Casey wouldn't have hurt a hair on Justin's head. He loved the man, always has."

Elizabeth watched the woman to assess the nuance of her meaning. Casey said she knew about his past, but how much?

"How long have you known my brother?"

"Ever since those two came home with degrees in their hands but no clue what to do with them. To be honest, I think your brother had it easier, a clean slate. No offense."

Elizabeth shrugged.

"When you have family around, you are always trying to meet arbitrary expectations, be something to someone other than yourself. Without that kind of pressure, your brother could take his time figuring out what he wanted to do. Justin, God rest his soul, was born with a list of accomplishments to meet, his life plan in his father's hands. That's serious pressure."

"It is." Elizabeth remembered her brother decrying Justin's family responsibilities, the man's own dismissal of family concerns. "Casey told me Justin didn't want to work the ranch, that he only stayed for his mom."

"That's the truth. If only that old windbag hadn't also let Roz stay, when all of that fell out. I think Justin would have been a lot happier, home more often, if he didn't have to see his ex at every turn."

"Roz still lives there?"

"She had asked, just until the divorce goes through. Says she needed to save money to move out with her sister, which is true. Now, she's a widow."

Elizabeth thought of Nick. "I couldn't have done that, no way."

"I never wondered why he kept a stack of wood by that old line shack, though others did. The man needed an escape."

Elizabeth pictured Justin splitting wood on the stump, stacking it with precision by the door. An heir to a fortune and he preferred a rickety one-room space to a sprawling ranch. "People have been splitting wood since at least the Neolithic period."

"At any rate," Jo continued, "Charlie is a good lawyer. He'll get things going for Casey, help him out. Don't be too mad at Clint. It breaks his heart whenever he has to arrest one of ours."

"To a swift investigation, then," Elizabeth said.

"Okay. Well, let me know if you need anything. I'm just down the road, you know."

"Jo," Elizabeth interrupted as the woman opened the car door. "Is there anything about the case you can share?"

"All I can say is that it's clear that whatever happened to Justin involved cattle, horses, and at least one human in size ten-and-a-half logging boots. There aren't many around here who wear those, Liz."

26

ELIZABETH DRAGGED A BASKET of clean clothes to the living room, knowing folding laundry would give her twitching hands something to do while they waited for Casey's return. She watched the news out of Billings, the volume low as screen images flickered past her consciousness until a shot of her brother came up. Listed as a person of interest, the news anchor said the investigation was ongoing in the murder of Justin Hart and that all leads should be called in to the Sheridan Country Sheriff's Office. She switched off the screen.

Casey stumbled through the door, hours later, shirt rumpled, circles under his eyes.

"Hey," Elizabeth opened.

"Hey. Thanks for calling Charlie. Thanks to him, I've been released until trial, but I have to stick close to home."

"When is this trial?"

"Charlie said a few weeks, October. There's a tax fraud case up now. Shouldn't be long."

"Is that enough time to sort out your defense?"

"My defense is easy. I didn't do it."

"You know what I mean."

Casey sighed, pushing all the air out of his lungs and into the room. "Can we just give it a rest for a few?" Her brother reached for Rhett and swung the boy up into his arms, explaining the menfolk would be in the barn.

Elizabeth's phone rang, the number a local one. As she wedged it between her ear and shoulder, she flipped a dish towel over one shoulder as she folded another. "Hello?"

"Elizabeth?"

"Yeah?"

"It's Kade."

She frowned. "The mechanic?"

"Yeah. Look, sorry to bother you, but when we checked your spare tire under the cargo area, we pulled out your roadside emergency kit to get to it. I found the bag over here, behind a tool chest. I'll bring it to you, with my apology." A hint of worry licked at his tone, the sound of a man who didn't like to be in the wrong and would only feel better when all was made right.

"It's okay, I can grab it this week if you tuck it away somewhere."

"I'd prefer to bring it there, it's my fault, not yours."

Elizabeth pictured this hulking man tossing and turning in angst over a first aid kit and smiled. Casey caught her eye, and she dropped the grin.

"It's your gas. Know where the ranch is?"

"Yep. Be there in half an hour."

Elizabeth ran a brush through her hair and a swipe of balm across her lips. "Force of habit," she said to the woman in the mirror.

Kade had been blunt, curt, and efficient when she'd picked up her car. That day, she'd been so focused on the grilling at the Sheriff's Office it was strange to realize she hadn't paid much attention to the car exchange. He'd presented her with the bill, she'd paid with plastic and left.

Twenty minutes later, a rap on the door was quick and sharp. Kade held out the small, red bag, and she received it. He continued to stand on the welcome mat, staring.

This is awkward. "Thank you," she said, instead of other comments floating around, waiting for the opportunity to make it past the politeness goalie in her head.

"Look. Again, I'm sorry. If there's anything I can do to help the situation, let me know."

"Not a problem, really, it's fine. Coffee?" She gestured over her shoulder with her thumb.

"No, thank you. I, uh, did want to add that I'm glad you came to the school. Polly says Benny loves his new teacher and has been asking her about all kinds of things. He didn't used to do that. Kind of kept to himself, nose always in a book, you know?"

"Must be nice to have family close by," she prodded.

"You know how cousins are. You lose track of some, keep in touch with others. Stay close. Polly is the best kind. Well, her and Roz."

Elizabeth was curious about their family, how they fit in line. While Kade was all auburn and brown, heavy eyebrows and a Roman nose, the two women were blondes with tiny features, slight builds. The hair could be from a bottle, Elizabeth reasoned, and she did see something familiar in their jawlines. This also explained the mutual dislike the three cousins had for Justin.

"Benny is a good kid. I enjoy working with him, learning with him. With all of them."

"Well, it matters to me. His father was a useless piece, if you get me. I was glad he skipped out on Polly, in a way. Just sad for his kid, you know?"

What was happening here? She held only impressions of dislike for this man, thoughts bordering on contempt, yet he was now telling her his family drama, ruining her previous image.

"That's hard on any kid," she said, to buy herself time while she considered this exchange.

"If there's anything you need for the school, let me know. We usually sponsor a baseball team in town, but I want to do more. For Benny. And his classmates. Help them get out of this corner of the world, make something of themselves."

Elizabeth was stunned at this exchange. Her prior opinion of the man fought against a new curiosity, an opportunity for understanding and appreciation.

Kade interpreted her silence as a dismissal, shifting his stance on the mat, and backpedaled out of the conversation. "Look, I ought to let you get back to things. I just wanted to drop off the bag and say thanks. Anyway, yeah. If you're ever back at the Inn, the beer's on me."

He waved before she could reply and strode over to his truck. She watched him drive off, remained outside until the cloud of dust could no longer be discerned in the dim.

Inside, she found Rhett digging in Casey's trunk. The wooden box looked handmade, brass fastenings gleaming with care. Rhett had his hands around a rodeo trophy, attempting to free the statue from its trappings in the trunk.

"No, no, that is not yours. That is Uncle Casey's." Elizabeth used her mom voice and raised brows to convey this new limit, and Rhett's face screwed up in protest.

"It's okay, Liz," Casey called from his bedroom. "I told him he could look at my old stuff while I look for my baseball cards. He can't hurt anything."

Elizabeth attempted to replace the trophy among her brother's paraphernalia, stacked haphazardly in the recesses of the trunk. As she did so, a rubber-banded packet of letters toppled over, exposing the return address—Justin Hart in Banner, Wyoming. A quick glance at the postage date gave the summer between her brother's freshman and sophomore years at college. Casey hadn't come home that summer or any other. Instead, he took a summer job on the mountain—"to help pay for his dorm," he'd written in his letter to her. She knew back then, somehow, that it marked the end of any plans of his to return home.

The letters in her hand were uniform in envelope size and penned in the same blue ballpoint. Justin's words, weighty against her palm.

A handful of letters, a story. A relationship.

27

THE SUN RECEDED INTO the western sky, painting rainbow streaks in pinks, oranges, and purples as it sank behind the Big Horn Mountains.

Despite the risk, Casey had gone out when Elizabeth had tucked Rhett in for the night. She suspected he didn't want to be left alone with his thoughts. Neon lights and liquid therapy were the friends he wanted around.

Elizabeth freed some carrots from the confines of the refrigerator and stepped out the back door, seeking company in the barn. The motion lights clicked on at her approach, the door squeaking as she slid it open in the floodlight. She ran her hands down the side of the horses' soft faces as they chewed.

A flip of a latch and she'd locked the barn behind her. Elizabeth paused in the still night to tilt her face upward. She sought out the sliver of moon, a crescent above, surrounded by endless stars in the inky sky.

Headlights woke her from a doze on the couch. After shucking her outerwear indoors, she'd turned on a comedy, tucked her feet under a throw blanket, and proceeded to nod off. The blanket fell from her lap as she rose to peer through the curtains into the night. A midnight blue car arced its lights over the house before releasing its passenger, Casey. He leaned in to say something to the driver, then closed the door to approach the house, head hanging low.

Elizabeth waited, unsure of her greeting.

"Hey. Lizzy-beth. Thanks for staying up."

"I had no idea when you'd get home, so I put on a bad movie and had too much wine."

"Any left? I could use a glass."

She gestured to the bottle on the counter, cork jammed a third of the way back in. Casey selected stemware from a rack and poured the remainder of the pinot noir into the glass.

Elizabeth's internal questions nipped at the inside of her lips like piranhas after their prey. "There's a bit of a cork taint."

Casey wrinkled his nose and sniffed at the goblet before he took a swig. He abandoned his phone on the countertop.

"Liz, I'm guilty until proven innocent. Everyone is treating me like I'm the murderer or like I could have done it, at least."

"Who brought you home?"

"That would be Roz. She said she believes me, even though her mother-in-law doesn't. Or at least isn't willing to cross me off the list."

"Does she know about you and Justin?"

"Roz? Or Marg? Neither, which is likely why I'm still on any kind of footing with them." He palmed his face, then dragged his hand upward and over the top of his head. "At least, they don't know yet."

"Are you going to tell me what happened today, or do I have to keep sitting here, fighting off the urge to scream?"

"Sorry," he said. Looking away from her, he continued, "Involuntary manslaughter. I had to wait for my lawyer to sort out the bond. I—"

He put his hands back over his face and let out a sob. Elizabeth, still shocked at the charges, froze, uncertain, then moved to wrap her arms around her sibling.

Elizabeth remembered being seven, believing the world was kind and just. Her parents gave her a bike and Casey took her out to their cul-de-sac to practice riding. After an hour of wobbling and asphalt contact, she could make a shaky loop on the pavement track. She would see the world from between the handlebars.

That night, she heard an argument in the kitchen and peeked into the hallway. Casey and her parents argued about the bike. Her brother had used his own money to buy it for her, not her parents.

"You think you're better than us. You've got things easy. How would it have looked if we gave her nothing and you gave her this fancy bike?"

"Maybe I care about my sister enough to give her something for her birthday."

The return slap had been swift. Casey's jaw popped with the contact. He didn't yell, he didn't start crying. It was a moment before anyone spoke.

"We're her parents," their mother said, weakness shredding her rationale.

"A title means nothing," Casey said, and stalked off.

Elizabeth felt her lip quiver as she bit back tears, the image of her new bike and its shiny handlebars and basket souring in her mind.

"Shhh...hey, it's going to be all right. Let's get you back to bed, Lizzy-beth. You've got more riding to do tomorrow. A girl needs a good sleep to stay upright on a bike."

He'd tucked her back into bed, and she heard soft movements in his room followed by the slide of the window opening. He was sneaking out, sneaking away. Elizabeth wished he would take her with him one of these nights.

Now, decades later, she held her brother as his aching wretchedness slowed. With a squeeze, she released him and stepped back to give him air.

"I used all my prize money for the bond," he said, sobered. "I'd planned to buy some new milking machines, help production. Especially now that I won't have...well, guess that's on hold."

"Once I get paid, I'll see what I can do, too, to help. I'm paying you rent."

"No. Absolutely not. You are still my guest. Don't take that from me."

"What does your lawyer think?"

"He says it's a weak case. They have footprints that match some of my boots and my own admitting having seen him. As for a motive, that's where Charlie thinks I'm set. Yes, if need be, he guesses they will paint the courtroom with my and Justin's dirty laundry, but we broke it off a while ago and haven't shown any animosity toward each other since. Hell, we are best friends."

"Wait, you said prize money?"

"From rodeos. I socked it away to start my businesses. I don't have a lot. I've loaned out some, spent some on equipment, things like that."

"Are you sure you can manage the bond?"

"I can for a while, especially if the cheese deal goes through. I have a few design clients in the wings. There's a new development going up in Big Horn, and I've got clients there. I can get by all right."

"When is the next hearing?"

"Two weeks or so, Charlie thinks."

"Let me know what I can do. I think I put the animals up for the night right, but double check."

"Will do. Actually, I'll do that now. I'm a bit torn up, I need a shower and sleep. I've got another meeting with Charlie in the morning to strategize."

"Cognition is at top levels in the morning hours."

"Knock it off, Liz. This is serious."

Elizabeth bit her lip to fight her urge to inform and distract. "Kade stopped by to drop off my roadside bag. He said he wants to help if there is anything we need."

"Kade, huh?" Without further comment, he shoved at the door.

Elizabeth thought about the letters and willed herself not to race over to reopen the trunk to read their private contents. One at the bottom of the stack hadn't been in an envelope, just folded. She's seen some of the handwriting. Read the missive, interpreted its meaning.

"...then I think of you..."

28

DAWN ARRIVED TOO EARLY that Monday morning, like an unwanted relative. A barrage of phone calls lit the screen of Casey's phone. The story of his arrest as a suspect made local news, was printed in the Sheridan Press. Most of the calls were conciliatory, Casey doing more assuring callers than they did for him. "Yes, I'll be okay, Charlie's getting things sorted out for me. Thank you, I'll let you know. It will turn out fine."

Others were problematic.

"Casey Blau." He paused to listen before responding. "I see. Wow. Okay. I understand. I will call you in November, then, okay? To check back. Yes. No. Thank you." When he hung up, he said, "That was one of my clients, canceling their contract. They said they can't have someone connected to a murder working in their house. What would people think and can't I understand, nothing personal and all that."

"Oh, no, I'm sorry."

"When people ask who did their house, they need to be able to tell them it was not someone accused of murdering their best friend. I get it. What if I went and murdered them while I was in their house, making it look nice?"

"I don't know what to say. That's incredibly unfair." Her brother lost his best friend and had simultaneously been accused of the man's murder. Now he was losing work. The hits kept coming.

"On that note, I need to meet with Charlie. I'll be home before you today, likely."

On her way to work, Elizabeth turned over the facts of her current situation like rocks in a field, looking to see what crawled out. She dropped Rhett off with a tight-lipped Jo. Elizabeth was at work in this small town, exposed to raw sides of its living and yet required to function within the confines. Casey seemed confident in his lawyer, but she could find none of his relief, however she tried.

As she entered the small school building, her phone buzzed in her satchel. Hoping it was Casey with news, she withdrew the device from the leather confines. Nick had sent her a *Call me* text. Elizabeth rolled her eyes.

"Maybe after I deal with the rest of my life, I'll find time for you," she said to the device.

"What's that?"

Elizabeth hadn't heard Polly and Benny approach from behind.

"Oh, hi," she mumbled, shoving the phone in her jacket pocket before smoothing her hair and plastering on an approximation of a welcoming smile. Stewing in her internal monologue would have to wait. "Come on in."

"Sorry, I know we're here a bit early."

"It's all right, come on inside. I was planning on making a pot of coffee. Join me for a cup?"

Casey had a top of the line espresso machine at the house, but Elizabeth never wanted to risk angering the metal behemoth while her brother slept. The classroom had a long countertop with a sink and a few cabinets, and in one, she'd found a small coffee maker and a canister of ground beans still in range of its expiration date. The beverage called to her, like a siren.

Polly, in a burgundy tunic over leggings, tall boots, and a puffy coat, hesitated only a moment before accepting. "Sure, sounds good, actually."

While Elizabeth puttered at her preparations, she watched the mother and son. Polly followed Benny around the room, listening as he described the learning they'd done, showed her some of his work, and pointed at sights out the windows. His mother nodded at all his commentary yet looked exhausted, dark circles under her eyes. Her limp, blonde-streaked hair was braided back in an elastic band, adding severity to her haggard look. *Must have been a weekend of late shifts.*

From the warming carafe, she poured two mugs, one bright green, emblazoned with a mountain scene, the other a hand-maid ceramic with eggplant and navy striping. Polly accepted the drink with reverence, cradling it in two hands before venturing a sip.

"There are some packets of sugar and creamer in the cupboard," Elizabeth offered. "Seems I inherited them along with the coffee pot."

Polly shook her head. "Thanks. I like it black, believe it or not."

"I believe it," Elizabeth returned. "My grandfather was the same way. Used to say all that junk ruined a perfectly good beverage."

"Sounds like mine. Said coffee today has too many flavors in it."

"I think our grandfathers would have been friends. Benny is a wonderful student, by the way. I saw him showing you his work." Polly's son had out his favorite work, the microscope, and was using nimble fingers to change out slides. "I can only peel him away from those books to work on science."

"He's always loved books, and he adores your little library here," Polly said, smiling into her cup. The grin faded. "His father used to send him a book for his birthday each year."

"Children who have book-loving families know up to forty percent more vocabulary words." Elizabeth wanted to ask about Benny's father. There were boundary lines she wouldn't— couldn't— cross in prying into students' home lives. Still, she was curious and a little worried. Benny's file held only his mother's information with Rosalyn Hart listed as the emergency backup. She'd toss out a line, see what she caught. "Benny's father reads to him?"

"Oh, no, he's long gone. Otherwise out of the picture. Said his life had no place for a kid, a family. Funny thing is, two years after we broke up, he got married."

Elizabeth stayed quiet, sipping. She knew a little about how things could go with fathers of sons.

"How is your son doing? Rhett, right? Jo adores him, says he's a cherub."

"She saved me, wanting to watch him like she does. I had no idea how remote this job is when I applied. I'm not sure I would have been able to pull this off if she hadn't offered. He loves his uncle, but Casey's been busy with his businesses during the day and..."

She trailed off as she remembered Casey's new existence, his new identity as the accused.

Polly's face reddened. She knew. The moment verged on awkward, teetering toward problematic. How much did everyone know? Or think they knew?

"I'd better go. Let you get going with the day," Polly said, standing. She moved over to the sink to rinse out the dregs, tipped the mug upside down over a paper towel, gave Benny a quick hug, and slipped out the door with a brief wave and a, "Thanks for this, it was nice."

Elizabeth glanced at the clock, wondering when the rest of her class would show up. For the first week of school, the Brown and the Ramirez cars practiced a synchronized arrival. Their mothers were friends and relished the convenient morning gossip time.

She fired up her computer before opening her planbook to the students' current reading lists. When she opened her emails, twin messages from each family excused their students from school for the day. Elizabeth marked the absences and closed the machine.

"Well, Benny, I guess it's just you and me today."

After a morning of math, a picnic lunch, map reading, and a rabbit hole on cattle breeds, the school day wound to a close.

Polly returned to find Elizabeth reading to Benny from a vintage animal husbandry text, the little boy's attention rapt on the diagrams of cattle breeds.

"Hey, Benny," Polly said to her son, bending down to appraise his work. "Those are great drawings."

"Mama, did you know cows have four stomachs?"

"I think I've heard that somewhere." The excitement in the boy's voice was palpable, and his mother smiled.

"It's because they only eat plants, that's why."

"Right," Elizabeth said, returning Benny's grin. "Benny is just like me—he loves facts. He's welcome to take this book home with him. It's a little bit higher level jump than I would typically assign, but he is picking up details and loves the diagrams."

"Thank you, I bet he'll love that. Benny, what do we say to Ms. Blau for letting us borrow her book?"

"Thank you, Ms. Blau. I can't wait to read more about the highland cow. They are the shaggy ones, right?"

"Right. You can come back tomorrow and tell me all about it."

"Where are the other kids? I didn't think I was late today."

"You weren't, they called in," Elizabeth said.

"Huh. Well, we'll see you tomorrow."

"See you!" Benny tucked the book under one arm and gave her a salute.

Elizabeth hoped they were right.

29

ELIZABETH AND RHETT WERE barely in the door when Casey rushed at them, phone in hand, cheeks flushed, and gesturing.

"Someone told," he started. "It's all over."

"Someone told what?"

He looked at her as though she were dense as a brick wall, attempting to reason.

"That I was *arrested*."

He hissed the last word as though Rhett could comprehend their meaning.

"It was on the news."

"Two clients called to cancel on me today. Two. Good ones, too. Not just the people who only want a new back-splash. People who want the works. Now they're gone."

"That super sucks, but what does it have to do with what happened to Justin?"

He gave her an exasperated look. "They said just about everything short of that they couldn't have an accused murderer in their house, busting down walls, painting molding, secretly thinking about killing them, you know."

"Damn."

"Yeah. And if they know, others know, and then I'm worried it's just a matter of time. What do I do, Elizabeth? I can't wait for my name to be cleared. I could lose everything."

"Case, I'm so sorry. We can do this. We can run damage control. We just have to get you some new clients, that's all. Big names. Better ones. People not obsessed with a turquoise and salmon-flavored southwest decor."

He'd regaled her with stories of the poor taste rampant in the county. These weren't the ranchers who grew up here and made their money off the land. These were people who would buy retirement spreads, sight unseen, then move from places like New York, Pennsylvania, and Florida. Incapable of distinguishing the southwest from the Rocky Mountain states, he was constantly tasked with a "New Mexico feel," whatever the hell that was.

"Liz, I'm freaking out here."

Rhett ambled into the living room, carrying his plastic horses. Casey offered a hug and hoisted him up, whispering that if he wanted, they could go see the babies in the barn.

Elizabeth took the diversion to drive to the closest tiny market in Story. They needed milk. She needed a chance to call her ex-husband.

"What did you want, Nick?"

"I just wanted to tell you that my mother is looking into specialists in Portland. She says that if you bring Rhett back here—"

Elizabeth cut him off. "I am not going back. I have a job and a family—here."

"But part of Rhett's family is here, too. Mom thinks you're trying to punish me."

"I really don't care what she thinks. This is my home now. Our home."

"Fine. You think you always get to dictate how things will be. Well, not this time. I'm done trying to balance both sides of this mess."

When he hung up the phone, she leaned her head against the seat back for a moment, flustered by the storms she'd weathered, before crossing the small dirt lot to the building.

Inside the store, she grabbed milk before pausing to consult the ice cream containers, promising within the frosty coolers.

"Elizabeth, hey." Kade had rounded the end of the aisle to find her gazing at labels, undecided, frozen.

"Hi, Kade," she replied, too distracted by her real problems to erect walls against this relative non-issue.

"Polly told me about the farm book, said Benny wouldn't shut up about milking machines and that now she's going to have to read the thing when he goes to bed just to keep up with him."

She turned to regard the man, noticed his uncharacteristic spotlessness, the lack of a mechanic's coverall. Instead, he scanned the few cereal choices before tucking a box of granola under his arm and turning back to her. He'd caught her watching him, and she blushed.

"Are you doing okay today?"

"Could be better, could be worse." In this moment, she felt all the shades of worse.

"Ain't that the way of it."

"Well," she said, noticing the shadow of stubble across his jaw, a thin scar at his chin. "See you around."

"Hey," he said, reaching out to brush her sleeve. "Would you ever be interested in grabbing a beer or a glass of wine sometime? I've got a good view and a fire pit."

His invitation hijacked her quest for chicken noodle soup, a Blau Family comfort food. This man with a rough attractiveness, like an unpolished gem, who had all but growled at Justin, was now asking to spend time with her. A date. Elizabeth narrowed her eyes.

"Thank you, but now's not a good time," she said. "Besides, drinking increases your risk of dying in a fire."

Kade's eyes followed her until she rounded the corner of the aisle. She knew how those stories turned out, the ones where a woman let her guard down.

"What do you know about Kade?" She'd returned home to find Casey at the island, paperwork covering the surface, while Rhett worked through a pile of cereal and pear cubes at his highchair close by.

"Kade Michaels—the mechanic?" Casey held a pencil between his teeth as he dug through the sheets in front of him. He tapped on a calculator and scribbled notes onto a desk pad. "What about him?"

"I don't know. I was just curious what you knew about him. I ran into him at the store."

"He grew up here. I don't know much more than that, to be honest. We've never been close. Justin couldn't stand him. It was like there was an old wound there."

"Like they had an argument or something?"

"I never asked. It's not the kind of thing I do with my friends, grill them about everyone they've ever known."

"You think they had a relationship?"

"No. Nope, not Kade. I do wonder if he knew about all of Justin's...interests. But no, I just assumed they'd had an argument long ago that stayed raw. I take my truck to the dealer, so I've never been to his shop. Sheridan is small, but it ain't that small. You can avoid people if you want to."

"Point taken."

"Wait, are you thinking he had a part in Justin's death?" Casey dropped his pencil to laugh. "Liz, that's rich."

"What? I was just asking. That night at the bar, Kade practically shoulder-checked Justin, and they glared at each other like two dogs ready to fight."

"That's the thing. It was open animosity. I don't know much about Kade, but I don't get the feeling he's stupid, let alone random enough to come down to Banner in the middle of the night at the exact time when Justin would just happen to be outside, in order to run him over with a couple dozen cattle because of some old beef from high school or whenever."

"Okay, okay, I was just thinking. Hoping to help you out."

"I know, thanks. Trust me, I need all the help I can get right now. I can't lose more clients. I've got to land that distribution deal. It will be okay, though, it has to be."

Elizabeth could see the numbers on his pad, see the $10,000 bond circled several times. Tying up his cash flow at a critical time in business expansion was not an optimal situation, and here she was mooching off his good graces.

"They told me I'll get paid at the end of the month, and I'm contributing, no arguments."

Her brother rubbed at his temple and sighed. She saw the crows' feet anchored on either side of his eyes, a few pock marks on the side of one cheek, old acne scars. There'd been so much life they'd shared and yet so much she missed. She was surprised to note the oncoming of age. "We'll work something out. How was school today?"

Changing the subject was a conversational dance move, and she accepted his lead. "It was just Benny Michaels and I today, but we made do. Quieter, though."

A shadow of thought crossed Casey's face, and he shook it free. "Huh."

"While I love having a small class, a class of one is a little too small. I'm hoping the other kids feel well enough to come back tomorrow."

<hr>

Polly dropped Benny off in a rush, with little more than a hello. Elizabeth knew the woman worked two jobs and wondered how often she got to spend time with her son. This was the life of a single mother, and Elizabeth knew it all too well.

The thoughts reminded her of the newest barrage of texts from Nick and one voicemail from a number she didn't recognize. *Save it for after work*, Elizabeth told herself. She didn't want to be distracted with news from her ex.

Beth Ramirez's car inched up the hill and parked. Jo stepped out of the passenger's side. Beth stayed in the car, a pair of earbuds to keep her company inside the vehicle.

"Hey, Elizabeth," Jo said.

"Hi. Is something wrong? Where are the kids?"

"They are going to stay home again. Maybe for the rest of the week. But I hope not."

"Are they okay?"

"They're fine. It's just..." Jo hesitated, glancing in Beth's direction. "Well, the Ramirez family and the Browns feel that, well..." Jo stumbled over her message like a sputtering engine.

"Out with it, Jo. I've got a single kid to teach today."

"They don't feel comfortable having the kids here while you're living with Casey. What if he needs to drop something off, or pick you up? I know it's prejudice, believe me—"

"But?"

"But I kind of get it. People need to think of schools as safe places for kids."

"Are you kidding me? I'm the teacher, not Casey. "

"Sorry, Liz, that's the long and short of it. Once the charges are dropped, things can go back to normal.

"I see." *If things go back to normal.* Elizabeth's lips pressed together, and she crossed her arms as she rolled the situation around in her mind. She knew how much the school meant to the small community, how so much was riding on this school year to keep the building going. "Chronic absenteeism decreases achievement, you know."

"Look, it's just how people get out here. Protecting their kids and all. Anyway, Beth and I—" Jo gestured at the car. Beth, who'd been surreptitiously watching the exchange, gave a half smile and a little wave from inside the vehicle. "—were wondering if you'd reconsider moving into the teacherage. Give Casey some space to get it all sorted out."

30

SORTED. JO SPOKE ABOUT THE case as though it were a mix up at the grocers. The neighbor picked up the wrong mail. Not a murder case.

Elizabeth had forgotten about the little cottage, once the original schoolhouse. She'd preferred Casey's farm even if it meant a short commute.

"That way if Casey is found guilty—"

"He won't be."

"Of course he won't. Still have the key?"

Elizabeth, not trusting herself to speak without swearing, nodded.

"Think about it, please? The kids really do love you. I'll tell Beth and Mirabel that you'll consider, at least."

"He's my brother, Jo. I'm not abandoning him."

"No one is asking you to do that. They are just asking you to consider the bigger picture."

Before Elizabeth could work out a response, the woman slipped back into the car and the two were gone.

Elizabeth didn't like confrontation. She didn't like being bullied. Nick would still be her husband and she would be cowering under the pressure of his mother's wishes had that been her game.

Yet Elizabeth hadn't outright told her no, hadn't told the woman it was wrong to treat Casey as a criminal before they'd even finished the investigation, let alone held a trial. Guilt settled in her heart, however, because if roles were reversed and she was in Beth's or Mirabel's shoes, she wouldn't have left Rhett in the care of someone living with an accused murderer, either. Double damn.

Polly hadn't hesitated to drop Benny off this morning. The woman peeled out of the driveway as soon as he hit the welcome mat. Elizabeth guessed she didn't have a choice to consider such protests. She needed to work, needed the money, so her son needed to go to school.

After some work with the scales, plant identification guides, and making homemade wax candles, she parked Benny in front of the microscope. They'd found a box of prepared slides in the closet: onion skins, a bee leg, and a fish scale, and made some of their own after a nature walk. Solemn in his work, proud to be trusted with the serious apparatus, Benny sketched the intricacies of an aspen leaf on his notepad. What his fine motor skills lacked in detail, his interest balanced. She pictured a grown-up version of Benny in a graduate assistant's lab, hair uncombed and wild, a latte abandoned on a desk, laboring over samples and his notes.

When his mother arrived that afternoon, a half-length apron still tied around her waist, he ran to show her his drawings. His cheerful chatter was bittersweet to Elizabeth, anxious to hear Rhett talk about his schoolwork one day.

"He was awesome," she told Polly. "A true scientist."

Benny grinned at the compliment. "She taught me to turn the knobs until I could see right."

"That's so cool, Benny."

"I wanted to talk with you about him, if you have a quick moment. It won't take long."

"Sure. Should Benny hang out or wait in the car?"

"I think it's okay if he gets to hear, but that's up to you."

Benny, blue shirt emblazoned with a shark wearing sunglasses, jeans, and tennis shoes, looked up, volleying his attention between the two women.

"Benny—you okay with that?"

"Yes, Mama."

"This is the first time I've had students on the younger side of things. I usually teach high school, though I did middle school before that. Never kindergarten."

Confusion spread over Polly's face, but she nodded, putting a hand on Benny's shoulder.

"I'm not starting well. Look, I know I haven't been working with him long, and I'm not an expert on five-year-olds, but since I've had a couple days to focus on Benny, I've noticed that many of his skills seem advanced, especially compared with the curriculum they've given me."

"I'm always saying he'll be smarter than his whole family put together in no time."

"Well, I'd like to do a couple of things about what I've seen, support him. I think I should get your permission for that. I'd like to give him some of the second-grade work that I have here for Rachel. Normally, I'd go to first grade, but they only sent me books for the kids I have."

"Do you hear that, bud? You get to try second grader work!"

The shy smile that spanned Benny's face belied both his humility and excitement at the prospect.

"And, as I'm new, I'd like your permission to call the district and ask whether they have testing for abilities, or maybe even a program, or something I could use to make sure he gets what he needs. Back home, I knew who to call, what to do. Here, I'm kind of on my own, so I'd have to do some research."

A tear slipped down Polly's cheek, and she wiped it away with the back of the fingers on one hand. "Thank you. I don't know what to say. No one has ever...his father..."

Benny held his mother's hand, looking down at his feet, uncomfortable with the outline of emotion.

"I don't think you'd have to take him anywhere or do any-thing different. I would just be working with him on different standards, advancing him as he is ready as opposed to waiting for the end of the year."

"Can I do it, Mama?"

Both women looked surprised at Benny's request, the complacent boy in a moment of self-advocacy.

"Of course you can," Polly said, her usual creases of worry replaced with hope as she bent down to clutch him to her chest. Then, to Elizabeth, she said, "Do I need to sign a paper or something?"

"No. Or rather, not at this point. Let me find out who to get in contact with, and I'll let you know. I'll call them today."

"Thank you. Really, thank you. I don't know why you are being so nice to me, since—"

Polly clamped her mouth shut before the words escaped, and Elizabeth wanted to pry them back open. Since my brother's been accused of murder? Since the guy I had all of two dates with was the one murdered? What was she missing?

"It's for Benny. I'd do it for any kid. School should meet them where they're at."

"Can I at least buy you a beer? I'm at the Inn most nights this week. Come by if you can, the next one's on me."

Elizabeth thought of the phone call she needed to make after calling the district. She'd need a drink after that train wreck. "Thank you. I'll take you up on that."

As the mother and son walked to their car in animated chatter, Elizabeth's mood dipped as she turned to face her task list.

⋆

A phone call to a program manager allowed Elizabeth to share her observations of Benny. She received a rundown of the gifted program and the promise of resources in the next material drop off. She hung up that call and readied herself for the next.

Before she called Nick, she tapped at the voicemail. A clipped, efficient voice informed her that she was the attorney for one Nick Thompson and would Ms. Blau please return the call at her earliest convenience to answer a few questions.

Elizabeth's hands shook, her fingers numb as a chill raced down her spine. Nick's attorney.

He'd warned her, but she'd lost track of the comments, assuming he'd back down. They hadn't used a lawyer in the divorce, preferring to work it all out on their own. This smacked of a trespass, a violation of their agreements to function as a calm, however reluctant team. This was a tactical move.

Rage pulsed through her veins. Elizabeth hit the speed dial for Nick and began talk-yelling before he could utter a greeting.

"What the *hell* Nick? A lawyer? Explain, now."

"Hi, Liz." She could picture him, seated in front of his laptop, a half-eaten sandwich on top of a pile of files, coffee cups littering every surface. He had worked from home as long as they'd been together, taking up as much space as possible in the occupation. When they argued over domain, he'd said he was an artist, that architecture required the ability to spread things out, take a look from all angles. "I take it you got the message from Delilah."

"On a first name basis with this woman, are you?"

"We've known each other since we were kids and I—look, that doesn't matter. I asked you to call me. I told you my mom has been concerned Rhett isn't getting the care he needs out there away from the resources of a city. She doesn't think you are taking this seriously enough and—"

"*She* doesn't think I'm taking this seriously? Aren't *you* his father? You told me you were okay waiting until he is two, following what the actual doctors said to do."

"Yes, but—"

"Yes, but what? Let me guess, she convinced you otherwise." The fact that Nick rolled over anytime his mother disagreed with him was a sore point that had plagued their relationship. If his mother didn't like their furniture, their choice of vacation spot, the menu for Sunday supper, she would goad Nick until he relented. Elizabeth had learned long ago that Nick only had independent thoughts if his mother allowed them.

"Liz. Casey's name was in the paper."

31

"IN THE *OLYMPIAN*, MOM READ an article about a man being trampled under a herd of cattle, a freak accident, then a sudden murder charge and an arrest."

"I can't believe you. You know this is a bullshit charge that won't make it through court."

"The lawyer is calling to verify that you live with Casey, Liz. Take it from there."

"You can tell your lawyer—and your mother—that they don't know what they are talking about. Not about Rhett, Casey, or me."

Hanging up on people on a mobile phone didn't have the physical finality of the old telephones, but cutting him off before he could spout more terrible news was a temporary satisfaction. Elizabeth slammed her laptop shut, too, grabbed her bag and coat, and stormed out the door.

At the Wolfs' house, she knocked with more force than was necessary, the reverberations through the wood announcing her presence and her mood.

When Jo opened the door, Elizabeth spat, "I will move into the teacherage this weekend, but not for you or Beth or Mirabel or anyone other than for Casey, to give him the freedom to do what he needs to do without us underfoot."

Jo's cheek twitched as she gave a perceptible nod, indicating she heard, loud and clear. Elizabeth regretted the sting of her words, if just for a moment. Jo came to her in kindness,

Elizabeth responded with acidity. She had a right to be bitter, though, she thought. She was the one who had to adjust her life to fit the needs of others again and again, exhausted from the effort and brokenhearted over the circumstances.

Rhett toddled up, brandishing a stuffed lamb Jo had given him. Elizabeth scooped him up and without a word, left.

Back home, she mulled over how to break the news to Casey. His truck was gone when she arrived, but he came through the door just as she and Rhett finished their soup. He dropped his gear at the doorway and slumped onto the couch, turning on a game to lose himself in the blue light.

"Hey, there's something I need to tell you."

"Please tell me your new boyfriend is a distributor for Whole Foods and wants to fund my cheese operation. I just closed my last contract and don't have any others on deck, yet."

"Not yet, but you've given me a good goal for my online dating profile."

Her attempt at a joke fell flat as Casey continued staring at the screen.

"Look, Jo suggested I move into the teacherage at the school for a couple weeks until things die down. A couple of the families—"

"Go ahead."

"What?"

"I said, go ahead. You were going to tell me that the families would feel better if their kids weren't in the same room all day with a woman who lives with a murderer, and I get it."

"You do?"

"It's always something new in this place. They've been pushing me out since the day I got here. I'm good enough to redesign their fancy vacation homes but too gay for the parties they hold in them. This is just one more excuse to shove me out, tell me I can only get so close. So, go right ahead, I'll be fine."

His works stung her, like fat raindrops on the sidewalk. This was another rejection, and she was torn between saving her own reputation and saving her brother's.

"Casey, I'm coming back. It isn't permanent."

"Sure. It's fine."

"Hey, could I get your lawyer's number? Nick called and I—"

"Help yourself, it's on the fridge," he said to the screen before turning up the volume on the remote.

The dismissal raked at her heartstrings. Elizabeth zipped her lips into a determined line, ordering herself not to cry.

The metallic melody of Casey's phone punctured the silence between the siblings.

Elizabeth planted Rhett next to herself on the couch with a sturdy picture book, cocking her head toward Casey to eavesdrop as he muted the television and tapped at the phone.

"Hello," he said into the receiver, his voice dusty and hoarse.

A pause for a voice, male, rambling, and then, "Oh, really?"

Elizabeth could hear a stream of garbled uttering from the caller on the other end of the line, explaining something in detail as Casey listened, his intense gaze fixed on a spot on the wall in front of him.

"On the flank? Interesting."

More sounds on the receiver. Elizabeth tried to care about the duckling pond dilemma as she read the colorful pages to Rhett but faltered, not wanting to miss a word Casey said.

"Yeah, I'd seen that. Hadn't told Elizabeth, yet. You know, it could be something or nothing. 'Tis the season."

Her ears all but reached out to him, beyond starving for details.

"Saturday, then. I'll be waiting."

In the light of the television, a flash flood of relief painted his expression as he ended the call.

"Who?"

"Charlie."

"And?"

"Apparently, they found a strange mark on one of the cattle. On her hip, so to speak. They think it's from an electric prod. A little semicircle of singed fur."

"Don't make me connect the dots, brother. What does this mean?"

"The Harts' cattle had been rounded up the day before, penned for the vet visit. Sheriff Wolf questioned the hands, and none had used any prods, nor had they seen any of the others use one."

"So, they think someone used a cattle prod to cause the stampede? I don't see how that's helpful. Everyone around here probably owns one."

"Everyone except for this goat herder."

32

ELIZABETH SQUEEZED THE NEXT few days out of Casey's good news.

Jo dropped off a basket of muffins with an offer to help her move, an olive branch. Elizabeth missed the easy friendship with the woman as she corralled her and Rhett's meager belongings, once again preparing to decamp to a new location. Despite the sheriff's discovery, Casey's mood sank as she prepared to move. He told her that his demons should be ignored until she had a chance to end this business with the lawyer. Elizabeth wasn't so certain.

No one had visited the house since the accusations.

Friday night, Elizabeth painted on her jeans and drove herself to the Crow Bar. Casey had shooed her out the door, claimed a need for solid uncle-nephew time with Rhett while they were still in the house. Elizabeth, happy to relinquish mothering for a couple hours of adult time, left the pair examining a farming catalog, her son's preferred chicken nuggets in the oven, broccoli steaming on the stove.

The sound of a local blues band met Elizabeth in the gravel parking lot. She tucked her tiny car among a row of oversized working vehicles and a few motorcycles. Neon signs beckoned her to the front door.

Inside, the place was packed. People leaned on every surface, table or otherwise. She headed for the bar where Polly, flushed like a runner, held a pitcher up to a tap.

"Hey!" The bartender grinned at Elizabeth, perspiration tracing her brow. "Glad you came out! What can I get you?"

"Busy night. I'll take an IPA, thanks."

Bread in a bottle, Nick called beer, empty carbs. Elizabeth preferred the big and wintery beers, the stouts and barley wines. The hoppy bitterness of tonight's choice would keep her from downing the cold liquid in one gulp. It had been a stressful week. While she was tempted to try every brew in the house, she also had to drive herself home. Better to linger over something she could only stomach in slow motion.

Elizabeth rotated in her seat, the bar stools designed for conversational flexibility, and faced the room.

An ersatz dance floor held a few couples who leaned on each other, shuffling to the music in their heads as the band, a decent one out of Casper, the flier on the door proclaimed, played. Servers ducked between tables, dropping off pizzas and collecting glasses, but it seemed to be Polly who was the busiest.

Elizabeth held the pint glass to her lips, the cold, creamy foam tasting of neon lights.

When Kade entered the bar, she heard her own sharp intake of breath, a tiny sound in the musical din. Was this a good turn of events or a bad one?

The man looked good, damn good. A tight black T-shirt with the shop logo over his chest with dark denim jeans and black boots. Elizabeth cooled her inner engines as Kade and his buddies approached the bar. She feigned giving the Cowboys vs. the Rams her full attention on the wide-screen.

Kade ignored Elizabeth and delivered a full wattage smile to the bartender. "Hey, Poll, it's slammed tonight."

"Kade, Isaiah, Eric, how are things?" Polly leaned over the bar in front of where they stood, a few stools away from Elizabeth.

"I'll take an amber and look for a table," Isaiah or Eric said and walked through the archway to the next room.

"Bourbon and water for me," Kade said.

"Crown and Coke," the other Isaiah or Eric said. As Polly worked the taps, Kade's friend leaned back, elbows on the bar, and spotted Elizabeth.

Damn. Here it comes.

"Well, hello there," the man said. "I don't believe we've met. Are you new in town?"

Elizabeth stuffed down every urge to roll her eyes and instead swallowed the sarcastic remarks on the tip of her tongue. With a tight-lipped smile, she opened her mouth to reply when Polly jumped in, her savior.

"Easy there, Isaiah, that's Casey Blau's sister. The new teacher. I'm not about to let you scare her off."

So, the super tan, sandy-haired one was Isaiah, Elizabeth noted.

Newly labeled Eric said, "Casey is a good guy. I'm Eric Roundhouse, welcome to town. Don't mind my idiot friend. We're not all like him."

"Nice to meet you both," she said, her generous side winning out.

Kade sipped his drink in silence, ignoring them for all intents and purposes, watching the game on the screen in the corner of the bar.

Polly stoked the conversation as she poured drinks. "Benny is a changed kid with her help."

"Benny makes my job easy. He's a great kid."

She glanced at Kade. So, maybe a little piling admiration.

"He's not the social one," Isaiah explained. "And hey, I didn't mean to come on too strong."

"No harm, no foul," Elizabeth acknowledged, tipping the mouth of her bottle toward him in a brief salute.

"Your brother did a fantastic update on my folks' cabin. Opened it right up and installed a huge stone fireplace. Looks great now."

"I've seen some photographs. He's got an album on the coffee table I've paged through. Some of those buildings were stunning to begin with."

"Did he show you the work he did on the Arrowhead Lodge? Rehabbed the whole place. Used to have a zillion tiny, dank rooms and now it has a huge entryway. Bookings have doubled. Shame all that's happened. For what it's worth, I don't believe it."

Polly shot Isaiah a murderous look. Elizabeth took another sip and tried to calm the clenching of her gut. If she went out in public here, she knew it was only a matter of time before their family business was up for discussion.

"Yeah, my brother is paying a price for something he didn't do," Elizabeth said, setting down her beer and peeling at the label. "If that's not messed up, I don't know what is."

"They'll clear that up, right quick," Polly said, wiping glasses she then shelved. "It's terrible, the charges and all."

"I heard there's some new evidence," Eric said. "Might help."

Polly paused to put both hands on the bar, towel in one. "You on the sheriff's investigative team now? They run all the leads through you since you have all that experience watching crime shows?"

"Funny," Eric said. "Alls I'm saying is that they think they know what caused the cattle to stampede in the first place."

Elizabeth tried to picture a dime-sized circle of black on brown, the gagging smell of searing flesh. She hadn't thought this was public knowledge, but if there was one thing she was learning, it was that secrets didn't stay secret long in a small town.

"It's not like it's that hard," Polly said, bending into the coolers to grab bottles for a couple at the bar. "Just about anything will do it. Look at what happened to poor Harry."

Elizabeth wondered at the fate of this Harry person.

She also wondered at Kade's continued silence. He reached for a bowl of corn nuts on the counter and tossed a few into his mouth before chewing. Like a moth to a flame, she ventured a risk.

"Either way, a great guy is dead, and Casey is wrapped up in it."

"Yeah, a real great guy." Kade snorted.

He *was* listening.

"Yeah, he was."

"Oh, and you knew him so well?" Kade asked. "Why don't you ask Roz about how great he was? Or half the people here? Hell, even his mother wasn't his biggest fan."

"Kade, we don't speak ill of the dead."

"God forbid anyone say out loud what we're all thinking about Justin Hart, that he was a spoiled, selfish, washed-up team roper who didn't know a good thing when he had it." He took the bowl and his glass and stalked off to a far table.

"Don't mind him," Eric said. "He and Justin haven't gotten along since high school football."

Elizabeth's pinky twitched as she absorbed the vitriol in Kade's voice, a long-standing practice from her years with Nick.

"Hey, Liz," Polly said softly, putting her hand on Elizabeth's arm. "Can I get you another?"

"This one's on me, Poll," Isaiah said. "To apologize for our grumpy friend. It'll give us a chance to change the subject to something else."

"A toast to a new subject," Eric suggested, holding up his bottle for clinks. "How do you like the band?"

Elizabeth accepted the second round and the kindness from Kade's friends.

"They're good," she said, tapping out the rhythm with a foot on the rung of her barstool. "I was at the Occidental last week. Bluegrass is more my style, though."

Eric and Isaiah exchanged a look.

"It just so happens we like to play at the jam sessions, too."

"That we do."

"Mandolin," Isaiah said. Then, pointing to Eric, "Fiddle."

"Don't forget Mr. Grumpy Guitarist over there," Eric added.

"I'd pay to see that." Elizabeth wasn't sure she meant this. She'd loved the music, but could she make it through a set without thinking of Justin? Dancing with him, tucked in close. The way he tipped back in his chair, a wide smile crossing his face. Walking, hand-in-hand, to the creek bank.

"Hear that, Polly? Eric finally found us a groupie."

Elizabeth's laughter was a hollow sound in her chest. The stress of the last few months kept her laser focused. To have a moment for idle chat, let alone with a couple of cute guys, was a luxury she'd forgotten.

More conversation led to the discovery of a mutual love of soccer. Elizabeth lamented the loss of her season tickets to the Portland Thorns to a captive audience.

When Eric and Isaiah ran through the roster of Real Madrid, she excused herself to find the restroom. The memories of Justin tugged at her, disrupting the ease of the evening.

Elizabeth side-stepped the group gathered around a foosball table planted in front of the ladies' room. She sensed the stare of one of the players.

Kade. He watched her weave through the bodies, not bothering to cloak his vigil.

Decoding his expression was impossible. *I bet he makes a damn good poker player*. He set down his glass and stood, as if to approach. She ducked inside the door to the ladies' room before he could.

When she came out, having lingered over hand washing to steel herself for a confrontation, he was gone.

Elizabeth settled her tab, handing Polly a crisp bill. Her envelope of savings wouldn't last long if she depleted it at this rate, but she'd needed this. Needed to be a single woman out having a drink.

"Need someone to walk you to your car?" Polly handed over change which Elizabeth stuffed in the tip jar.

"I'm right out front, but thanks." Elizabeth waved to Eric and Isaiah, promising to attend a soccer watch party some night, and made her way out to her car.

Veiled moonlight streaked out from behind the mountains and toward the prairie. The search for daredevil deer would consume her drive home. The animals often bolted in front of cars, pell-mell, eyes wild, hooves flailing. In those scenarios, no one wins.

"I checked your tire pressure."

Elizabeth yelped, and her purse went flying.

33

KADE HOVERED NEAR HER car, tire gauge in hand. He twirled the skinny, metal tool between his fingers. "Your front driver's side is low. You'll want to get that looked at. Might be a slow leak."

Elizabeth stooped to pick up her bag and collect the lipstick, keys, and book scattered in the gravel.

"How dare you touch my car!" She twisted her fear into indignation before it got the better of her ability to breathe and think. The parking lot was empty. She needed an escape route.

"Hey, I was doing you a favor. I noticed—"

"I don't care what you noticed. I don't care if it was flat. I don't want you to touch my car. Ever. Again." She punctuated her last two words and glared at Kade.

A flash of vulnerability crossed his face before he narrowed his eyes into slits. "Why is it always about Justin Hart with you?"

"What are you talking about?"

"This." He held up a hand to her, waving at her as though she were a slate to be cleaned. "Hostility."

It was about Justin. She wouldn't admit this, though.

"I don't know what you are talking about." *Liar*, she thought.

"Last time I'll be your friendly mechanic. Got it."

Maybe people here did the neighborly thing. Looked out for each other. This wasn't working for Elizabeth, though. She needed boundaries.

"I'm asking you not to touch my car, my things."

She watched his face harden from confused to bristling. "Fine," he said, stepping back and sweeping his hand in a wide arc. "Don't let me get in your way."

Stomping forward, she wrenched open the car door, threw her purse on the passenger's seat, and started the car. Her reverse was deft, kicking up rocks and dust, before she shifted gear and exited the lot. Kade watched as she left, a statue of judgment.

On the approach to Cloud Nine, Elizabeth lifted her foot from the accelerator and exhaled, the spite leaching from her veins. Why did Kade matter? Why did she let him get under her skin? She needed to focus on her family, the people waiting inside the beautiful ranch house in front of her. She would miss this view, a poor trade for the teacherage, cold and lonely on the hill.

On Saturday morning, she loaded their suitcases and a small box of Rhett's toys into the trunk and added a small bag of groceries.

As promised, the lights, plumbing, and heat worked. Jo had put a small vase of flowers on the tiny kitchen table with no note, but Elizabeth knew her mark, knew the woman was of two minds about the situation.

Rhett explored the connected rooms as she unpacked their few belongings. A front area served as kitchen, dining, and sitting spaces, with a couple windows facing west. The former classroom had been converted into a bedroom space, shelves added to the coat closet. There was a trundle bed and a squat dresser to finish out the furniture, a prairie landscape dotted with buffalo hanging on one wall. *Like a motel.*

"It's just for a little while," she said to Rhett, hoping she spoke the truth.

Casey had made Rhett a stack of building blocks out of some lumber he had, polished smooth. Her son stacked the blocks to form first one wall and then a second, on his way to a full structure.

"Mac and cheese work for you?"

Rhett regarded her, brown eyes saucers. He held out a block, a pine tree burned into one side, a bison on the other.

She busied herself at the small cookstove, a two-burner operation Jo had warned her to regard as armed and dangerous. "We filled the gas tank, so you shouldn't have any issues with cooking or heat, but it's not the newest equipment, so if anything, and I mean anything, acts strangely, let us know."

Later, after tucking herself into the overstuffed chair to read from a bodice ripper, convincing herself that somewhere there may be a man who would seduce her over Parisian picnics if only she would give him a chance, she heard a tap on the roof. Another page in and she heard it again. Two minutes went by, and a series of three startled her.

The roof of the old schoolhouse building was tiled in green shingles, layered over each other and anchored with nails. The steep pitch was designed to negate the snowstorms that battered the structure each winter. Anything that hits the roof should roll off.

Two more taps. Like hail, an unnatural force among the gentle patter of rain, the sounds disrupted the night. Elizabeth slid into her shoes to peek outside.

Wrapping her arms around her torso, as much for comfort as for warmth, she beheld the night sky in all its glory. *Light pollution is all but a myth in this part of the world*. Endless tiny stars pin-pricked the blackness, a few thin clouds chasing the moon.

She scanned the landscape in front of her, the glow from the sky crescent giving little hint but shadows.

Nothing.

In the distance, she could see the yard light on at the Wolf house. A copse of trees blocked the view of Casey's place, but she thought she saw the faint glint of a silver roofline behind them.

A rush of vulnerability raced up her spine. Elizabeth shivered. Whatever it was loomed outside the door.

Inside again, Elizabeth double checked that she bolted the lock and drew the remaining curtains closed, turned on a second lamp, and went back to reading.

Tap. Thunk. Tap. Tap.

She sat up. Must be rodents. Or raccoons. Were they in the rodent category? She would ask Jo about them in the morning.

Elizabeth reread a page about the heroine, leaning on a balcony overlooking Sacre Coeur for the fifth time. The character, a headstrong woman who'd left everything behind to move to France, debated whether to risk it all for a museum curator with a bad boy streak.

Elizabeth couldn't focus. She closed her eyes for a moment, picturing herself in her twenties, back in Paris in the spring. Adulthood rolling out ahead of her like a red carpet. The adventure had required saving every penny from lifeguarding for two summers in trade for a week in a hostel. She'd loved every minute.

Paris seemed a lifetime away from this tiny house on a hill, thousands of miles from the City of Light.

Thunk. Thunk. Tap.

On impulse, Elizabeth reached up to turn off one lamp and then the next. She became a statue, breathing only as necessary to remain upright.

Silence.

Slinking along the wall, Elizabeth moved toward the bedroom door. She turned the knob until it clicked and pushed the door inward to create a crack of light. Through it, she caught a glimpse of Rhett, sound asleep on the bed. Thumb in his mouth, he looked like the cherubim, content in their airy castles.

Back in the hall, she switched off the light.

At Casey's, there were two adults, motion lights, and the old rifle above the door. Here, she was a sitting duck. Exposed.

Elizabeth readied for bed in the dark, trembling.

Getting changed was a quick process—clothes off, pajamas on. She paused her toothbrush, a mouthful of foam, to listen for percussive interruptions.

Nothing.

A sleepless night sloughed off to reveal a new dawn. Before she woke Rhett, Elizabeth wrapped herself in a dark robe and headed out in the lingering cold. A walking tour of the exterior revealed nothing other than an old tire, an ancient swing set, and pinecones littering the yard.

Pinecones.

Three aspens shook their golden leaves into the yard, and the branches of an old cottonwood stretched outward toward the sun. The closest conifer was back at Casey's house where a spruce and a Ponderosa shaded his driveway.

Elizabeth picked up one of the cones and studied it before chucking it onto the roof.

Thunk. Tap.

34

"CAN'T YOU DO ANYTHING? EVERYTHING is on the line now!" Casey yelled into the phone as she stepped through the front door, Rhett in tow.

Muffled talking came through the phone. Casey held up his pointer finger to her, a hold for silence. His brow was damp, his hair a shaggy mess.

"How quickly can we get this dropped?"

More talking.

"I am going to lose my business. I won't be able to pay you. You have to get this gone, now."

This time, the voice continued for a few minutes as Elizabeth watched her brother's face melt into hopelessness.

"Call them. Call anyone. I don't care. I have to get my name out of the damn news."

He had to have lost another client. The farm was still in its infancy. Stacking these small blows against each other made for big problems.

"I could just kill whoever leaked my name! Why should anyone in Seattle give a damn about where their cheese came from and whether or not the maker is accused of murder? Just look at that bread guy."

This was one of those moments when no response would help.

"Dammit!" Casey hung up the phone and put his hands on his hips, a gesture Elizabeth remembered from childhood when he became frustrated.

"If you don't feel like watching Rhett today, it's okay. I can take him with me."

Her brother sighed. "No, it's fine. I'm good. I'll stop yelling around him."

Rhett clung to Elizabeth's leg, face half-buried in her jacket.

"Hey, buddy," Casey said, kneeling on the tiled floor. "Sorry. I'm so sorry for talking that way. That was not cool, not okay. Can you forgive me?"

Rhett twisted his face away, farther into the folds of fabric. Casey extended a hand and tried again.

"I could really use a junior cowboy to help me feed the goats. Would you know one?"

At the mention of the animals, the little boy looked to his uncle, fingers of one hand in his mouth. Casey held out his hands to snuggle his nephew.

"Thanks, little man. I needed this."

Elizabeth mouthed, "What happened?" Concern made her face heavy, slack.

Casey made no pretense of hiding the ugly truth. "I lost the distribution contract. They won't launch cheese partnerships with the future of my business in question, as they put it."

"Oh, Casey, I'm so sorry. Will they reconsider when this is all cleared up?"

"Liz, I'm lucky if I can last that long. I sank just about everything I had into this place. I'm wondering if I can make it to next week."

Elizabeth watched her brother, her protector, falling apart. She had to do something to fight the powerlessness reaching for them all. She added another stop to her list of errands.

35

THE HUM OF A pop machine in the hallway was the only sound audible in the sheriff's office. When Elizabeth entered the small lobby, the secretary clicked out of a game of solitaire on her screen. The woman made a show of scrutinizing her schedule book before sharing the obvious with Elizabeth.

"Sheriff doesn't have you down for today."

"I know. I'm here to get on his schedule." Elizabeth took a seat on the couch and reached for a magazine abandoned on a side table.

"I see."

After a few mouse clicks, the woman picked up the phone and said, "Ms. Blau is here to see you."

A pause.

"Mmhmm. Yes, I told her that."

Elizabeth recrossed her legs and tapped her foot, listening.

"Not until two." The woman scrolled through a schedule on her screen as Elizabeth fumed with growing impatience.

"You know me. I just do what I can."

Elizabeth pressed the tips of her fingers together, hand to hand.

"She sent along something in a container. Want me to reheat it for you? After? Got it."

Returning the handset to its cradle, the woman sighed. She turned to regard Elizabeth, as if annoyed to still find her rooted to the couch. "Head on back. He has a few minutes before lunch."

"You know, crossword puzzles have a greater positive effect on cognitive abilities than computer games." Elizabeth flashed a smile at the woman behind the desk before picking up her purse and heading down the hallway.

Sheriff Wolf didn't look up. Instead, he squinted through reading glasses at this computer screen, his eyes pin pricks behind the reflections in each lens. "Ms. Blau, this is...unexpected. What can I do for you?"

"Sheriff."

"It's Clint unless this is official business."

"It's business."

"I see." He removed the reading glasses from the bridge of his nose and rubbed at his eyes. He lifted a few stacks on his desk until he found a notepad, clicked open a pen. "All right."

"Two things. First, what is the hold up with the investigation? My brother is losing all his clients. He hasn't even been convicted. Where is the justice here?"

The sheriff set the pen down, interlaced his fingers, and rested his chin on his knuckles. "Ms. Blau, I cannot comment on an active case, and I think you know that. I can tell you that this department is following all procedures when it comes to exacting justice as we've done the last thirty years I've been here."

"But Casey didn't do it. You have to know that!"

"One of the hardest parts of my job is keeping my personal life out of my professional duties, but I assure you, I would not have the reputation I do if I were not a fair and just lawman. Now, as to your other concern?"

Wolf picked up his pen and raised his eyebrows in encouragement.

Elizabeth knew he was right. The entire point of the law was so that rules couldn't be altered to suit a situation or the accused, but dammit, this was taking too long. She sighed. "Someone or something threw pinecones onto my roof last night. A bunch of them."

"Pinecones?" Wolf held his pen above the surface of the yellow memo pad.

"Yes. You know, the stabby holders of seeds from conifer trees such as spruce, pines, hemlocks, and the like? Coniferophyta. Make great fire starters, bird feeders, and Christmas decor."

Wolf read each word as he wrote them. "Someone was throwing *pinecones* onto the roof of the teacher's cottage."

"Teacherage."

"Right." He crossed out two words and wrote above them. "Did you see this someone?"

"I went outside and checked but didn't see anything. When I came back inside, they started up again, so I turned off all the lights, and it stopped. In the morning, there were about two dozen of them on the ground. As you know, there are no pine trees near the school."

"I see." The cursive scratchings paused. "What time did this happen?"

"After ten. I'd fallen asleep reading and woke to the sound. They sounded like rocks."

"Two dozen, you say?"

"About."

"How long did the barrage of nature's grenades continue?"

Elizabeth raised an eyebrow, imitating Vivian Leigh appraising his level of jest. Over his shoulder loomed a bookshelf crammed with the western requisite Louis L'Amour and just as many Kerouac, Angelou, and LeGuin interspersed. The man just appreciated descriptive narrative, she reasoned.

"Maybe five or ten minutes before I went outside. Nothing happened when I was outside, and then after I came back in, they started up again for about five minutes before I turned out the lamps and they stopped."

"Why did you turn out the lights?"

"I don't know, really." Fear had been edging into her conscious thoughts at that point. She was exposed in that building, even more so with the lights on. At least without illumination, anyone outside would be unsure of her actions. "I guess I thought if someone was out there, they might think I'd gone to bed and wouldn't be paying attention."

He leaned back in his chair, arms crossed, tip of the pen resting against his lip. "Tell you what. I'll stop by tonight and look around. It is an odd thing, but my guess is it's just some kids messing around."

"Okay."

"I'll be home tonight. Jo, too. Call if it starts up again."

Elizabeth watched the hills along her drive, the perceptible undulation of landscape. The western sky hung above them like a blanket, edged in gray. Autumn flirted with snow long before welcoming her in for the winter. Elizabeth made a mental note to test the heat in the cottage before the first dumping of powder. If the clouds opened up with something intense, she didn't want to be isolated and frozen out on the prairie. Better snag a load of firewood from her brother's house, too.

The old schoolhouse had a fireplace that could use a sweeping out. Half a bird's nest sat in the hearth alongside crumpled newspaper advertisements meant for kindling. She'd have a purpose for those pinecones.

It wouldn't be a bad idea to lay in a supply of canned food and some bottled water. If a storm blew in while school was in session, she would have to think of her students. *The average*

*person doesn't have supplies to last a week in their home after
a disaster, let alone enough for others in their care.*

When a familiar SUV rolled into Casey's driveway, Elizabeth swore under her breath.

36

"H EY, LIZ."
The voice made her skin crawl. Her emotional
wall of protection crumbled into dust at her feet.

Nick sat on Casey's couch in full ex-husband glory. Beer in
one hand, a children's book in the other, he snuggled Rhett in
his lap. Her son's rapt attention broke only to extend a hand
out toward his mother, as if to say, look who's here. Casey gave
her a strained smile from his perch in a chair.

"Nick," she began, his name grinding out through her
teeth. "What are you doing here?"

"I came to see my son, of course," he said. "Casey has been
updating me on his situation."

"Oh, really?" Elizabeth replied, the ice behind her words
lowering the temperature of the room. Elizabeth shot her
brother a look that would fell a doe at three-hundred yards.
"I would think Casey would want to keep information close
with all the trouble the false accusations have caused."

Her brother flinched as though she'd hurled each word his
way, seeking purchase.

"Relax, Liz. I haven't told him anything that's not already
public knowledge."

"Are there things not in public knowledge?" Nick's question
sounded innocent, but Elizabeth would never trust a snake,
once bitten.

"Wouldn't your mother like to know? Is your lawyer on speaker phone or something?"

"Hey. Not too long ago, I was a part of this family," Nick said, drawing a circle in the air among the three adults. "I can actually give a damn about people regardless of our arguments, Liz."

She stood staring at these men in her life, too furious at the invasion to trust herself with a retort. Hands on hips, she willed her pulse to slow, her emotions to unknot themselves from around her lungs. After an extended exhale, she turned to Casey. "Did you know he was coming? Did you call him?"

Casey held up his hands. "Of course not. What was I going to do, turn him away?"

"Yes."

"Liz, I was here with Rhett."

Elizabeth looked to her son. The little boy tucked up against his father, alternating between watching the pages and the face that read them. When she moved out here, leaving all of what she knew behind, she divorced the familiar. She had struggled with the decision to move her son away from the most important man in his life. It was a gut-wrenching choice to make, and there would be no winning.

"I'm going for a walk," she said, shrugging back into a parka. It hung on the coat hooks with the others, above the umbrella stand near the bookrack.

"Now?"

"Yes, now. And don't let Rhett out of your sight," she said to her brother.

"Liz, I'm here to talk, that's all."

Elizabeth clenched her jaw. "I mean it, Casey."

"Understood. Take my flashlight, the light's on its way out."

Elizabeth stomped toward the road and turned away from the schoolhouse, toward the Hart ranch and the highway. A breeze whipped a few loose strands of hair around her neck, and she shoved the flashlight in her coat pocket before zipping her jacket up all the way against the cold. The thin soles of her tennis shoes announced each rock, and she regretted not pausing her reactive rage long enough to put on her hiking boots.

How dare Nick show up, unannounced. Elizabeth couldn't believe his nerve to drive a thousand miles and expect contact, expect an audience, expect...whatever it was he wanted.

Elizabeth hadn't given Nick a chance to explain himself. She would go back and allow him that, on a technicality, and then she would tell him to leave. While she couldn't force him out of the county, she sure as hell could get him out of the house.

A quarter mile down the road, Elizabeth paused for a breath and to take stock of her surroundings. Off the roadside, she spotted a worn path through the grasses leading toward the creek. Jo had mentioned that prior teachers had taken their charges down to the water on hot days. This might be the pathway.

The stream, deep enough to wet her ankles, snaked along the ranch land before emptying into the larger Prairie Dog Creek. Fed primarily by snow melt, the water was crisp, clear, and cold. She followed the trail down to the bank, letting her hands brush against the dried, golden grasses, stiff and forsaken. A red-winged blackbird landed in the branches of a bent and twisted ancient cottonwood and chirped for its mates.

Elizabeth picked her way across the rocks along the bank with care. The thin trickling of the water called to her, soothing the flames that raged within. Despite the cold, she wanted to sink her hands in its depths and allow numbness to take over.

Rocks under the water shone with brilliant hues. Amber, yellow, green, and gray, striped, dotted, and mottled were jumbled in display. Once the bottom of an ocean and then a land of ancient volcanic activity, Wyoming told colorful stories of origination and composition. She picked up a split piece of chert from the bank, turning it over in her hand to examine chips of quartz among the mauve.

She reached for another, then drew her hand back. The granite was streaked with a red-brown smear, angry and thick. Elizabeth leaned toward the mark, noting with growing horror that this was no inclusion.

For blood, mammalian blood, blue inside of veins, dried to that exact shade of burnt red.

37

ELIZABETH'S HEART POUNDED IN her chest as she tried to think over what she'd been told.

A ravine. Cattle in, cattle out.

The narrow walls around her would prevent an easy exit. More probable would be that this area acted as a chute. Quadrupeds would struggle to climb these sides, especially in a hurry. Around her in the sandy clay, there were shuffles that could be more than her footprints but nothing that represented nearly a hundred hooves running through.

This place was tougher to get to, a nestled, narrow bend in the water's path. A large gray boulder hulked, bench-like. The path indicated a place visited often by humans. A thinking spot.

Elizabeth backed up from the site, then half jogged up the hill. At the road, she spotted a telephone pole with an orange tag nailed a few feet from where she'd entered the brush. She needed a marker to find her way back.

Her cell phone was in her purse, back at the ranch. As one ankle complained about her panicked scramble, her pace quickened to match her heartbeat.

Inside the house, she told the three surprised faces that she'd be back in just a moment. Digging in her bag for her phone, she ducked outside with it. Her fingers shook as she punched in the numbers.

"Sheridan County Sheriff's Department, non-emergency line." Elizabeth could all but see the woman, interrupting social media scrolling to answer the phone.

"This is Elizabeth Blau, I need to speak with Sheriff Wolf."

"He left a while ago. If I recall, stopping by to see you was on his agenda."

"Yes, I know, but that's not going to be until..." Elizabeth paused to think. There'd been no sight of injured animals nearby, no other blood. It could have been from anything or anyone. The sunlight waned as she stood on the doormat, facing west. A hint of pink edged the mountains. "Can you get him a message? It's getting dark, and I need to show him something before it's late. He has my number."

"I'm sure he does," she said, Elizabeth catching the slight. "I'll tell him."

The line went dead.

When she entered the house, she took control. "I have to go. The sheriff is meeting me at the schoolhouse." Seeing suspicion on Nick's face, she added, "Perfectly rational for him to do. He and his wife are the caretakers."

"It's only four. I'll hang out with Rhett here until you finish up with the sheriff."

Elizabeth volleyed her glare between Nick and Casey. The two sat, with beers in hand, a game on the big screen.

"Nick. Where are you staying?"

"I figured I'd find a place in town. Casey said they have a few hotels."

"When are you leaving?" Elizabeth would deal with the treachery of her brother later. She needed the basics from her enemy, posthaste.

"I head out Tuesday. Unless, that is, there's a reason for me to stay longer."

"There won't be," she said, and left.

The sheriff was parked at the school when Elizabeth angled her car alongside the patrol vehicle.

Circling the house, she found him on the south side of the building. He tossed a pinecone into the air and caught it.

"Well, your description was accurate. Can't figure out their source." He waved the pinecone at the building. "This place is covered in footprints. I walked out into the yard a bit but didn't see much in the bushes, either."

"I found blood."

"What?"

"Down by the creek. On a rock. There was blood."

"Where?"

"The pathway, near the telephone pole, the little one off the road. The spot where there's a big gray rock on the creek bank."

"Lovers Lounge," he said.

"Excuse me?"

"You know. Where couples go. I've had to chase many teenagers home from there. Hell, Jo and I were frequent visitors back in the day. Small fire pit off to one side, a little shelter from the bank?"

She nodded.

"Did you see any animals around? Hear anything?"

"No, but I didn't offer myself as bait." In fact, Elizabeth had all but run from the scene to call him. "Are you telling me you usually find bloody rocks in all your creek beds?"

"We found Justin upstream from there."

Elizabeth swallowed. "I didn't know, but I guessed."

"Still, I'll go have a look in the morning, in case. Get Ryland to bring the kit, maybe his old hound, too. If it is blood, it was likely a kill spot for a coyote. Either way, I'll take a look at first light."

Venus winked at them from the sky, ahead of the advancing twilight. The sun started to slink off, unnoticed, over the horizon.

"Thoughts on the pinecones?"

"No reason they should be here. Their fall lines indicate they rolled or bounced off the roof. I'm leaning toward a prank but not sure who'd bother, to be honest. Your students aren't exactly at the delinquent age."

"Yeah." It was hard to picture any of them coming up with a nefarious plan, let alone escaping out of their beds late at night to make it happen.

"Keep the doors locked tonight. I keep my mobile on, and Jo answers the house phone at all hours. Let us know if anything happens.

38

"NICK, YOU ARE BUYING me a beer. Casey, you are babysitting. I've had a long day with too many problems and zero resolutions. Let's go."

Coat over one arm, she led the way, a bewildered ex-husband trailing behind.

At the Crow Bar, they made their way to the bar and claimed two stools. Polly's face lit up like a firework when she saw them.

Nick, a city giveaway in his fresh outdoor gear and too-clean shoes, was uneasy under the scrutiny of the room. Elizabeth relished in his discomfort as she greeted her friend.

Polly wore cut-off shorts and an oversized green sweater hanging off one shoulder. While the temperatures continued to drop outside, running back and forth to the kitchen kept her blood flowing. Nick eyed the woman, appraising her attire. Elizabeth needed to warn Polly about Nick. She was exactly his type. Friends didn't let friends date cheaters.

And they were friends, she and Polly. Or at least on their way to that status. She liked the woman, could see the two of them having wine on a deck while their kids played in the yard, at soccer games, holding coffee in travel mugs as they cheered for their sons.

"Hey, Elizabeth! You saved me. JD would not stop talking about some new video game he got. Apparently, he's some kind of warrior with a clan, and it involves meeting up with people in South Dakota to play with real swords or something. My brain turned to mush and started flashing warning lights behind my drooping eyelids."

Elizabeth laughed. "I saw it all over your face. Happy to serve as an escape."

"Any longer and I would have passed out behind the bar of boredom. You'd have had to do CPR to raise me from the dead."

Nick held out his hand to the woman between him and a beer. "Nick Thompson," he said to Polly. "I'd love a stout."

Elizabeth watched him amplify his grin, used to charming women with charisma. Nick was good-looking, to a fault. Brown eyes a little wide for his features, full lips, and a decent build from time at the gym. His hair was a little long. He had shades of the big bad wolf. Someone who would romance his prey into vulnerability.

"Polly, meet my ex-husband, Nick."

The bartender raised her brows at Elizabeth who returned the inquisition with a covert eye roll.

"Hi, Nick. One stout, coming up."

Elizabeth watched Polly at the taps, filling two glasses with a dark liquid brewed with a hint of Montana cherries. Tiny bubbles floated to the top as Nick slid a twenty over the polished surface. Nick waved back the change, winking at Polly.

Her friend palmed the cash, then raised an eyebrow at Elizabeth. *I have to get him somewhere we can talk. Not give him free rein to flirt with locals.*

Roz sidled up to the bar and leaned over to talk to her sister. Nick watched her, tracing Roz's curves with his eyes. If Elizabeth could smell Roz's perfume from here, Nick was inhaling it in clouds.

"Poll, I'm heading home. Call me later?"

Roz Hart was a taller version of her sister, more legs than torso. She had her hands stuffed in the pockets of a navy coat, dark jeans ending in black boots. Her ash blonde hair was loose, streaked in highlights.

"Will do," Polly replied, setting full glasses in front of Elizabeth and Nick.

Roz looked their way, and her eyes widened, betraying surprise. In a flash, this was transformed into a semblance of confident aloofness, a smirk on her lips.

"Elizabeth, right?" Roz smirked. "You sure don't hesitate much. Not getting any younger, I suppose." With a dismissive shrug, she flounced away, giving Nick a clear view of her retreat.

Nick blanched at Elizabeth's icy glare. "What?"

"Let's get a table, so I don't have to share your attention with every female who walks in the bar. We need to talk."

Elizabeth led Nick to the back of the room. Sundays were quieter by a few decibels. No live band but full of people avoiding the weekend's impending demise. She chose a table near the back of the room.

Nick sat in one of the captain's chairs and sipped from the pint glass. A vintage sign for Hamm's beer blazed on the wall next to a rodeo poster left over from July.

Elizabeth's ex-husband tipped back into his seat, craning his head to look around.

"Nick. I am broken-hearted over waiting to hear Rhett's voice. I think you are, too."

Nick blew out the air in his lungs and set the glass on a coaster advertising a domestic beer. He laid both palms flat on the table before looking up at her.

"I am worried," Elizabeth continued. "Worried that every choice we make is wrong. Scared we won't find the right doctors or enough doctors or that I am not mother enough to handle all of this to begin with."

Nick waited for her to continue with his chin resting in one hand, fingers wrapped over his mouth. She looked him in the eye and took a deep breath.

"At the same time, I know I am doing the best job I can, with what I have. Rhett loves it here. He's happy. He interacts with me, with everyone. He's eating, thinking, growing...he's doing everything he should be doing—except talking. He isn't in a city, breathing extra fumes or toxins or whatever other crap some books say can exacerbate the problem. He isn't around fighting and yelling. Here, people look after him."

This last point was a blow designed to draw a clear line in this fight. Nick sucked in his lower lip and held up a finger.

"Before you tell me why you are here, let me be clear. My family is here. My job is here. My son is healthy and happy. Here. I will fight tooth and nail for him to stay. You have zero proof that I have not followed the doctor's recommendations. If you let your mother pursue this crazy lawsuit and make our lives a living hell, I swear I will come after you with everything I have to fight it."

Emails. Late night texts. Irregular bank statements. A backpack stuffed with cash and a black book of phone numbers. The lying, the cheating, and the neglect.

"Your turn."

Nick took a sip of the dark liquid in his glass as if to give him a chance to gather his thoughts. He returned the glass to the shiny wooden surface rubbed smooth by a thousand patrons before him. Her ex ran a finger through a drop of condensation that pooled there, stalling. After a deep inhale and a measured exhale, he spoke. "Look, Liz. You're right. I've been...well, I was a terrible husband. A terrible father, at times. I just...miss my son."

Too little, too late. "Well, your son lives here now."

"Mom thinks the doctors are better in Seattle. He'll get speech therapists and whatever else he needs. Do they even have those out here?"

"Of course they do. It's not a remote island. Also, he's my kid, not hers."

"And mine, Liz. When do I get a say in what he does, where he is?"

"You gave up that right in court, remember?"

"That was then," he said, a tone of irritation in his voice. "I've changed. I want another chance."

"You can visit, Nick, whenever you want," she said. "I'm not coming back, at least not this year." Guilt creeped its way into her conscience, and she fought to stamp it out. "I signed a contract."

"Will you at least think about it? For after this year?"

"Will you drop this lawsuit?" Elizabeth had been gulping down her drink to keep herself from flipping over the table in frustration, and now the liquid salve was almost gone. Its heaviness sat in her stomach as her head swam. The skin behind her ears went hot, anxiety disrupting her calm.

Nick spun his glass in a slow circle. "I will call the lawyer in the morning."

At that moment, Elizabeth remembered what drew her to him. What kept her strung along for the almost decade they were together. He would mess up, she would catch him, and he would change. For a little while.

A group of bow hunters bustled into the bar. All in camouflage, one wore a fluorescent orange hat. They circled a table near the jukebox. One dragged over an additional chair. Polly set a pitcher and a stack of glasses on the table. The group settled in to compare shooter gloves and field binoculars.

"I dropped that buck at twenty yards."

"You got lucky, that was a slammer."

Elizabeth didn't see Kade until he entered last in time to perch on the extra chair.

39

KADE'S EYES LOCKED ON hers, all fire, then made loud work of rotating his chair to face away from her.

Fine. It wasn't like she wanted a hot and grouchy mechanic's attention. At least not one who spooked her in parking lots.

"How is Casey, really?" Nick asked.

Elizabeth met his question with suspicion. "Why do you ask?"

"I always liked your brother, the few times we heard from him. He doesn't look so good."

"Being accused of murder will do that to your complexion."

"That's not what I meant."

"We're under a little stress, you know."

"This isn't about Rhett, Liz."

"Isn't it though? I moved all my stuff to the schoolhouse, so you can tell that snake of a lawyer that I'm not endangering the well-being of my son with his innocent uncle."

"Even though he's home alone with Casey as we speak?"

Elizabeth pushed back from the table, the chair legs scraping the ancient wood floors. "Shove it, Nick."

"I'm just pointing out the facts."

"You wouldn't know the truth if it bit you!"

"Everything all right here?"

Elizabeth jumped at the sound of Kade's voice.

Kade waited at the side of the table, eyebrows lifted. He faced Elizabeth, giving a shoulder to Nick.

"We're fine," she said through gritted teeth, unnerved. "Who are you?"

"Seems it's you who are the stranger in my bar."

"Really? You own the place?"

"Kade Michaels, meet my *ex*-husband, Nick Thompson."

Kade's lip twitched. Nick crossed his arms.

"Can we help you?" Elizabeth asked.

"Seems like a car with Washington plates," he paused to look at Nick, "which I'm guessing is yours, is causing us some trouble. Isaiah needs to back out his trailer. I said I'd go ask if the owner would be so *kind* as to move it."

"Sure," Nick said. "Wouldn't want Isaiah put out." He stood, zipped himself back into his sweatshirt, and headed outside

"Does Isaiah really have a trailer to back out?" The man in question sat among a hunting crew, ensconced in a riveting debate over preferred bow brands.

"You're welcome," Kade responded and returned to his friends.

Nick returned after a few minutes, shivering. "The wind picked up. It smells like snow."

"Snow doesn't smell. Hydrogen and oxygen have no aroma."

"That's what my dad always said back in Illinois. It's freezing out there."

"What idiot drives over Idaho passes in nothing but a sweatshirt?"

He drained his glass, took her now empty one, and said, "The idiot who's going to pay for our beers so we can get out of here."

Nick approached the bar and set the glasses in a bus tub for Polly.

Stillness wrapped the vehicles and settled into the trees. Nick started his car, cranking up the heater.

On the drive back, Elizabeth detailed her job, the students at the schoolhouse, and even the pinecones.

"Don't you get freaked out with all this...space?"

"Not really. Well, not anymore. Other than the odd pinecone incident, it's peaceful. You feel like a part of the landscape."

"I don't think I could have been a pioneer," he said to the steering wheel, his eyes on the road. "They had to be crazy to give up everything for what looks like a whole lot of nothing."

"Many were banking on finding better. A new start. Others...well." Elizabeth thought of Justin. "I think if you try to ignore your sense of adventure, you will regret every minute afterward."

They were quiet as the darkness leaked into the car and their thoughts.

"Liz, do you think we will ever forgive ourselves enough to really move on?"

"I don't think that's something I can answer for another person."

Elizabeth thought of motherhood. Casey's guilt about leaving her to escape to college. Justin shackled to the family business. They spent so much energy on the things they couldn't change, attached to their hold over them.

"I tucked him in bed a half hour ago," Casey said. "He kept rubbing at his eyes, poor kid."

"Thanks, Case. I should have watched the time."

"Not a problem. You know I miss him. Should I try to bring him to your car?"

"No, he'll just wake up. I'll go get him a change of clothes. He can stay here with you."

"You sure?"

"Shoot. Actually, no, that might freak him out." Elizabeth pressed her hands together under her chin.

Casey said, "I'd volunteer, but my animals need feeding, and unless either of you wants to get up at four…"

"Don't worry. No one wants to take over your choring if they can help it."

Nick said, "You don't want me within ten feet of something with four legs. I wouldn't know which end is which. Better off giving you your space. Wouldn't want your boyfriend to get ideas."

"Boyfriend?" Casey's eyes ping-ponged between his sister and ex-brother-in-law. "Clearly, I missed something."

"How about I sleep at the schoolhouse, and you two stay here."

"Thanks, Nick," Elizabeth said. "I appreciate this."

"I'm going to hit the hay now that my babysitting duties are relieved. Night."

Casey shuffled down the hall as Nick got up from the chair, patting his pockets. "How about I run you down there to get Rhett's clothes? No sense in us taking two cars."

"I'll need to get to school in the morning. Should I drop Rhett off at his sitter, or…" Elizabeth didn't know how to ask if he'd act the part of a decent father.

"I'd like to hang out with him, if that's all right. I only took off the week and spent two of the days driving."

Elizabeth glanced at the clock. A call to Jo could wait for the morning. "All right, be back here by seven, then."

"I'm ready to go when you are."

40

"**I** 'M GOING TO BE late. I knew this would happen. I could just kill Nick!"

A light snow had fallen overnight and draped the prairie in white. Elizabeth had gone out to brush off her windshield, freeing the wipers. She'd started the car to give it time to warm up.

"I'm sure he's almost here, Liz. It'll be fine."

"It's anything but fine. This is so like him. I can't leave Rhett with you, the accused murderer, to go hunt Nick down. And I just got my students back. What will their families do when they see a random man stumbling out of the place and no teacher? March their kids right out of the school again, that's what."

"Do you need me to stay?"

Casey had planned to drive to Billings and pick up equipment. He'd offered to delay the trip to serve as a buffer between her and Nick.

"No. It's fine. If he's not here in five minutes, I'll take Rhett to Jo's."

Twenty minutes later, Elizabeth parked behind Nick's car, willing the parents to be late. She grumbled as she stamped over to the schoolhouse door, stepped inside long enough to turn on the lights and drop her bag, and then continued along the footpath to the teacherage.

Elizabeth wore her indignation like a wool jacket. Snug, itchy, and hot.

On approach to the smaller log cabin, Elizabeth froze. A tang scented the air. A half inch of snow dusted the ground, and the thick silence was wrong, early. Cold clinched at the capillaries in Elizabeth's fingertips, turning them white. She pressed forward, entering the house.

"Nick? Nick!" Elizabeth ducked into the bedroom and the bathroom before turning a slow circle in the kitchen. "Where the hell is he?"

Wind seeped through the crack in the back door that led to the scrub brush and open prairie. The door wasn't closed. It fluttered, failing to latch.

Elizabeth's fingerless glove wrapped around the ancient brass knob, swinging the door inward in order to step out.

Red, red snow greeted her.

Bile rose in Elizabeth's throat as she beheld a grisly scene. In a pool of liquid, nearly carmine in the morning light, a lump of prey lay sprawled, life force leaching out into the fresh powder.

Elizabeth's eyes strained to focus before her knees gave out. The figure wore a green jacket. Her green jacket.

Then it moaned.

"Nick?" The words came out in a hoarse whisper as she choked on the word. "Oh my God, Nick!"

Adrenaline clicked her joints into gear and propelled her forward to assist.

Nick lay on his side, half-covered, the wind having blown the hood of the jacket over his face. He breathed in ragged huffs, eyes vacant.

A quick glance toward the source of his pain revealed a carbon-fiber shaft sticking out of one thigh. Electric pink fletching mocked the severity of the moment.

"Stay here. I'll get someone. I'll be right back."

Elizabeth had left her phone in the bag sitting on her desk. Her feet slipped on the snow, which had already begun to melt in the new sunlight, as she ran for the school. The soles of her boots found purchase on the shale driveway as she scrambled inside.

Polly and Benny were at the front steps when they saw Elizabeth. Their moon eyes took in the blood on her shoes and hands, the wild in her eyes.

"It's Nick. He's hurt. I need to call 911."

"I'll call Jo," Polly said to Elizabeth's retreating form.

Elizabeth ripped her phone from the bag. Her hands shook as she dialed before pressing the device to her face. "Hello? Someone has been shot. I'm at the school in Banner—"

41

"I NEED TO ASK how you found Mr. Thompson."

Sheriff Wolf watched Elizabeth, a crease between his brows.

"Ms. Blau? I know you're worried. The nurses say he'll be sleeping for a while yet, and that's a good thing."

Elizabeth succumbed to the need for coffee and vengeance. Ex-husband or not, this was the father of her son, and she would not have him taken from this earth. She followed Wolf into the waiting area of Sheridan Memorial.

"All right now," Wolf said, settling the two of them in plastic chairs with Styrofoam cups. "Walk me through when you left your house to when you found Mr. Thompson."

Elizabeth recounted her morning. The irritation at Nick for not showing up, her flustered arrival at Wolf's house, the search for Nick at the school, and the blood. All that red.

"We've got the arrow from the doctors. Depending on the tip, they are designed to do varying degrees of damage which would explain why Mr. Thompson is in this state."

A hunting accident. That was the talk between the ambulance drivers as they'd collected Nick onto a stretcher. They'd strapped Nick down for the ride, the arrow shaft still protruding from his leg like a beacon.

"We see this all too often," the emergency response person in the ambulance had said. Her brown hair was tucked into a bun at the nape of her neck, mascara swiped over sparse lashes, a plain gold band on one hand.

"Especially during hunting season," the other technician said. "He's stable. We'll get him there, and the doctors will get to work."

The bright lights and measured temperature of the Emergency Room had been a welcome sterility. A nurse yammered placating mumblings as she ushered Elizabeth into the waiting area. The roaring in Elizabeth's ears failed to dissipate. She was unable to hear anything until she knew Nick would be okay.

"Ms. Michaels is going to tell me what she saw, too, and I will speak with Mr. Thompson as soon as he is able."

"So, that's it?"

"It?"

"You aren't going to ask me who I think did it? Whether we had an argument at the bar last night? Because we did. That's why he was even at the school."

"You have evidence this wasn't an accident?" His question, chosen to knock some sense into her rant, fell without effect.

"I'm just saying someone shot him. With a frigging bow and arrow. And I can't believe this is the extent of your questioning."

"Ms. Blau, while I appreciate your fervor, as always, and I know you started your day with quite the shock, we are investigating this to the absolute, I assure you. I will say that, as it is late September, Mr. Thompson was walking in the brush, and he wasn't wearing orange. It doesn't take a badge to put two and two together and question whether this is an issue of a misfired hunter's shot. One meant for a deer or an antelope."

"But he was outside the school. Who is hunting there?"

Wolf told the nurse to alert him as soon as the patient awoke and to allow no visitors outside of the family. Elizabeth returned to Nick's side.

Her ex looked small, beaten. Sheets up to his chin, the blips of a monitor marking time like a metronome. A faint sheen of sweat painted his split upper lip.

"We've given him meds to ease the pain, stop infection, and help him sleep. The doctors stitched him up. Nasty shredding those broadheads do. He'll be okay, though."

Elizabeth wanted to believe the woman in lavender scrubs. Her name tag identified her as Denise, and a thin, gold cross on a chain ringed her neck. She flipped her French braid over a shoulder and patted Elizabeth's hand. "I'll leave you two alone for a bit."

The institutional-blue walls pressed in on the two of them. A print of a sailboat on the ocean hung near the window of the second story room, teasing the viewer with a sight never seen in the landlocked state. A large plastic jug of ice water, complete with bendy straw, waited on a wheeled stand. Notes hung on a clipboard near the door.

At the window, she watched the traffic on Fifth Street.

My students. Elizabeth smacked herself on the forehead and slipped into the hallway to call Jo.

"Elizabeth."

"Jo, I'm so sorry."

"Clint said they're fixing up your friend and he will be fine, but I've been wondering how you're handling things."

"Fine," she replied, though she knew the hollow, incessant growl of her stomach was half hunger, half nerves. "I'll be fine. This morning was...a lot. How is Rhett?"

"He's good. We were just sorting the farm animals from the toy box. He really likes the chickens. We're staying busy. He keeps looking at the door as if he knows something is off. Smart boy you have here."

"I called because of the students. Benny. I—" She let the rest of the sentence hang in the air as she knit a picture in her memory of the boy's horror when she approached, panicked and bloodied.

"He'll be okay. Polly said he didn't see anything other than you, which shook him, but he's tough. Been through a lot."

"The others?"

"I got a hold of them before they got to school."

"Their first day back." Elizabeth preferred to blame herself for being unable to open school rather than examine the sickening turn of her stomach.

"We'll get it sorted. Focus on Rhett's father."

"Okay. Thank you."

"All right. Farmer Rhett and I are going to rustle up some lunch. You should eat, too. Get the chicken salad. It isn't half bad. But check the date on that little sticker."

In the cafeteria, Elizabeth over-chewed her food, fork in limp hand, eyes vacant. Visitors and staff buzzed around her, occupying and abandoning tables in her vicinity.

She couldn't shake the visual of the wound. Elizabeth could see the arrow's shaft when she closed her eyes. Forget sleeping tonight.

One thought kept running through her mind, on repeat, until the volume was so loud she couldn't ignore it.

It could have been me.

42

NICK ROUSED, GROGGY, WHEN she was on her fourth magazine full of casserole recipes. He mumbled a request for water and to watch the Seahawks game. She pressed the button for the nurse who brought another visitor.

"Hello, Sheriff."

"Ms. Blau. Mr. Thompson, how are you feeling?"

"Oh, I've definitely been better," Nick croaked. The nurse raised the back of his bed, and he groaned.

"I'd like to ask you a few questions about what happened this morning, if that's okay. Is it alright with you if Ms. Blau stays for the questions?"

"Of course it's all right," Elizabeth snapped.

"She's fine to stay."

"Thank you. Can you tell me, in your own words, what happened this morning?"

"Not much to it. I got up, walked outside to check out the snow, felt a stab to my leg, and dropped to the ground. The next thing I knew, Elizabeth was yelling my name."

"Did you see anything unusual outside? Any movement, like animals or people? Or hear anything at all?"

Hunters, Elizabeth thought. "Or the Doppler Effect of someone firing an arrow at you?"

"I'll ask the questions, Ms. Blau."

"I was checking out the snow. We don't get much where I'm from."

"Can you tell me what you were wearing?"

Elizabeth pulled her hands into the sleeves of her sweater and crossed her arms. The hospital had to have the clothes Nick had worn in and turned them over to the sheriff.

"Pants, shirt. Gray Seahawks sweatshirt. Guessing they're trashed now."

Elizabeth would have to bring Nick's suitcase. A change of clothes. Rhett couldn't see him like this.

"Oh. And her jacket. Big poofy thing. Green."

"What kind of green? Kelly? Olive?"

"More like a hunter green."

"What does this have to do with anything?" she asked the sheriff and then turned to Nick. "And why were you wearing my jacket?"

"I was freezing. It was on the coat rack, so I borrowed it."

"I loved that jacket!"

"I'll get you a new one. It's not like I planned to get shot in it."

"I'll verify the evidence," the sheriff said. "Were you wearing any bright colors? Orange or red, maybe yellow? A hat or scarf or anything?"

"No."

"I see."

"Of course he wasn't wearing orange. He didn't go on a hike, he just stepped outside in my—"

Elizabeth paused, mouth open. He'd been an easy mark at the school, standing in front of the building just before students would have arrived, the thick coat the color of lush forests, a contrast to the tan-gray of the early autumn prairie.

Her green jacket.

"What am I missing here?"

"They think you were shot by a hunter."

Nick burst out laughing, then swore and reached for his wound. "That's ridiculous. Like someone thought I was an elk or something? I was just relieving myself in a bush."

"You were peeing outside a school? Are you nuts? You could have gotten me fired!"

"Hey, it was early—how was I supposed to know someone would try to take me out?"

"Which brings me to another question. How tall are you, Mr. Thompson?"

"About five ten, give or take."

Give, thought Elizabeth. She was almost eye to eye with her ex. Her heels had languished in the closet throughout her marriage except on an occasional girls' night. She'd packed a few choice pairs for the move, for future nights out. Enough trying to make herself appear smaller for someone else.

"Ms. Blau, it sounds like Mr. Thompson would appreciate some of his own things. I can give you a ride back to your place in about an hour or so unless you have other plans."

━✦━

Casey didn't answer her call. She dialed another number, and Polly picked up.

"Hey there. How are things?"

"Nick finally woke up from the drugs they gave him and is talking to the sheriff."

"Oh?"

"Sounds like they think he was shot by a hunter. Stray arrow."

"What was he doing outside?"

"Not sure." Admitting her ex-husband had his zipper down outdoors was not something Elizabeth planned to do.

"Hate to say it, but it happens. There's a reason hunters have to wear orange."

"Nick isn't the hunting type."

"Gotcha. Wouldn't hurt to get yourself a hat or something. You are kind of on the edge of nowhere out there."

"It's on my to-do list now. Can I get a ride back to Casey's place or my car?"

"Anything for a friend."

43

THE PASSENGER SEAT OF Polly's car was dusty, sprinkled with glitter and the odd, escaped French fry. A few cans and bottles rolled at Elizabeth's feet on the turns.

"Thanks again for this. I can't get a hold of Casey."

"Anytime." Polly flicked on her turn signal for the onramp. "Where's Benny?"

"I left him with my sister. She watches him when I close."

"That's kind of her."

"Not sure many call Roz kind. She adores Benny though."

"Casey loves watching Rhett. They have become best buddies." Elizabeth would take any opportunity to remind everyone he wasn't a monster.

"Roz just loves Benny. She really wanted kids of her own until...well. Anyway, I tell her she can have her pick of future fathers when things settle."

Settle. Elizabeth's own life kept getting swept into storm clouds, and she found herself envious of Roz Hart, a woman looking forward to the future.

"So, what's the status of your husband? Er, ex."

"He's stable. They took out the arrow."

"He say what kind it was?"

"Something about a broadhead, maybe? I don't know, Casey's the archer. My parents did all their hunting at the grocery store."

Polly nodded. Her slim fingers held the wheel at nine and three. She had a tiny tattoo of a horseshoe on the inside of one wrist. "Hunting accidents do happen."

"Even to vice presidents."

They both laughed. Elizabeth had forgotten what female friends could be like. When she was with Nick, every woman was competition, someone to be distrusted. In hindsight, it was Nick she should have watched.

"Sheriff say if they have any leads?"

"Not sure. He was talking to Nick for a while."

The two of them watched the field slide by the windows. A herd of cattle perched on a hillside, a magpie cut the air in flight.

"Hate to say it, but it would be pretty tough to find the hunter."

Elizabeth turned to Polly. "Why do you say that?"

"Arrows. It's not like people write their name on them. Some do, but usually only for big target shoots."

"Can't you tell what kind of bow people used?"

"It's not like guns where you know the caliber. Arrows are simpler. The shaft might tell you if it was a compound or a bare bow. That's about it."

"What about the broadhead part?"

"That just means it's for hunting, rather than target practice. Broadheads are meant to pierce flesh."

"The feathers?"

Polly squinted into the waning sunlight. "Color?"

"Two were hot pink. One was white."

"The white one is the cock feather. Shows you how to notch your arrow."

"You know a lot about archery."

"We don't have as many grocery stores out here," Polly said to the windshield.

"Not your favorite activity for family bonding, eh?"

"Hah. No, that's Roz. She bagged our Thanksgiving turkey. I liked shooting, sometimes. Just targets, though."

Elizabeth let the past hang between them in the cramped space in the car. Waited for Polly to lead forward.

"She and Casey go all the time," Polly continued. "Your brother used to run hunting camps up into the mountains with Justin, too, before his business took off. Pretty sure Casey is the best shot in the county, after Roz. Don't tell the guys at the bar that, though. I let them think I don't play favorites."

"Your secret is safe with me."

"It doesn't bother me, by the way."

"What's that?"

"You and Justin. Before he died."

Elizabeth swallowed. This had gotten awkward. "Uh...thanks? Not sure what else to say to that."

"I just wanted you to know there are no hard feelings with me. I mean, it's not like Roz wanted him back, so it's cool."

"Well, he's gone."

"I know, and I'm sorry."

"Me too."

She said, "Kade's our cousin, so that's not an issue."

"What do you mean?"

"He's my dad's sister's son."

Elizabeth shifted in her seat. "The average person has four first cousins and sixteen second cousins. Goes up from there."

"Liz, I spend hours behind a bar every week, watching people. Watching how they interact and with whom. Folks are always trying to talk each other into or out of something. Alcohol fuels some of the risks—people doing or saying things they shouldn't, or maybe not taking advantage of what they should. I've seen many matches made under those neon lights, and in case you didn't know, Kade Michaels doesn't take his eyes off you."

Kade. The man rankled her. Yet here she was, her cheeks flushed.

"I know you liked Justin," Polly said. "But as my mom would always say, it ain't healthy to pine after ghosts."

"Did she speak from experience?"

They'd turned off the highway onto the familiar dirt road as Elizabeth wished time would slow, allowing her longer to get to know her friend.

"She passed after Daddy did, yes. But he was lost even when he walked among the living. That man drank himself awake each morning and asleep every night. My mother worked herself to the bone after he died, trying to keep us fed and clothed. Roz swore she would never end up like that, a woman making up after a man's mistakes. Then here I am, walking right along in Mom's footsteps."

"I didn't mean to—"

"I know I'm a classic story. Fell for a worthless drunk, stayed with him until both our savings were gone. Now I miss too much of my son's life to make just enough to get up and do it all over again each morning. I'm too tired to be bitter. Too tired to be ashamed."

"You've got nothing to be ashamed about."

"That's why I like you, Liz. You get it. You know what it is to be a single mom, on her own."

When the going got tough for Elizabeth, she'd run away. Moved here. Polly was a warrior. Elizabeth was a trainee.

Polly stopped the car in front of Casey's door and idled, watching Elizabeth, eyebrows lifted in concern. "Are you going to be okay?"

"I think so. Thanks again for the ride." Elizabeth swung open the door and reached back for her purse.

"Sure. And Liz?"

"Yeah?"

"Just my two cents, but give Kade a chance. He's a good guy."

"Noted. Will we see Benny tomorrow?"

"If you're up for it, count on it."

A note on the counter stated that Casey went to pick up Rhett for a bite to eat. In response, Elizabeth's stomach growled. She opened the fridge and leaned in to examine its paltry contents.

The phone rang, Jo's number on the screen.

"Elizabeth, hi. How is Nick?"

"Stable, awake, and talking. Even laughing about it all a bit. Listen, Jo. I can't stay at the teacherage anymore. I just can't, not with my son. It wasn't part of the contract and I—"

"Say no more. I've already called the families. We understand."

"I'll be there tomorrow."

"You sure?"

"I am."

44

THE BOYS RETURNED IN a jumble of coats and containers of leftovers.

"I got you a club sandwich, in case you hadn't eaten," Casey said.

"Thanks. I was eyeing the box of mac. You're saving me from myself."

Rhett clung to her in full koala mode. Elizabeth relished his snuggles and the warm scent of his skin. "Hey, Buddy. Daddy hurt his leg, so he is sleeping at the hospital tonight. He will be okay, but he has to stay a little longer."

Her son's eyes searched hers, lip protruding as he tugged on the fingers of one hand with those of the opposite.

"He'll be okay, I promise."

❧

Elizabeth hustled Rhett into a bath with extra bubbles. After warm pajamas, a storybook, and lots of kisses, Elizabeth returned to the living room, exhausted. Casey sat at the kitchen island, scrolling on his phone. His jacket was over his lap, keys resting on a knee.

"Headed out?"

"Yep."

"Any news today?"

Casey sighed. "Nope."

"Sorry. Be careful."

"Will do."

An old movie on the television, Elizabeth stared blankly at the screen.

She needed to plan for the week, for her students. Each time an idea came to mind, her brain vacated to visions of red and white, shaft and sinew. Nick on the ground. The emptiness, his vulnerability.

Scrolling websites didn't help, and social media was off limits while she needed to focus. As was the wine. Maybe not all the wine.

Elizabeth crossed to the cabinet for a goblet to pour herself some merlot. Bringing the glass to her lips, she spotted a second sticky note, yellow on the gray and black granite countertop.

M. Hart — Tuesday @ 2.

M must stand for Margery. She plucked the note from the surface.

The memorial was Sunday. Casey had debated whether he should attend. Would he be able to celebrate Justin's life with accusations over his head? That is, if he was allowed inside the door.

45

ELIZABETH AWOKE TO THE sound of a car in the driveway, her neck stiff from her awkward nap. She rotated her head and her vertebrae popped. She winced at the release.

Singing could be heard outside, the sound closer by the minute.

The door swept open and in came Casey, bellowing George Strait at the top of his lungs, half hanging off the shoulder of Kade Michaels.

"Amarillooooo by morning—"

"Casey," she hissed. "Quiet, you'll wake Rhett."

"You be quiet. No one interrupts King George!"

"Easy there, Big Shooter," Kade cautioned. "You wouldn't let me talk to your sister that way."

"He sure as heck would not." Elizabeth scrutinized her brother. Rumpled clothes, bloodshot eyes. The smell of alcohol coming from his pores. "Beer? Whisky?"

"Tequila," Kade said. "Shots. Plural."

"Can you help me get him to his room?"

Kade nodded. Elizabeth shoved her shoulder under Casey's other armpit and wrapped his arm around her. They walk-dragged Casey down the hall.

"Everythiiing that I got, is just what I got on—"

Elizabeth clapped her hand over Casey's mouth as they neared the hallway. She didn't let go until they'd deposited him on his bed in a heap. Kade removed her brother's shoes.

Casey looked young, lost, and vulnerable. She left him snoring.

Kade followed her out the door, closing it with a snick and depositing Casey's shoes at the front mat.

"He'll be himself in the morning. Maybe brew a strong batch of coffee. Toast with a side of ibuprofen."

"Thanks for bringing him back. His truck still down at the Inn?"

"Yeah. I can get one of the guys to bring it back tomorrow."

Elizabeth rubbed her forehead with her hand, considering a complicated tomorrow. "I might take you up on that. At least he didn't drive."

Kade stooped to slip his own boots back over his feet. The man wore crisp jeans, a black leather jacket. He looked good. Elizabeth knew she shouldn't ask him to stay.

But she didn't want him to go.

"Have time for a drink? In thanks. For King George. And the truck."

Before she could second guess her motives, she jumped up to pour them each a glass from the open bottle.

Kade nodded and perched on the edge of the couch, clearly uncertain. She handed over a glass.

"Thanks." Kade sipped. "Tempranillo?"

"Bingo."

"It's decent."

"I wouldn't take you for a wine snob."

"Definitely not. I know just enough to be dangerous at a liquor store, that's about it. Can't ruin a date over a wine pairing."

"All I have to offer is some goldfish crackers and applesauce, so you can blame me for this pairing."

"I've had stranger dates," he said, grinning over the glass.

Flirty, indeed. "What happened with Casey?"

Something hardened in Kade's eyes, and he hesitated. "He got into it with some people from town. Got drunk enough to need me to drag him out, the idiot."

Elizabeth swallowed. "What were they saying?"

"You don't want to know."

"Oh." The mood shifted into a gray area, one in which a part of Elizabeth ached for her brother, his dreams, his past. "I know he'll thank you in the morning...or maybe the afternoon."

Kade smirked behind his glass. "He seems like a good brother."

"He was. He is. It's complicated. There was a time there when we didn't see each other much for a few years. Now I know it wasn't me. It was our parents."

"Running from family doesn't work in the long run. Even the ghosts come after you until you deal with each other." Kade pressed his lips together before taking another sip. "At least mine do."

"You're onto something there."

"I think we make too many promises in life. The more we care about someone, the more promises we make to them. And when you're around another person long enough, you won't be able to keep every promise you make. We can build up disappointments that way. Bitterness."

Elizabeth thought of Nick, the late-night phone calls, waitresses slipping him their number. "We all have our limits."

"Fair." Kade rolled the empty glass back and forth between his palms. "So, who broke their promises to you?"

Elizabeth bought time by refilling each glass, a tiny splash on the glass tabletop. She wiped at it with her shirt sleeve, stalling.

"My parents, back home, same as Casey. Rhett's father. Classic sob stories."

Kade leaned back into the couch, crossed one ankle over the opposite knee. "Any news on your ex?"

"A hunter mistook him for a deer."

"A punishable act. Anyone to blame?"

"Not yet." Investigations took time but in the interim, lives were ruined. Lost. "I'm trying to be patient. Everyone thinks my brother is a murderer, and now I'm back to taking care of my ex. I'd give anything for them to solve either case."

"Waiting is the hardest part."

"Tom Petty." Her insides felt warm, the wine tasting of caramel and cherries.

"Two points for you." A corner of Kade's mouth turned up, then fell. "I'm sorry, I don't mean to make light of things. Some days, it seems like you get going on a solid track and someone rips it out from under you."

"Was having a business a dream of yours?"

"Yes and no. I love the business and I'm good at it. Being my own boss is great, but it's a lot of work some days."

"No one needs a mechanic when things are going well."

"Exactly. How is school going?"

"Only five kids means more individual time to work with them, and I can get to know their families. Focus on their needs."

"Poll says Benny loves it there, with you."

"He's great. They all are." Elizabeth ran her finger around the lip of her glass until it made a tone, then stopped. "At the same time, it's hard being the only one, carrying all the responsibility. This thing with Nick made me think if an emergency happened, what would I do? Where could I go? The school is so isolated. No coworkers with whom to share stories and chocolate stashes."

"Well, I'm not much for chocolate, more of a gummy bear guy, but I am a good listener if you ever want to vent."

Kade met her eyes, his gaze deep and steady. His prickly external shell repelled this kind of intimacy. This new side was inviting, a little raw. Elizabeth was similar. A wall kept people out so when they disappointed her, it hurt less.

"You seem far away," Kade said.

"Must be the wine, and I'm up late."

"That's my cue, then. This was nice, thank you. It's not often I get to spend time in good company."

At the door, Kade slipped back into his jacket and shoes. Elizabeth felt a tug of longing, of not wanting the night to end but knowing it needed to, if only to be closer to the next.

"Thanks for bringing my brother home. And for the company."

"Can we do it again?"

"You hauling a drunk out here or sharing a bottle of wine?"

"Both, if the former is what gets me to the latter."

A wide smile stole across her cheeks. "Sounds like a date."

Kade's crinkled at the edges, and he held her gaze. "I'm keeping this promise." He brushed a kiss on her cheek and went out into the night.

Elizabeth, starry-eyed from wine and talk, swooned. Justin had been a breath of fresh air and freedom. He hadn't required anything from her, almost too easy. Kade evoked a slow burning fire, closeness, an exchange. She replayed the evening in her mind, allowing herself the luxury. Unsure what to make of it all, she relinquished the need for everyone to fit into neat compartments in her life. If only for an evening.

Reaching to turn out the living room lamp, she heard a crash in the barn. The motion light blinked on, flooding the back yard in a washed out, blue light.

46

I N A SMOOTH SWEEP, Elizabeth took the rifle from above the door, stepped into her boots, and then out into the yard. She kept her back to the door and regarded the darkness, rifle at her side, her shoulder ready to meet it.

A sliver of moon winked through the smattering of trees around the house. All was quiet.

I've seen too many cop movies. Elizabeth ducked out of the light and eased into the warm barn.

Casey's horse Gypsy, a chestnut Tennessee Walker, leaned into the aisle from her stall. The light flashed against her pupils, green and eerie, until Elizabeth blocked the beam with her body.

"You spooked, old girl?" She stroked the horse's neck, assuring herself in the process. "Kick something over?"

Her phone flashlight flicked shadows across the wall from the goat pen. Several of the herd stood at the railing, heads extended. In front of their enclosure was an upturned milking bucket.

Elizabeth crossed to the metal container and righted it, scooting it out of the way with one foot. "Sorry, ladies. I'll come feed you if His Royal Highness sleeps in, promise."

The goats watched her, plumbing her commitment, their horizontal pupils probing, invasive. Elizabeth turned to leave and stepped onto a bundle of soft matter. She aimed the beam of light on the otherwise earthen floor and found a wad of plants, mashed under her foot. Purple flowers with fans of leaves. The name swam in her consciousness.

"Don't give them that!"

Elizabeth dropped the poseys and swung the rifle toward the doors.

Casey ducked behind the opening. "Liz, it's me for Chrissake!"

"Casey?"

"You were about to feed my prize milk producers lupine!"

Lupine. Lupinus polyphyllus. "I just found it. I wasn't going to give it to them."

Casey took the handful of plant matter from her and tossed it in the trash barrel. "Where was it?"

"Right here. I heard a crash. Found the bucket."

Casey looked around and rubbed at the back of his neck. "There's no way."

"No way what?"

"I would never have brought lupine in here."

"Why did you get up?"

"Is that your way of asking if I'm hungover? I heard the crash, saw the light flick on through the blinds. I may have a raging headache but I'm not dead."

The barn shrank around Elizabeth, both fortress and stage of exposure at once. There were nooks in which someone, a person who knew about poisonous plants, could be waiting, watching.

"I'm going to check on Rhett." Her thoughts raced—had she locked the front door when Kade left? "You search the barn."

"I'm going to lock up. I'll comb the place in the morning."

Elizabeth jogged to the back door, wrenched it open, and dashed down the hall. Rhett slept, alone in the guest room. She checked the window lock and then backed out of the room to check the other locks. Assured, she waited at the back hallway to watch for Casey out the window.

"Didn't find anything," he said, nose pink from his time in the cold.

"We'll look again tomorrow."

"Hey, Jo. Sheriff around?"

Rhett ran a train around a wooden track. Elizabeth sat next to him on the floor, back to the couch, eavesdropping.

"I know. I wouldn't call unless it was important...yep, I'll hang on," Casey said.

Elizabeth rolled her head in a circle, stretching out taut neck muscles. Casey hadn't said much that morning. He'd made coffee and scrambled eggs and stared out the window, counting down the minutes until the socially polite hour of seven to make the call. A threat to his person was one thing. A threat to his livelihood, the animals he treated almost like family, another.

"I wondered the same. Nope, Liz didn't see anything. Uh huh...uh huh. Got it. See you in fifteen."

"Keep me posted," Elizabeth told her brother. "I'm off to pretend I can focus at work."

"Sis, I'm starting to wonder if you're a bad luck charm."

Elizabeth had dropped her bag on the threshold when Rhett ran over to hug her, hands sticky from his snack.

"Welcome home to me. What did I do now?"

"I just know a hell of a lot has happened since you showed up."

"No good news?"

"Sheriff thinks someone tried to poison my goats, and Marg Hart suggested I skip the memorial."

"I thought she didn't know about you two."

"She doesn't. Didn't. Doesn't. This is about the murder charge. While she didn't outright tell me not to come, she suggested people would be less upset if I stayed home."

"So, you're skipping it?"

"Oh, I'm going. Roz told me I'm invited. Said Justin would have wanted me there."

"But I thought Justin and Roz—"

"Split? They did, but she was widowed before the divorce was finalized. She and Marg get along, but they don't always see things the same way." Casey's eyes went gray, as though clouds passed in front of his irises. "Marg is a bit like Jo. Likes knowing everything about everyone but isn't as...inclusive."

"Should I go?" The request was part duty, part curiosity. "I guess I'd have to bring Rhett."

"Might help. If I know one thing about Margery Hart, she loves kids. Wouldn't leave Justin alone about it."

"Did Roz want them?"

"She did. Does. She had baby-fever like I've never seen before. Picking out colors, talking about names...until that stopped."

"Changed her mind?"

"I think she started to question what kind of father Justin would make."

Elizabeth knew that pain. She didn't regret Rhett, not one minute, but she could empathize with Justin's widow.

"What to wear to one's married date's memorial at his mother and widow's house?"

"Black."

47

THE HART RANCH HOUSE appeared after a winding drive through rows of poplars, standing like sentinels. The expansive, stone-fronted home was more than adequate for two women.

Half the county, judging from the field of automobiles, was in attendance. The long driveway was lined with trucks, like a sales lot, huge vehicles of every color, wheels parked on the lawn.

Elizabeth, with Rhett on her hip, and Casey took the steps to the wide, wrap-around porch at the back of the building. He greeted people ensconced in scattered rocking chairs, leaning against pillars, and chatting in small groups. Elizabeth gave out an awkward smile or two, knowing to most, she was a stranger there.

Rounding the porch, they found the gathering.

"Okay then." Elizabeth shifted Rhett to her other hip and looked to Casey. "Not your average memorial service, is it?"

"Subtle isn't a Hart trait."

The tableau was one part garden party, one part barn dance. The memorial aspect seemed to have stopped at the dress code.

People in various states of dark attire dotted the lawn. Twinkling lights wrapped around a pair of wizened cottonwood trees. Notes from a string quartet escaped the open barn doors.

Inside the massive structure, the bulk of guests gathered in heated comfort. Bouquets of peonies and roses rested in glass decanters over lace tablecloths covering the dozen round tables scattered across the immaculate wooden floor. Many were occupied with mourners, others stood among wired tree shapes entangled with tiny white lights. Mourners chatted in front of a food truck parked under the massive barn roof, its side promising the best barbecue in the area. On the periphery, a half dozen kids climbed hay bales or played corn hole. Somewhere, a dog barked.

A woman with a long, silver braid snaking over one shoulder approached the two of them, a silver Concho belt slung across her hips and silver-tipped alligator boots.

"Mrs. Hart," Casey started. "I am so sorry for your loss. This is my sister—"

"Save it for someone who will buy it, Casey Blau. This is a fresh hell for a woman approaching the end, and I'd rather not play the part of the dowager in some English novel." The woman's words came out like pea-sized hail, biting and disruptive. She turned to Elizabeth. "I know who you are, but who is this young man?"

"This is my son, Rhett."

"Ah, the one whose father fell like a tree from a stray arrow, I'm told." Marg turned her attention to Rhett, stooping to shake his small hand. "Young man, we have a new colt I think might be right up your alley. Be sure to hand his mama a carrot. She's got a soft mouth." Her eyes crinkled as she chucked a wrinkled hand under Rhett's chin. "And as for your mama—"

"Elizabeth Blau, nice to meet you."

"Divorce wasn't a thing we considered in my neck of the woods. Ruined the best of reputations."

The words rang like a slap. Elizabeth faltered, her softened expression shifted, defensive. She'd be damned if this stranger would be given judgment privileges.

"Bet many folks would have died a lot happier."

Margery Hart leveled her gaze at Elizabeth before bursting into laughter.

Casey and Elizabeth watched, startled.

"Oh, I like you. No wonder Justin was sniffing around. This event has been hell. I needed some levity." She patted Elizabeth on the shoulder as she passed, heading toward the door. "This old lady needs some of the good Scotch. Casey, if you are committed to making this about you, at least hold the door so I can get a proper drink."

Margery grabbed the doorframe before stepping over the threshold and away from the crowd.

"Wow."

"Consider yourself introduced. I need a drink." Casey left Elizabeth standing with Rhett.

"Well, buddy, I guess we should go see a colt."

Elizabeth's black and white floral dress, a thrift store find, flowed around her boots as she walked Rhett toward the barn's recesses. A lit hallway took them past a dozen stalls and then a dozen more. Horses of all sizes and colors chewed at the contents of their feed, an occasional occupant turning to regard the interlopers.

Rhett held a hand out toward every elongated head that drooped over a gate toward him.

"So many pretty horses. I wonder where..." They ambled down another corridor and found a stall with an extra light and a stool supporting a small bowl full of sliced carrots over ice. "Even the horses have it good here," she said to Rhett.

Casey was a tidy rancher, keeping his barn space swept and stalls cleaned, but this was a new level of immaculate. As she wondered if someone cleaned the moment any animal dared foul the shining, yellow hay, a movement along the hallway caught her eye.

Roz Hart stood near a stall, watching one of the horses eat. Long strands of tiny pearls draped over a loose, black sweater. If Elizabeth hadn't seen her before, she would have recognized the woman from the framed wedding photos peppering a table displaying scenes from Justin's life. Diamond bands still circled her left ring finger.

When Roz saw the two of them, she froze. Recognition and irritation flashed in sequence across her face. The woman rearranged her features into an expression of reluctant welcome.

"Hello, big guy." She smiled at Rhett.

"I'm so sorry for your loss."

Roz's smile faltered at the edges. "I'm so glad you all could come." Was this a dig at Casey? Roz watched Rhett, who hadn't taken his eye off the colt. The little horse wobbled on its new legs and stayed close to its mother's side.

"Want to help me feed his mommy a carrot?" Elizabeth selected one of the peeled orange sticks that looked like they belonged in a photo shoot from the bucket and held it out.

Rhett pushed her hand toward the mare's nose and her lips found the treat. As she crunched, Elizabeth and Rhett stroked the horse's muzzle, soft and brown.

"Lady was Justin's favorite," Roz said.

"She seems to be a sweetheart."

"One of the few women who would put up with him." Roz flashed Elizabeth a curt smile. "The service will start soon."

The taps of the woman's heels faded around the corner. "All right," Elizabeth said to Rhett. "How about we get you a snack? I think these carrots are spoken for."

Elizabeth found Casey near the makeshift bar, talking with Polly. Benny leaned against his mother, her arm wrapped around his shoulders.

"So glad you guys could come," Polly said. "Roz wanted to get everyone together to celebrate Justin's life, and she went all out. There's a band from Buffalo coming in to play after the service."

"Service?"

"The pastor from Our Lady of the Pines came over, and there are a few speeches planned."

"I'm going to need another drink."

"Get me one too, please." Elizabeth set Rhett down and held his hand. Benny showed the little boy a toy horse he'd brought, explaining its origin with much animation.

"I got to ride in a Jeep all the way to the feed store to pick him out with Aunt Roz. There were hundreds of horses, and I had to choose the best one. His name is Jack, and he is painted."

"A paint," Polly corrected.

"A paint," Benny repeated. "You can hold him if you want."

Rhett took the figurine in reverence and examined it, turning the miniature with his fingers. Benny watched the younger boy with patience.

"I know he'd like a brother," Polly said, reading Elizabeth's mind. "I don't want him going through life alone, but it's hard to think about trusting another human again. Especially a male one."

Elizabeth nodded. Another kid, another relationship, was a lot to fathom.

The quartet paused its songs for Roz to step to the microphone. "We're about to begin our service with a prayer from Pastor Carrey, followed by a few words about Justin. If everyone could gather here, we'll start in a few minutes."

As people shuffled in from outdoors, Elizabeth locked eyes with Kade who was making his way through the crowd. With a nod, he greeted her before making his way to a seat.

"Polly?"

The woman shifted in her seat, crossing and uncrossing her legs as she scanned the crowd. "Hmm?"

"Why did your cousin hate Justin so much?"

Polly looked behind her, as if to check who was listening. "Who, Kade? Hate is too strong a word."

"I don't think Justin liked Kade, either. Casey said it went back to high school."

"You can imagine how it is when people grow up together in small towns. A little too much togetherness, sometimes."

Elizabeth doubted the darkness in Kade's eyes was an old high school tiff. She watched Kade swirl the amber liquid in his rocks glass before taking another swig.

A compact man in a gray suit, bolo tie, and cowboy hat took the stage, Bible in hand. He read passages from the book before expounding on the good man lost too early to the Lord. She watched as Kade smirked into his glass when the preacher spoke of Justin's generous nature and kind heart. Just as she began to think him tolerable, maybe even date-worthy, he was acting like an ass.

Margery Hart took the stage. "Thank you all for coming. I won't stay up here long as the last thing any of us wants is to see an old lady cry, so suffice it to say that I loved Justin for his beauty and his faults. He was the best son I could have wished for, a lover of animals, and a man dedicated to this community. He would have given any one of you the shirt off his back, and I think in more than one case, he did. I miss him and his father every day and I..." Margery wavered, bringing a tissue to dab at her eyes and then the whisky to her lips. "What I am trying to say is that it isn't right for a mother to have lost her child, but that's the hand I'm dealt. Justin came into my life when I'd given up hope for a son, and I'm eternally grateful for the time I had with him."

The captive audience remained silent as she stepped down from the small stage and made her way to a back table.

Heads swiveled from her to Roz Hart who'd crossed back to the mic and cleared her throat as if commanding attention toward herself.

Elizabeth scrutinized the woman as she removed a folded paper from a jacket pocket, making a show of unfolding it, smoothing its surface, before taking a breath and beginning to read.

"Justin Hart was the kindest, most wonderful man, both husband and son. Had fate been kind, he would have been a loving father. Instead, his life was stolen—"

Was Elizabeth imagining it, or had the woman's eyes flicked to Casey, brief and accusatory?

"He gave everything to this community, whether through his good works at church, sponsoring the championship county softball team, or helping out a friend. He was a rodeo star, a horse breeder, and no one knew cattle ranching like Justin."

Elizabeth was curious if Roz had ever actually known her own husband. The affirmations she piled on his memory were thick with ignorance of his true feelings.

"Justin was the kind of man who treated you like you were the best thing that ever happened to him. He knew how to make everyone feel loved, cherished, special. He believed in the ranching lifestyle as something good for our country and good for the soul. In his name, I am honored to announce the creation of the Justin Hart Rodeo Scholarship, a fund for students on collegiate teams majoring in agriculture, for which I will be the initial Chair. Mrs. Hart has provided a sustaining endowment in Justin's name that will ensure his memory lives on."

Elizabeth dropped the spoon at the burst of applause. She clapped one hand against the inside of the wrist holding her fork, a slight percussion.

Rhett continued to scarf bites of artisanal mac and cheese Casey had offered. Elizabeth had tucked a stiff, white napkin into his shirt front. The little boy's outfit needed to stay clean of cheese sauce or she'd be wearing it, too.

"Thank you, thank you," Roz gushed. She slipped into the role of benevolent widow like a skin, a costume to don with pride. "Justin would have wanted more joy than tears tonight, preferring storytelling over regrets. Would anyone else like to say a few words?"

⟞⟋

Seeking Casey's attention, instead she watched him mount the stage and swallowed hard.

"I've been asked," he started, stooping to speak into the microphone, "no, *urged*, not to speak tonight, but Justin would have been disappointed in me shirking responsibility, would have given me shit for sleeping on the job."

A titter pulsed through the crowd.

"Justin was my best friend. I was the best man at his wedding, his roping partner, his right-hand man when he needed help, and he did the same for me. I wouldn't have half the success I have without Justin. He believed in me, helped me make connections in a new place, and would even muck stalls if it's what I needed because that's who he was, a giver."

This was the Justin Elizabeth had glimpsed, someone who drained himself for others.

"I know what you've heard about me, and I'm not going to say anything about that other than that I loved Justin Hart and wanted only happiness for his future, not the quick end he was dealt instead. Rest in peace, brother." Casey kissed two fingers and held them up to the sky before stepping off the platform and reclaiming his spot a few feet behind Elizabeth.

"Thank you, uh, everyone." Roz resumed emcee duties before others could get ideas. She still held the wadded handkerchief in her hand, squeezing it into her fist. "Now I'd like to welcome Highway Five to the stage. Please stay and make yourself at home, just as Justin would have wanted."

Elizabeth bounced Rhett on one knee. Steam fizzled out of the evening, pressure released with Casey's statement. Like a spent balloon, the memorial lost its tension and folks relaxed.

"I'm about ready to split," Casey said. He'd appeared at her elbow, finishing a beer.

"Same."

"I need to say goodbye to Margery and apologize again."

"Why are you apologizing to that woman? She treated you like the plague showed up at her event."

"She's a force to be reckoned with, all right."

"You feel guilty, don't you?"

"No, I—well, yes. That and I need what little support she's willing to give me, if any."

"What do you mean?"

"The only reason I have any customers at all is because of the connections of that woman. If she openly shuns me, if I give her any tangible reason—"

"Or if you are found guilty—"

"Which I *won't* be because I'm innocent. I can't afford to be anything other than a grateful subject. So, can I borrow Rhett?"

"What?"

"He's a shield of an adorable child. She has no choice but to accept our graceful exit."

"Okay, but be quick. He's tired out."

Casey held out a hand to Rhett while Elizabeth rose to carry the remains of their meal to the bus tubs. The sounds of a slow country tune filtered through the dissipating crowd.

After setting the bowl and silverware into a wicker-wrapped bin, she stood against the wall, anxious to go. Elizabeth squeezed her eyes shut and took a deep breath, willing herself not to cry, telling herself she could hold out a few more minutes, at least.

Her eyes shut, her ears picked out the crowd shuffling around her. People asked after each other, told stories about

Justin. Then, a bitter smell entered her nostrils, and her eyes flew open.

Frantic, pulse racing, she sought out the source. Tendrils of smoke came from the entryway to the horse stalls. Her mouth moved, speechless, unable to form words for a second before sound finally came out. "Fire!"

A few people stopped what they were doing to stare at her, this unknown woman screaming words so out of context in this venue.

"The horses! Fire—in the stalls!"

48

LIKE A STALLED ENGINE, the crowd roared to life, people running in every direction. Half a dozen of the brave ran for the stalls while the others took the nearest exits. Elizabeth willed her feet to move but not before she saw Roz and Polly consulting together at the corner of the barn. Roz crossed her arms as Polly gestured wildly as she talked. Roz reached out and grabbed her sister by the sleeve to drag her out the side door.

Out in the fresher air, Elizabeth searched for Rhett and Casey. She found them on the porch of the main house, watching the barn with Margery Hart. The woman had both hands over her mouth. Rhett covered his ears with his hands and buried his face in Casey's chest.

She swam through the crowd to their side, taking her son. Casey ran for the barn to help.

Horses streamed out the back of the barn, filling an attached corral, stamping and whinnying in the dark and smoke.

Elizabeth cradled her son's head with one hand, unable to do much other than watch the scene unfold like a nightmare. Margery stared at the melee.

A man mounted the steps, out of breath. "Mrs. Hart, we got all the horses out."

Margery audibly exhaled, putting both hands to her rib cage. "And the fire?"

"Still burning, but we're working on it. All hoses. We called for the truck—" The sound of a siren interrupted his report.

"Okay. Make sure everyone is safe. Get the horses out to a pasture, away from the smoke. Bring extra water troughs, and call the vet."

"Yes, ma'am."

"How is the colt?"

"Casey Blau led him out with his mom. He's fine."

"Good, that's good. I think I'm going to lie down. Tell Mrs. Hart to come tell me when there's news." Without a word to Elizabeth, the woman left for the confines of the ranch house.

Elizabeth waited on the steps for Casey. When he made his way over to them, he was covered in dirt and soot, his forehead striped from wiping away sweat with grimy hands.

"I need a shower."

"You do."

"Let's go."

In the car, Casey blinked, and whether from the smoke or the emotion, tears began to fall from his eyes.

"I'm sorry, Casey. This was...a lot."

"She wants to see you. Tomorrow."

"Who?"

"Marg. She said to tell you to stop by after church."

"But we don't go to—"

"Her church, not your schedule."

"Will she want me to, after..."

"When Margery Hart gives you an appointment, you attend."

"I haven't given anyone that kind of power over me, last time I checked. I'll go, but only because of what you said about needing her in your corner."

"She may surprise you. At any rate, I can't go back. At least not for a while."

"What? Why?"

"Charlie was furious with me, said I'm lucky Marg didn't call the cops."

"Cop."

"Cop. At any rate, he told me to stay away until the trial."

"So, I have to brave the waters myself, then."

Kade waited in the driveway when they pulled up.

"I'll get Rhett ready," Casey said. "Then you have to tap in so I can shower."

"Thanks."

"Casey," Kade said, as her brother passed him.

"Kade."

Elizabeth faced the man when the door closed. "That was some memorial."

"It was."

"It was good to hear from all the people who appreciated Justin."

"Good to see you, too."

"Is there a purpose to this visit? I'm not in the mood for more wine and conversation." She moved as if to brush by him.

"Wait. Elizabeth. Just a minute." He didn't reach out to stop her, his words acting as footholds in their stead.

She turned to face him, the weight of the day dragging on her ability to focus. "I'm listening."

"Justin owed me money. He never paid me back."

"What?"

"He borrowed money. A lot. I never should have leant it to him, that's my fault. He didn't pay me back, almost costing me my business. That part is on him."

"You're kidding me. You want me to believe that the heir to the Hart ranch borrowed money from you?"

Kade had been leaning against his truck but stood upright at her rebuke. "You calling me a liar?"

"I just think it's an easy thing to tell stories about people who aren't here to defend themselves."

"You know what? Fine. Continue to put a dead man you barely knew on a pedestal. *Saint Justin.*"

"Kade, I—"

But he was in his truck, the door slamming. He didn't look back.

49

ALL EVIDENCE FROM THE night before had been scrubbed clean when Elizabeth rapped on the giant, walnut door with an iron, horse-shaped knocker. The porch rockers sat, occupied only with ghosts. A barn cat was the lone living thing in the yard, cleaning its orange pelt with a rough tongue and front paw.

A man in a polo shirt and slacks answered the door, wavy silver hair and trimmed mustache accenting a weathered face. Elizabeth tried to place him among the dressed-up guests from the night before.

"Hello," she said. "Elizabeth Blau. Mrs. Hart wanted to see me." Elizabeth felt subservient to the whims of Margery Hart. This wasn't cool.

"Oh, yes. Come with me. Coffee? Tea?"

"Coffee. Cream, if you have it. Please."

"Of course. Mrs. Hart's in here." He gestured to an open door that led to a spacious room with clearstory windows, exposed beams, and a huge iron chandelier. Several chairs circled a massive, stone fireplace. Margery Hart sat in one, paging through a photo album, champagne flute in hand.

"Mrs. Hart, hello."

"Ah, Elizabeth. Thank you for coming. Enough with the formalities. Call me Marg. After all, if Fate hadn't been a fickle thing, I might have been your mother-in-law."

An audible gasp came from behind Elizabeth before she could choke out a reply to the presumptuous comment. Roz had just entered, purse under one arm, a portfolio under the other, with car keys in hand.

"I was headed to the lawyer's office, and I just wanted to ask if there's anything else you wanted me to bring him." Roz glared at Elizabeth and turned to Marg with pursed lips. "I didn't know we were having guests."

"He should already have everything he needs, thank you. If not, he knows how to get a hold of me."

Roz's nostrils flared before she stormed back out the door, clouds of perfume following her retreat.

"Ignore her," Margery said. "I always do. Sweet girl, smart enough, but she's resisting change, that's all."

"Change?" Elizabeth sipped her cup.

"She'll be moving out." Margery Hart dumped the fact in Elizabeth's lap as though it were as banal as a grocery list. "It's beyond time. I let her stay a bit to get sorted, but she needs to spread her wings, decide what to do with the rest of her life. To tell you the truth, I'm not even sure they liked each other toward the end, let alone loved each other, but that's how many marriages turn out."

"Oh, I'm sure that—"

"Says the divorced woman."

Elizabeth met the woman's steel gray eyes. "I still believe in love."

"Time will cure you of that soon enough, if you didn't learn last round."

Elizabeth studied the woman. Marg held the slim glass to her lips for a healthy swallow. What could have happened in her life to create such bitterness? What kind of marriage had Justin seen, growing up?

"I hope not."

"Well, let me know how that turns out for you. Fairy tales are always possible in the pages of a book." Margery drained the flute and dangled her wrist over the arm of the chair. "Justin liked you, and I see why. You don't accept the word of others as gospel. Nor do you grovel, flattering me with some false agenda."

"Agenda?"

Marg waved vaguely at the house, her surroundings, as if not wanting to vocalize her obvious advantages. "You saw him and liked him for his truths. He told you things, I think. Things he wouldn't tell just anyone."

"Mrs. Hart, I—"

"Marg. Please. Since I see you did not bring your son with you, we might as well get to business."

"If this part was supposed to be the pleasure part, by all means yes, let's change it up."

"Cheeky you are. Anyway, Randall told me it's all in order, and the check is signed." She handed Elizabeth a slip of paper before reaching behind her chair. "Oh, and Justin would have wanted you to have this."

Marg revealed an off-white Stetson, circled with a horse-hair band that she placed on the side table next to Elizabeth.

Elizabeth sat staring at the paper in her hands, didn't notice the hat, and couldn't focus for all the zeros. "I don't understand."

"It was his current, favorite hat. He bought a new one every time he...well. He thought new relationships needed new hats, for luck. This was his latest hat, so, it's you. Yours."

"Justin left me a hat and ten thousand dollars?"

"Well, to be precise, he left you nothing. It is I who bestows these gifts on you."

"Okay." That made a little more sense to Elizabeth except that it didn't at all. "I don't know what is going on here, but I think you must have the wrong person. We barely went on a couple dates, we didn't even...um. Well. I can't accept this."

"You can, and you will. Use the money to get your life back in order."

"Excuse me?"

"I was you, once. I made choices, allegiances, because I thought they would get me somewhere, anywhere, away from the mess I'd made at home. I didn't have the resources to do otherwise."

"But you can't buy my—"

"I grabbed the wrong keys. Do you have—" Roz burst back into the room. She saw the hat in Elizabeth's lap, a check in her hand. Roz's eyes narrowed, cat-like, at Marg. "What are you doing?"

"What I told you I was going to do as the manager of Justin's estate. Following his wishes."

"She was not in the will!"

"You are right, there. The will did, however, give permission for funds to be distributed to estate interests and community projects."

Elizabeth had been reduced to a business transaction.

Roz spat through her teeth, "You're giving away all of our money."

"You got your money, dear. Now don't you have an appointment to make?"

Roz stormed out of the room, a frigid wake trailing behind her.

"I don't want your money. Her money. Justin's money. Whoever's money."

"She already got her payout. It's why she's buzzing like a hornet's nest. As I had the unfortunate luck to outlive my son, she received a portion of his estate. Half of less than half isn't the same as all. I think I'm going to need something stiffer if the afternoon insists on such upheaval."

Elizabeth held the hat in her hands and turned it over, remembering the man who wore it. "Thank you for the hat." She stood and crossed the Turkish carpet, swirls of reds, blues, and greens.

Marg called out behind her. "When you change your mind, come back for Scotch. You've only got a few weeks, though."

Elizabeth took the bait. Returning to their place in front of the massive, stone fireplace, she folded her arms and stared down at the woman. "Why is that?"

"Put your hackles down, girl." Marg's wrinkles deepened as she gave a bitter smile. "I'm selling the place."

The wind rushed out of Elizabeth's sails. Justin had painted a life in which his family loved the ranch more than anything, more than his wishes for a different life. He'd believed in the future of the ranch more than his own happiness, sacrificed his own well-being to attend to the family. Maybe without a son to receive a legacy, the value was gone.

"You aren't the only one Justin cared about. There's a list. You can see yourself out?"

"Goodbye, Mrs. Hart."

"Goodbye," she called to Elizabeth's retreating form. "Bring that adorable son of yours when you come back. You owe me a grandmother's fix."

50

ELIZABETH COLLECTED RHETT FROM a harried Jo. There'd been an accident on the interstate, and Clint was still out there, likely to be half the night before they got things straightened out.

"It's all specialists, math, and insurance adjusters anymore. It's even worse if someone dies," she said to Elizabeth, whose eyes widened in response. "I'm sorry. I think I'm still a bit shaken from the memorial."

Jo had been at the service, circulating. She'd waved at Elizabeth before the speeches, before the fire. The sheriff hadn't shown.

"I just came from the ranch. I didn't see anything."

"Sounds like the hoses helped hold off the flames long enough for the trucks to take care of the rest. Thank God the horses were okay."

"Do they know how it started?"

"Not yet. Could be anything. We had a dry summer. All you need is a spark, and the whole prairie would go up in smoke."

"I'm just glad everyone is okay."

"You and me, both. Tell that brother of yours to come by when he gets a chance. The lawnmower is choked up, and I can't get Clint home long enough to do anything about it."

"Will do."

≪

At home, Casey wore an apron as he stood in front of the stove and flipped pancakes. What passed for a plant-based, imitation bacon sizzled in a pan.

"A letter came for you," he called over his dishcloth-draped shoulder.

"Want to get your trucks?" Between Casey and Jo, Rhett was ending up with quite the garage of miniature entertainment. His latest favorite was a dump truck. The little boy added a tractor to the mix and held court on the thick living room rug.

Elizabeth collapsed onto one of the stools at the kitchen counter and picked up the envelope. No stamp, only *Elizabeth* across the thick, ecru paper in an even script. She tapped the corner against her palm, debating, before sliding it away from her.

"Randall dropped it off. I'm guessing it's from Marg?"

"Likely."

"You aren't going to open it?"

"Nope."

At this, he turned around. "She gave me one, too."

"You?"

"Don't act so surprised."

"You're right. You're accused of murdering her son, and she didn't want you at his memorial, but I shouldn't be surprised she offered you money."

"Gave. I accepted, which you should do, too."

"Casey!"

"What? This covers my bond and then some."

"You can't be serious."

"I am." He leveled a stack of pancakes on the counter next to a butter dish and syrup bottle. With a spatula, he lifted strips of faux bacon onto a paper towel, their printed pinkness betraying their status as imitators.

"Are these any good?" she asked, taking one of the limp strips in hand. She regarded the floppy facsimile and took a bite.

"I know an attempt at changing the subject when I hear one," he said, untying his apron. "It's fine though, I have some good news."

"Oh?"

"I'll get Rhett and then I'll share."

Elizabeth slid a single pancake onto a plate and cut it into a coordinate grid before drizzling the pieces with syrup, the scent of maple perfuming the air.

After Casey hoisted Rhett into the high chair, the little boy scooped up a couple rectangular chunks and stuffed them into his mouth. He chewed and then took up his cup with both hands, tipping water into his mouth.

Nick was scheduled to be released from the hospital tomorrow. They'd talked about how to explain to Rhett that his father would need crutches. Would need to fly home. Would need to leave his son. Elizabeth wondered if Rhett would notice his father's absence but wouldn't say anything to Nick. She didn't want to jeopardize the fragile peace they'd established.

Heartbreak of any degree would have to wait for tomorrow. Any more thinking about the lawsuit could wait too. Deciding what to do with the money from Margery—from Justin—tomorrow.

"All right. Here goes. I'm selling."

"What?"

"The ranch."

What was in the water around here? "Are you crazy? You love this place."

"Look, it will likely take a few months, between getting things in order and the market. I'm sure you'll find something by then. If you don't stay on at the school, you can move with me. No one would blame you."

"But where are you going?"

"Bozeman. I'm going to take the girls with me, start over. There are a ton of people who want artisan cheese and a kitchen facelift there. Why don't you come with me? You could start a brewery."

The check mocked her from its granite resting place, the envelope glowing with potential.

"But you have a life here."

"Had. Had a life here."

Justin. For all her brother's brave face, his acceptance of his friend dating his sister, he'd still harbored bruised feelings. Freed of them, only to have them replaced with a murder charge, what had been sweet turned sour.

"But Jo and the others. Won't you miss them?"

"I can't run a business in a community that's already tried me, Liz."

"They are still investigating. You said it yourself—there's no way you will be convicted because you didn't do anything."

"There's a trial by jury, and there's a trial by gossip. The latter, I've already lost. I can't afford to have goats and not sell cheese, not remodel ranch houses." Casey shoved a forkful of pancakes into his mouth, chewing. A dark mood sank down over his brow.

"Fine. Quitter."

"Quitter? That's rich, coming from you."

"What does that mean?" Her fork clattered to her plate. She picked up the napkin and wiped at her face.

"All you do is run away from hard things. You pretend you're all brass and fire when it's just a cover so you can deal with your own problems."

"Look who's talking!"

She looked at Rhett. Her son watched his mother and uncle, the tension fogging the room, his ears alert. He'd paused, a chunk of pancake halfway in his mouth. Elizabeth forced a smile and said, "Doesn't Uncle Casey make the best break-fast?"

Casey shifted his jaw before returning to his own meal in silence.

When Elizabeth tucked Rhett in for the night, they read the book about the little bunny on a big adventure twice through. She gave him a kiss on the forehead, smelling the soft scent of his bubble bath, and turned off the lamp.

Elizabeth wanted to apologize to her brother. Needed to apologize.

For what, she'd have to make a list. For not believing in his plan. For crashing his life. For not trusting him. For putting him on a pedestal and getting mad at him when he didn't live up to the status in her mind.

Instead, she did what she did best. She left, seeking air and a beer.

51

WITH CASEY A WILLING sitter, the highway was a black ribbon in front of her, distinguishable only by its white edging, yellow divisions. She followed it to the neon lights, seeking refuge among the tired, the jovial, and the desperate.

The Crow Bar was slow for a Thursday night. Polly held court among a few regulars, nursing longnecks, hangovers, and histories.

"Hey, Liz. Benny came home tonight talking all about letters standing in for numbers, excited because now he can guess correctly at math."

"I gave him a very basic introduction to algebra today. We were talking about herd sizes. He was all excited that he could predict how much a lemonade stand would make next summer."

"Your first one is on me, for having a future finance major on my hands. He'll be the manager of our future family business in no time."

"Oh?"

Polly handed her a glass. "Going to start my own bar one day. Sooner, rather than later, if I play my cards right. I'll call you when I do, so I can carry your beer."

Elizabeth gave her a wan smile, the sudden windfall looming in her mind. With that money, she could buy some serious equipment, materials. Get things started again.

She replayed the afternoon, recounted the ten thousand dollars. The hatred in Roz's eyes, the staccato of her exit down the long, tiled hallway.

"I saw your sister today, at the ranch."

"Really? What was she up to?"

"Something about seeing a lawyer."

"They say the paperwork after someone dies creates its own layer of grief."

"Marg...er...Mrs. Hart said Roz was upset by all that. Upset at her share."

"Did she?" Polly paused her busywork, flitting between tasks, to lean on the bar, wrists resting on the edge. "Roz has never been one to settle for less. She's a taker."

"It sounded like she was getting less than she thought."

"Yeah. Marg outlived Justin. Had she been dead, Roz would have gotten it all. Hard to walk away from a table that big. Kinda can't blame her for being tender."

Polly made an old fashioned and some sugary concoction in a martini glass for a young couple mooning over each other at a tiny table in the corner. When she returned, she leaned toward Elizabeth, a conspirator.

"Remember what it was like to be that young, in love?"

Elizabeth smirked into her glass. She did, before she was married, a mother, divorced. "Barely."

She remembered herself at twenty-two, falling head over heels for Nick Thompson from Seattle. He was sexy, out-doorsy, earnest in his declarations about the environment, his dreams, and his love for the nape of her neck. He'd kiss her, nuzzle her, and she swore she would follow him anywhere.

Things had changed. Time wielded a scythe in the field of big hopes and dreams, revealing who he really was. Who she'd become.

Elizabeth wondered if Polly thought of Benny's father, their dreams together. If they'd had any.

"Any chance you could give me a ride home?"

"Huh?"

"My car is in the shop. One of the guys in the kitchen would do it, but I'd rather ride with you, if that's okay."

"Sure thing." Elizabeth wasn't in a hurry to get back to her sullen sibling and his rodeo reruns.

"Thanks, Liz. I'll start closing out."

⤙

A half hour later, Elizabeth was behind the wheel. The bartender rode next to her, sorting cash in the thin light emitted from the mirror under the car visor. Polly stuffed the bills back in her wallet and leaned back, exhaling.

"Good night?"

"Eh, it was pretty quiet. Can't win 'em all."

With Polly's directions, Elizabeth navigated her car down the aisles of a trailer park. They pulled alongside a white home with blue awning. A strip of fake grass made a runway to the door, framed by several pots of fake flowers.

"Cute place."

"If you like living in a tiny, rundown metal box in a semi-sketchy area, sure."

"Sorry, I—"

"No, it's all me, I'm sorry. I won't always live here. This was my aunt's place. She left it to Kade. I want better for my son. We'll get there." She waved her purse at Elizabeth. "One crummy shift at a time."

"Benny is at your sister's place?" The dark windows of the trailer hinted at curtains, but no lights were visible.

"Yeah. In a way, I think she uses Benny to get to Marg. It's a bit sick, I know. She desperately wants to stay on the woman's good side, and I need an overnight sitter twice a week. We girls do what we must, right? Thanks for the ride."

"Any time."

On the drive home, Elizabeth turned over the day's drama in her mind. Justin's hat sat in the front seat, crown down. Polly had held it in her lap when she took over the seat, replacing it when she got out as though it was common paraphernalia. Elizabeth picked it up with her right hand and placed it on her head. The hat slid to meet her ears, so she tilted it back in order to see.

The urge to keep driving, past the ranches, past the hospital, past this life and into the next, burned deep within her, like magma in a volcano.

She could be packed in ten minutes, tuck a sleeping Rhett in his car seat, take the check, and...and what? Never talk to her brother again? Blow Jo and the students off? Not to mention her friendship with Polly...

Somewhere inside her, she was tired of always leaving. Tired of being the one to pick up and start over again.

It surprised her to realize she liked it here.

52

"To what do I owe this—early—pleasure?" Clint squinted at her from behind his desk but did not stand.

"My brother is about to sell his ranch. Tell me you've made progress on the murder case."

"You know I am not at liberty to tell you that."

"But the blood at the creek?"

"Not Justin's."

"Damn."

He gave her a curious look.

"I was hoping it was useful."

"It still might be. We don't yet have a match."

"Ah-ha, so you can tell me something."

"I can only tell you what is public record, that's all. We know it's human blood but not which human."

"And the fire?"

"Cigarette, according to the fire marshal."

"DNA on that?"

"Ms. Blau, will you let me do my job and kindly stick to yours? Or do you not have children to teach this morning?"

Elizabeth let the rebuke hang in the air, an ugliness hung out on the clothesline for the whole neighborhood to see. "Sheriff, I don't think you understand how much of my life is tied up in these slow investigations."

Elizabeth strode from his office and out the front door and onto the pavement without looking back, without acknowledging the call from his secretary. Her breath came in deep gasps, the grip of a panic attack taking hold.

There had to be explanations for the avalanche of horrendous circumstances taking hold in her life like a virus, spreading and invasive.

Hand to her stomach, she waited for her breathing to slow. Once she had a grip on her emotions, she steeled herself and marched back into the building.

"I want you to look into who got money when Justin died, even though my brother and I are on that list. I want you to find out who shot my ex-husband so his mother won't blame me. I want you to give a damn when I tell you my life is falling apart because I have to wait for things to be fair, to become just."

Clint Wolf watched her, speechless. Elizabeth was mortified. She'd all but yelled at an officer of the law and expected him to arrest her or at least admonish her and throw her out. So be it. It was past time for someone to light a fire in this department.

Instead, he picked up his keys from the desktop and said, "Come with me."

She followed him out the door as he called to his secretary, "I'll be back in fifteen."

"Follow me," he directed, getting into his patrol car. She hurried over to her own vehicle and started the engine.

They wound their way through downtown, taking Main south before stopping in front of a turn of the century building topped with an octagonal dome. The courthouse loomed, the embodiment of judgment.

The sheriff clipped up the steps, and she struggled to keep up, having parked a half block farther and jogging to catch his stride.

Once inside they proceeded down the hall to the records room.

"Emmalyn?" From the aisles of boxes and files came a redhead in a cream blouse and tweed skirt. She looked the part of librarian, missing only a pencil behind her ear for perfect association.

"Hey, Sheriff, what can I do for you?"

"Justin Hart's will through probate, yet?"

Clint leaned on the counter. He was comfortable here, Elizabeth knew, the courthouse and its happenings fully within his jurisdiction.

"Funny you should ask. Second person today or I'd have to look it up. No, it hasn't. Shame about him. Nice guy, and what a way to go."

"Ms. Blau is very interested in the information when it becomes *public* information. When should she come back?"

"I really can't say. Some make it through in a few months, others take a year or two."

Elizabeth's heart sank. If only she could wind time forward, know that an end was on the horizon. She should maintain hope instead of giving up, giving in.

"Thanks anyway," Elizabeth said. "Wait a sec. What about prenuptial agreements?"

"You mean are they part of public records?" The woman seemed perplexed but trying to follow.

"Yes."

"Generally, no."

"Damn."

Wolf watched her, calculating.

"Emmalyn, I may be back."

❧

On the courthouse lawn, he slowed his pace to face Elizabeth. "I think I know what that was about, and I'm going to tell you, ask you, to be careful about the ideas you throw around."

"What do you mean?" He wouldn't buy an innocent vibe, so instead, Elizabeth went for indignation.

"Were you to scatter accusations like wildflower seeds, you will gain attention. Not the good kind. Feel free to look around, fill out all the public records requests you like, but leave the detective work to those who've earned the right to ask difficult questions."

She watched his car disappear down Coffeen until it was out of sight. Every muscle in her body was tense with the dismissal.

"Sheriff, you didn't say I was wrong."

53

ELBOWS ON THE BAR, head resting in her palms, Elizabeth ordered a whisky with a beer back. Polly lined up the rocks and pint glass in front of her and frowned.

"Anything you want to talk about?"

Elizabeth held up one finger as she lifted the glass of amber liquid to her mouth and downed it in one go. Sliding the beer closer to her hunched repose, she took a sip and sighed into the glass. "My life is a bit of a mess. I decided to feel sorry for myself tonight."

She'd made it to Friday, skidding into the weekend with gratitude. Telling yourself everything will work out how it's supposed to is one thing. Putting on an "everything's fine" face for a handful of elementary students when you feel like your life has been run over by a steamroller is another.

Despite her hobby, Elizabeth didn't drink much. An occasional glass of wine helped her get through a hundred middle school essays, but other than that, she needed to keep a clear head. Being a single mom, a moment to herself was rare.

Tonight, she needed every moment she could get.

"You are in luck. I specialize in keeping people company while they feel sorry for themselves. I'm a bit of an expert."

Polly, always moving, cleaning, bending, stacking, organizing, was filling her prep tray with garnishes. Elizabeth watched her slice a few orange wheels, wedge some limes, and skewer maraschino cherries on bamboo toothpicks, the thin strip of wood knotted on one end. She refilled the napkin holder with black paper squares and pre-poured a couple bowls of corn nuts. The Friday night rush had yet to invade, and Polly was in preparation mode.

"Thanks. Not planning to make it a habit, but I appreciate the company." Elizabeth glanced around the bar to take in the other patrons. High school football streamed on one television, but the other regulars on the stools murmured quietly to each other, nicotine stained hands white-knuckling beer bottles during the recount of a dramatic fishing story. "How's business?"

Polly assessed the customers scattered around the bar. "We stay pretty decent, even when the weather settles in. We can't plan on the outside space much longer, but that's all right. People get snuggly inside, stay warmer that way."

Elizabeth took a sip of her beverage. "Fair enough."

"They hold a homebrewer's fest once a year, in town. Folks bring a keg or two for tasting, and the winner gets to brew with a local brewer, sell their creation. You should enter."

Elizabeth thought of her carboys, her kettles, and her kegs, now all in the garage of an old coworker, full of subpar pale ale. What started as a hobby to unwind from her day job as a biology teacher blossomed into a marketable skill. A couple of collaborations had gained her contacts in Seattle, but the split from Nick had cut eliminated that pathway. Being a single mom required a steady job with benefits. She'd sold all her equipment to move out here and couldn't settle for a bathtub version. Then, she remembered the check from Marg. Pure potential in paper form. Could she start over, get her recipes going again? Should she?

"If I'm here, I'll think about it, sure."

"If?"

Failure sank in Elizabeth's stomach like a rock. "If my brother sells his ranch and rides off into the sunset like he says he plans to, I won't have anywhere to live, and my only decent family member and male figure in Rhett's life will be gone. I could live in the teacherage, but I just can't seem to relax when I live next to work, even on the days when no one is shot. I'm not sure I'll even have any students to teach after the trial, to be honest. Then what would I do? Why would I stay somewhere that doesn't want me? Casey invited me to Bozeman, but I just moved. I don't know."

"That's tough, Liz. You've gone through a lot, and this is just one more layer on top of all the other mess you've dealt with. I wish I could tell you that you are wrong, but shoot, I'm a walking example of why you aren't. Hang in there, though. There's still time for it all to work out. I'd hate to have you jump ship too early. Be back in just a couple." Polly hung her rag over a cabinet handle, flipped her braid over her shoulder, untied her apron, and added it to the pile before heading down the short hallway to the kitchen.

Elizabeth rotated her glass in a circle, running her fingers along the condensation. The drips dove for the cardboard coaster that advertised last summer's rodeo.

Polly returned, flushed and smelling of cigarette smoke. She shoved her phone in a back pocket of her jeans and once again donned the apron. The woman seemed wound up like a top, zipping to the kitchen to deliver a few orders, stock a cooler, and dry glasses before lining them up on a shelf. She was a worker bee, buzzing from flower to flower in a manic attempt to cover them all.

"Ever get to a point in your life when you aren't sure what you are supposed to do with the rest of it? Like you had one plan, life nailed you with some curveballs, and now you're spinning?"

"No. I mean, yes. I'll be right back." The woman repeated her earlier motions to head outside again, phone in hand.

Elizabeth shrugged. As she reached again for her beer, a breeze whipped in from the front door opening. The hairs on her right arm stood, the ions from the presence of someone lurking on her side electrified her skin. *Fight or flight*, she thought.

"Polly will be right back, she just went outside," Elizabeth said to the rows of bottles in front of her. She wouldn't invite conversation with a stranger, not tonight. Their face when they found out she was the sister of an accused murderer was not something she wanted to witness.

"I'm a patient man," said a voice.

Elizabeth's mouth went dry—too many corn nuts, not enough water. At the same time her mind said flight, her body, alight with proximity to Kade Michaels, said fight.

"Don't you have some brakes to fix? Rumors to spread?"

"I did have an errand to run nearby, so I thought I'd say hi to my cousin, if that's okay with you."

Elizabeth regretted her words, kicking herself. Polly was back, and the energy shifted.

"Kade, hey."

Like the last time she returned, Polly was out of breath.

Kade's brow furrowed. "Everything okay, Poll?"

"Yeah. Was just talking to Roz."

"Benny okay?"

"Yep. Yes. He's good. Busy night."

Elizabeth laid a ten on the bar and pushed the stool back so she could get out.

Behind her, Polly called, "Elizabeth, wait—"

But she was out the door.

Snow fell in fits and starts as she crunched across the parking lot, white flakes catching in her hair.

Approaching the car, she froze. Both back tires were punctured, and the trunk sagged toward the ground.

54

"**Y**OU FORGOT YOUR JACKET, and I'm not sure you should be—oh my God!"

"So, you see them, too." The view swam before Elizabeth's eyes as her brain tried to make sense of what she beheld. She squeezed her eyes shut tight, willing the scenario to change, only to open them to the same view.

"Come on. Let's go inside. We'll get this figured out. I'll make tea."

Polly led Elizabeth back to the abandoned stool. The bartender disappeared into the kitchen to fetch hot water.

"You look like you've seen a ghost," Kade said. He dropped off a couple of empties at the bar and waited for another round.

"Leave her alone, Kade," Polly said, returning with a steaming mug, tea bag label dangling over the edge.

"What happened?"

"Someone took out her back tires."

"What? How do you know?"

"It's pretty simple, really," Elizabeth started. "When I arrived an hour ago, I had four functional tires. Now, when I go to leave, I have two flats."

"Wow. I'm sorry."

The concern in his voice sounded real, but she couldn't help but pop an eyebrow in suspicion. Someone had sent her a clear message. She would listen.

"I'm going home," she said, standing.

"How?" Kade asked with his infernal logic.

"Damn," she said, and slumped back into the stool. "I need to call the sheriff."

Polly bit her lip, glancing between the two of them. "I get off in a couple hours."

"I'll take you home," Kade said.

"Are you sure? Your tires could be next. Or your business. Or, you know, there's murder. Seems to be what happens to people I'm around."

"I've already taken one Blau home this week. What's one more? I'll take my chances."

Shoulders slumped, Elizabeth gathered her purse and followed Kade to his truck. He opened the door and gestured to the step plate and handle.

"Getting into your truck is like climbing into a saddle on a 17-hand horse."

"Hey, I got a deal on this truck. A rancher going out of the business needed to get rid of it."

"It suits you. Big and blustery."

The engine roared to life and Kade turned down the radio that blared.

"I would ask why someone would dislike you enough to stab your side walls but then you might just tell me."

"Funny."

Silence filled the car, vacuous, cautionary. When they turned off the red shale highway and onto the dirt road, panic seeped in.

"I can't go home."

"What?"

"Kade, my tires were slashed. Someone is trying to send me a message, a clear message. If I go home, I'm just bringing that target on my back home to my kid."

"I think that if someone wanted to hurt you, they could have. When you take out someone's tires, that's something else."

"A warning."

"Yeah, like a stay out of my life kind of note. Where do you want me to drop you off?"

"The Wolf Den."

Jo answered the door after the first knock, bird rifle in one hand. She wore a blue terry cloth robe, and her hair was down. The silver-streaked brown whipped around her face in the breeze.

"You two. I don't usually have tea ready to go at this hour, but I do have a nice Scotch open."

As they waited for Jo to return with glasses, Elizabeth stole a glance at Kade. Once again, he'd known just when she needed a rescuer, the very moment she was stuck without options.

Jo returned with a sweater buttoned up over her robe, a couple of mugs in hand. Elizabeth could smell the whisky, peat and bog singing to her frazzled senses.

"I called Clint about all this. He said he'll be by as soon as he can. Tell me everything."

While Elizabeth described the evening to her neighbor, Kade watched her. She was unnerved by the way he regarded her, not used to the scrutiny.

"...and Polly helped me stand up straight during all this. Without her, I don't know how I would have handled things."

The last comment was a barb aimed right for Kade. He didn't flinch. He let her words roll off him like beach sand.

"I will say, and I'm not a professional, but you do seem to have more bad luck than just about anyone else I know in the county."

"Whatever sign is on my back, I want it off."

"And you have no idea how it got there? Who could have pinned it to your jacket?"

Elizabeth shook her head.

"C'mon, let's get you home to wait. Goodnight, Mrs. Wolf."

At the ranch, Elizabeth retold the story to Casey. He'd spent the evening taking apart a milking machine. Lines of grease striped his forearms.

"Pretty quiet here, comparatively," he said. "Most exciting thing that happened all night was a car turning into the driveway before backing out and driving off."

"Where were they coming from?"

"From the west. It happens. People get lost out here all the time. Many at night. People who come in way too late from Lincoln and can't find anything in the dark."

"Wouldn't they have come from the highway, then?"

"Maybe they did, made it to the end of the road and had to turn around. At any rate, exciting stuff here at Cloud Nine."

"I'll have my guy pick up your car in the morning," Kade said. "I'm going to head out."

Elizabeth muttered a begrudging, "Thanks," to Kade as he ducked out the door, nodding at Casey.

Casey regarded his sister. Elizabeth saw her father's cheekbones in his teasing smile. "You like him. Like, really like him."

"What are you talking about?"

"Any man who riles you past the point of snarky comments has your attention."

"I was never that way with Nick. Am never that way with Nick."

"And look where that got you."

She shot her brother a look that would wither a dandelion, but he gave her a Cheshire Cat grin.

"Look, I liked Nick—I mean, except for him being a cheating creep. He didn't get you this fired up though. I think you just went along with suburban life because you wanted what we didn't get growing up."

He wasn't wrong. She remembered the last few months of her marriage, when attending neighborhood picnics, office parties, and moms' groups was torture. Pretending all was well. Talking with joy about her husband tasted like chewing glass. All she wanted to do was scream from the frustration. Let the whole world know her life was a lie, her home was a rotting place, and that the only joy she found was in mothering her son.

A tear slipped down a cheek, followed by another. Elizabeth wiped furiously at her face and willed herself to not let the rotted past affect her now. Kade was right. You couldn't escape your past, couldn't run from misery, or at least not for long. Truth would be heard, wanted or not.

"I need some sleep."

"Goodnight, Liz. I'll be up early. I have a meeting with a realtor bright and early." Casey yawned and stretched his arms upward over his head.

"Still putting it all up for sale?"

"I don't really have a choice." Casey started down the hallway toward his room.

"Well, Marg—," she said to his back.

Casey paused. After a beat, he reached out to press one hand against the wall, a steadying anchor. "I know what Marg is doing with Justin's money and don't even think about it. You are the best sister in the whole world for even considering me, but I can't let you. It would only keep me afloat for a bit, and then I'd be back in the same place."

"I'd say I'm surprised she didn't..."

He shook his head and turned to face Elizabeth. "Give me more? I'm not. Not when I'm on the hook for Justin's death. I'm lucky she gave me what she did. Anyway, you'll use it to decide where you want to go next. Wherever that might be."

"Nick gets out tomorrow. The danger of infection has passed, and he wants to do physical therapy back home."

"Are you going with him?"

"No. Absolutely not. No way in hell would I get back together with Nick. I just wonder if I should go back to Washington, though. Rhett would have both his parents to support him, no lawsuit drama."

"Go back to Seattle if you want, but only if *you* want, Liz. Don't let anyone take your choices from you. Not Nick, and not whomever ended those balding rubber Cheerios you called tires."

55

SQUEALS FROM A HYDRAULIC lift woke Elizabeth who, foggy, stumbled to the window to search for the source.

Ducking into a sweatshirt and stepping into Casey's new yard shoes, she left the warmth of the house to find Kade scrubbing at the side of her car in the chilly morning. His breath puffed out in clouds, vapor against the early morning backdrop.

"Hey," he said, standing up, cloth in hand, and gesturing at her car. "Your tires are toast. Even the two that weren't trashed are past the point of function. I wouldn't drive my son—"

"I couldn't afford—"

"Sorry. Look, sometimes I talk then think. Bad habit. In this case, I would replace all four. I would give you a discount and do it at the shop, but I can recommend another mechanic if you like."

"Thank you for hauling the hunk back here." She was grateful. Grateful for the moment to feel wanted, needed. Grateful not to have to carry every problem squarely on her shoulders, alone. Casey was right, she liked Kade. It was messy, she might be leaving, but she admitted that in a perfect world, another life, she might have seen where the energy took her. At present, she had to let it spark and die out. *Dammit, be nice.* "You didn't have to do this. It was kind of you."

"I'm not going to leave anyone stranded. It's just not my nature."

"Look, Kade, I should—" She went closer, saw what he'd been scrubbing. Several lipstick lines snaked along the doors. A pink-purple streak suggested a pattern, a letter. "What's this?"

"Either someone isn't your biggest fan or just wanted to see that shade over pearlized navy."

"Why would someone do this?"

"I was going to ask you if it was there when you saw the tires last night. I couldn't remember."

"I don't know. It was dark. I need coffee." Elizabeth pressed both palms to her temples, trying to think.

He stood there, watching her.

Elizabeth sighed. "I do need tires. You're here with a truck. Could I get some from you? Please."

He nodded. "Of course. I'll load 'er back up."

"Kade," she said, pausing on the front step.

"Yeah?"

"Thanks."

"Sure. Should be ready this afternoon."

Back inside, Elizabeth slammed the cabinet doors, hunting for coffee beans and filters before realizing she risked waking a toddler who would then require more energy than she had to give. She transitioned into quieter rage, a skill of the most adept mother. How dare someone treat her like trash, ruin her car, and write on it with lipstick? What kind of backwoods bullshit was this?

Outside the window, clouds hung low, gray, and sullen, like her mood. A cottonwood twisted up behind the barn, its sweet pollen long gone, the black ridged bark stark against the sky. Sage ringed the corrals, pale-hued leaves blurring in the backdrop of autumn, dry and sparse.

There, by the corral gate, a hank of summer blue disrupted the landscape. A token of summer, the shock of color was a beacon in the filtered daylight. Elizabeth set down the bean canister and headed for the back door.

She jogged to the bush in which the fabric was snagged, fighting against the winds which had ushered in the morning's clouds. Up close, the flag identified itself as a beanie, knitted, a single white strip along the bottom edge. Elizabeth picked it up, turning it inside out to look for a tag, a head, or who knows what else before searching outward, over the expanse for an owner. No one, hatless or otherwise, stared back.

56

"I 'LL SEND SOMEONE TO pick up my car," Nick said. Elizabeth stood at the wall as a nurse adjusted his crutches and played spotter as he ambled about the tiny room, like a colt with new legs. "Feel free to use it until then."

Today, she'd brought Rhett to see his father. The boy watched them both, wide-eyed and solemn in his support. Nick had booked a flight home, the drive hampered by a hole, now healing, in his thigh.

"Wolf said he'll keep me updated if they ever find the bastard who did this, but he also told me not to wait by the phone."

"Sounds like something he'd say." Elizabeth wanted to call the sheriff or storm back into his office to demand he investigate who vandalized her car—but what was the use? County justice was short on manpower. One could only do so much.

"Look. That neighbor of yours was here and she told me—"

"Jo was here? Or Margery?"

"The sheriff's wife. Said that moving out to that creepy building was all her idea, and she feels guilty as hell for what happened and that I was not to blame you."

"Blame me?"

"Jo said she talked you into moving out there, by yourself, to appease whatever version of a PTA exists out here."

Elizabeth shook her head. "She did suggest it. All but told me to go or I wouldn't have any students to teach. I went because I thought your lawyer would use my living situation to help you gain custody."

This was a showing of cards, and she wanted to test the waters of their unofficial agreement. Elizabeth crossed her arms and glared at Nick.

Nick sighed. "Given all that's happened, and if it were up to me, I think you should stay with Casey. At least for now."

Elizabeth spluttered, and Nick leaned onto one crutch to hold up a hand. "I'm not telling you what to do. I'm just saying it makes sense. I don't like the idea of you two alone out there."

"We might not be here for much longer."

"What do you mean?" Nick maneuvered himself back into the bed with relief, swinging the crutches to his side and tilting them against the bed.

"Casey is selling." Saying it out loud rang of a new finality, one that bruised rather than stabbed at her heart. "I hate to say it, but it makes sense. Being accused of murder seems to do a number on your client base. He's planning to move, likely to Montana."

"Are you going with him?"

Elizabeth looked at her ex-husband, tried to see the good behind the face she'd resented for the last eighteen months, the one she feared was hell-bent on separating her from her son. The face she loved, once.

"I don't know," she said. It was a risky response, but it was the truth. "I need a job. I like these kids, this school. I'm not sure about after this year, but I think I need to stay until summer, like I said I would.

Nick looked down at his shirt and nodded before meeting her eyes. "Okay."

"Okay?"

"I will call off the hounds until then."

She raised an eyebrow at him. "Am I supposed to say thank you to that?"

He exhaled. "I'll tell the lawyer to drop everything. Rhett will be two in a handful of months." He took his son into his arms and handed him some plastic implements from a wheeled tray. The boy began banging them like drumsticks on the surface. "He will be two, and if he still isn't talking, we need to seek the next steps. Right?"

"I'm not saying I will bring him back to Washington."

"I'm asking that we take him to a specialist. Do you agree with that?"

"Of course."

"You have a few months to choose the specialist. Then I think we will go from there."

"Agreed."

"And I want some weekend visitations."

"What do you mean?"

"I'll come here, or Montana, or wherever, but I'm not going to miss this couple of months."

"Fine. But they have to be pre-scheduled. No more showing up on Casey's couch."

"Deal."

She reached for Rhett after Nick gave him a tight squeeze. "Who sent you those flowers?"

"That cute gal I met at the bar. She liked my smile."

The card inside read *Come back soon* under which the sender had drawn a heart with an arrow through it.

Elizabeth's blood ran cold.

57

"**I** NEED TO TALK to him. Now."

"Ms. Blau, as we've discussed many times, the sheriff is not at anyone's beck and call, not even Mrs. Wolf's. You are going to have to wait until he comes back from his rounds. I can let him know—"

Elizabeth shifted Rhett from one hip to the other. He leaned as far forward as he could, reaching for the canister of pens on the desk. "We don't have time to wait. You need to radio and tell him it's urgent. Tell him I've figured something out."

The woman looked down her nose at Elizabeth, disdain dripping like viscous syrup from her words. "I'm sure that you have important things to discuss, but I will not be talked to like—"

Elizabeth didn't hear the end of the sentence. She pushed out the door and headed for Kade's garage.

"Your car is ready," he reported, removing a clipboard off the wall. "Craig is in the office. He'll get you closed out and on your way."

He handed her the paperwork and turned to address a sedan with a bowed bumper and cracked taillight resting on the lift. Elizabeth had been dismissed, she knew, in strict professionalism.

"I borrowed someone's car to come out here and pay my tab. Is it okay if I get a ride back later to pick up my car?"

"It's fine. I don't charge rent. Big lot."

Rhett watched in awe as Kade pressed a button on the lift and the car left the ground, hovering above in what seemed an impossible balance. Kade walked below it to inspect the damage from underneath. Rhett held his hand out toward the scene, as if reaching for the man with such power, willing it for himself.

"Kade?"

"Yeah?" The man reached up behind the taillight, using a slim screwdriver to angle in between parts. Half-listening, he continued his work, a signal of his attention.

Elizabeth assumed he would shut her down, refuse her information, ignore her curiosity if only to rid her from his sight and move on. She had to try, though. Her freedom, Casey's freedom, relied on it.

"Do you like bowhunting?"

He stopped what he was doing to regard her, a confused look on his face. "Bowhunting?"

"You know, the sport. Bagging elks, 3D targets, and all that."

Kade shook his head as if to ascertain the rationale of a perplexing woman, then went back to shining a pocket flashlight under the body of the car. "Nope. I've always left that to the rest of the family. I get what meat I eat from Sackett's. Never took to the sport part."

"But your cousin likes it."

"Lots do. In this part of the country, people understand where their food comes from. You can't always afford to be squeamish or you don't eat."

Elizabeth thought of a fawn, all spindly legs and tummy full of summer grasses.

"She a good shot, Roz? I wouldn't want an animal to suffer for my dinner table."

"One of the best. You should know that though. Your brother only wins every shootout she doesn't."

"Once I saw this event...mounted archery? That was wild to watch. It would be fun to see again."

"Not a big sport here. A deer would hear a galloping horse a mile away."

"Huh. Well, maybe they will make it one. My brother would be a natural."

"No doubt."

This last answer was almost inaudible as Kade worked underneath the car. The weight of messing this up flickered in a pulse.

"Thanks again," she said. Without waiting to see him twist his head out from behind a fender to watch her go, she left.

&

Elizabeth buckled Rhett back into Nick's car and debated where to go while she waited. Being alone wasn't a choice.

Casey was gone, so the house was out. Returning to the hospital would be a fresh ordeal. Ambling down Main Street was something best left for a warmer day. Elizabeth headed south.

Afternoon crept in like a cat; tentatively, first one paw and then the next, ears alert for welcome. A lone sandhill crane statued itself in the field just past the college, a few pronghorn antelope scattered beyond. Red shale highways fell away behind the new tires as she followed the curves in the road.

A turn off the familiar dirt road brought her to the Hart ranch. On approach, she tried to ignore the warming shack and the sight of Justin's truck parked near a barn. The mind is a fickle mistress, serving as a glaring reminder of the complicated and tragic past.

Before she could overthink the move, Elizabeth crossed the porch to knock on the solid door, Rhett snuggled in her arms.

"Ms. Blau," Randall said. "To what do we owe this pleasure?" The man wore a blue, striped apron over clean slacks, sleeves of his pressed shirt rolled up, spatula in hand. Elizabeth snorted. He looked like what happens when news anchors are forced into a cooking segment for viewer entertainment. An older cowboy, deep wrinkles, copper skin, and ropey forearms suggested he hadn't always been relegated to door and kitchen duties.

"I hoped Mrs. Hart was around. She said to come by anytime with Rhett." Elizabeth hoisted her son higher as if to make her purpose clear. Rhett stretched away from her, reaching toward a large, brass cougar on a pedestal by the door, stroking the extended paw as if it were alive. *Nice kitty.*

"Of course. She's in the stables. I'll let her know you are here. Please follow me."

Randall led them to a bright room on the south side of the house, and Elizabeth gaped at the fabricated Shangri-La. Solarium windows extended from the ground in an arch above to connect with the roof of the house, amplifying the sunlight. Several large plants anchored the corners. A dracaena, a monstera, and an organ pipe cactus created a lush escape from the bleak landscape outside.

Elizabeth selected from the wicker chairs draped with cushions and waited, her feet tapping on the plain, woven rug. Other, smaller greenery highlighted small tables. The stuffed, squat vases were cheerful and welcoming. While the rest of the house was leather, rich hardwoods, and Navajo rugs, this room resembled an English conservatory.

Randall presented a silver tray with two glasses of lemonade and a short stack of cookies—oatmeal, she guessed. "Help yourself," he said, setting the snack on a low glass end table, then leaving.

Elizabeth tested a cookie, taking a half moon bite. Warm, sweet, and indeed, oatmeal. She handed Rhett the rest of the disk and reached for a glass. The cool drink was sweet, tart, and to her surprise, came with a hint of salt.

Marg Hart swept into the room and removed her gloves to drop them on the table before collapsing into an over-pillowed chair.

"Vietnamese," Marg said. "Chanh Muoi."

"Excuse me?"

"Salted lemonade. My husband loved it during the war. Every time I have it, I remember him. He knew the whole mess was idiotic, did his best to bring home some positives alongside the PTSD."

"Justin's father."

She nodded. "A good man. Not perfect, mind you, but ambitious, brave. Successful, as far as those things go."

Rhett finished his cookie, a few crumbs tumbling onto the carpet, and reached for her glass.

"The other one is for you," Marg said. "I don't think I should put that combo in my stomach today. Not feeling my best."

"Rhett can use a glass, but I'm not sure I want to risk this one. It's a bit big for his hands. I can hold it for him."

"Nonsense. Randall," Marg called. "Don't we have a better glass for our young friend?"

Elizabeth shifted in her seat as Randall left the room. "I didn't mean to complain. We can manage."

"I pay him to do what I ask. It is his job, after all."

The man in question returned with a lidded travel mug. Before Marg could question his choice, Elizabeth jumped in, "That's perfect, thank you."

Rhett hefted the mug's opening to his mouth and took a sip before recoiling.

"You get used to it, young man," Marg said. "The regular stuff tastes like sugar swill to me at this point."

With a tentative renewal, Rhett took a second sip before pushing the mug away.

"Sorry to hear you don't feel well," Elizabeth stalled. She was so certain of her questions on the drive over but now, resolve faded like the sunlight outside the big windows, disappearing when faced with Justin's mother.

"Getting old is hell, but it happens to us all. Things flare up and remind me I can't race barrels anymore, let alone take in a glass of sugar, acid, and salt without consequences."

"Ah," Elizabeth said, the sheen on her forehead mimicking the condensation on the glass.

"Enough with the small talk, I'm not spending the rest of my life talking about aging, and I don't suggest you start. What can I do for you?"

As if on cue, Randall brought in a basket of toys which he displayed at Elizabeth's feet. An offering for Rhett. A triceratops, a locomotive, and a doll with twin braids and a gingham dress were the first items Rhett freed from the confines. He began puppeteering his own drama, and Elizabeth faced hers.

"I wanted to ask about Justin's inheritance."

58

"YOU HAVEN'T CASHED THE check."

Elizabeth's eyebrows shot up, and she sucked in air.

Marg continued. "Randall told me. He balances my books. If you are here to give it back in some grand gesture, then to hell with you. I don't take to sensationalistic statements. I've got enough of that."

"No. I mean, I'm not here for that. It's true, I haven't cashed it yet. It doesn't feel like mine."

"Well, it is. Justin would have wanted you to have it, would have wished something nice for everyone he cared about. He was sometimes a foolish boy with a heart on his sleeve, but he was impeccably kind, trying to save everyone he met."

"Thank you, I...yes." The tide of conversation had to change.

"Casey."

"What?"

"You are here about Casey."

"No, I—"

"There aren't many realtors up here. Secrets don't keep."

Elizabeth took the reins. "Look. Yes, I'm worried as hell about my brother. Yes, I think it's strange that you would give me, a woman Justin dated for all of a week, ten grand. I can't stop wondering why."

A smile played at the corner of Margery Hart's lips. "You'd be surprised at what is and is not on a body's conscience as they get near the end of things. I'd tell you to let me know when you finally get it, but I will be long gone, and with the good Lord's grace, will be with my two boys. If you aren't here about the check, then what do you want? More money? That's what most people want when they knock."

Elizabeth took a breath, steadying herself. She put a hand on her chest to feel her breath. The woman's accusations were barbs but not directed at her, just the world. At least, not yet.

"Mrs. Hart. Has the sheriff talked to you about anyone else being a suspect, other than my brother? Someone who might actually gain money?"

"Get out."

"What?"

Rhett looked up at the older woman's tone. His face screwed up in a silent pre-cry, and Elizabeth reached out to rub his shoulder.

"If you, for one second, are accusing anyone in my family, you will leave this house immediately."

"I...I..." Elizabeth stammered, seeking an excuse that would not come. "If you're sure it's not—"

"I think I've had enough visitors for today. Randall, the guests are leaving." Lines at either side of Marg's face deepened as her lips pursed, her eyes cold and unwavering.

The man appeared from the shadows to stand by the door.

Elizabeth stared hard at the elder Hart, as if to measure the exact sore spot she'd inadvertently prodded, before separating Rhett from his toys and departing as commanded.

In the hallway, she didn't wait for Randall. Elizabeth shoved at the front door and closed it with a solid clunk behind her. She heaved a great breath before hugging Rhett against her chest, smelling his hair. He wrapped an arm around her neck and buried his curls under her chin. Her sweet, perceptive son knew when his mother needed him.

The gravel driveways were littered with detritus from the copse of Ponderosas along one side. Elizabeth kicked at a cone with the toe of her boot. *Damn that woman.* Elizabeth was frustrated with her dismissal and annoyed at the respect Margery Hart had for Roz. Elizabeth had never inspired that kind of blind dedication from anyone except Rhett.

As she stomped to Nick's car, the sound of horse hooves hitting packed earth broke the silence. Roz approached the nearest barn astride a large palomino, all mane and legs. Slowing the horse as she approached the doors, she dismounted in an even swoop and walked the horse the last ten feet, reins as lead. The woman walked with the easy confidence of someone who rode in her sleep. Her boots, tight leggings, and camouflage vest hugged her like a second skin.

Instead of Roz entering the barn, a man came out and took the reins from her. Elizabeth's jaw hit the floor when instead of witnessing a polite thank you, the woman wrapped her arms around the man's neck and gave him a slow, deep, kiss.

Elizabeth looked around, but no other witnesses joined her in this observation. The property was otherwise devoid of occupants.

The man Roz kissed wore the ubiquitous, wide-brimmed cowboy hat and jeans, a lead rope looped over one shoulder. When he pulled away, the line of his jaw was familiar, the nose from a profile she knew.

As the gears of recognition clicked into place, the couple saw her watching them. The man steered the horse into the barn but Roz, fury painted on her forehead like a sunburn, stomped over to where Elizabeth stood.

Roz stopped a few feet from Elizabeth and planted her hands on her hips, eyes flashing. "What are you doing here?"

"I'd ask you the same thing, but I think that was pretty obvious."

"What I do is my business."

"Damn straight it is. If you want to ride off into the sunset with Isaiah, my opinion is the last one that matters. Not sure Mrs. H would agree, though."

"She doesn't give a damn about me."

"I know she has a lot of faith in her brokenhearted daughter-in-law, who appears to care far less about a deceased husband than she claims."

"You don't know the first thing about what I feel," Roz said.

"You're right. You claim to be miserable over the loss of Justin and meanwhile are making out with a man who's besties with Justin's enemy. I'm sure everything is copacetic."

"Keep your mouth shut or I'll...I'll—"

"What? Ruin my life? It's already in shambles, so let me save you a step. I don't give a damn who you're with. I just don't like liars. I'm leaving, so you don't need to throw me out. Enjoy your screwed-up, entitled life. I'm sure it will keep you warm at night when your conscience comes knocking."

Elizabeth whirled around to stalk off to her car. She'd had enough of this family, the secrets, the unfairness of it all. She would try another route. Wolf would have to listen to her. Being up front and honest was getting her nowhere.

Roz stared after Elizabeth as she buckled Rhett into the back seat and climbed into the front seat. Elizabeth started the car and rolled down the windows. Before she could drive off, Randall ran out of the house and called to Roz.

"Rosalyn! We need you to call Dr. Romacheck, now." His feet descended the stairs like an automaton. "I've called for an ambulance. Mrs. Hart is sick. The paramedics are on their way. She's pale and not keeping down water. She asked me to pack her a bag but I—"

"I'm on it." Roz pulled her phone from her pocket and dialed. Her movements were purpose-driven and exact. "I'll sit with her until they get here. You grab her overnight bag, her pills, her purse. Give me the bag, and I'll follow the ambulance into town."

Without a backward glance to Elizabeth, Roz and Randall rushed into the house. Elizabeth drove the short stretch home, watching the rearview mirror for emergency lights.

59

"WOLF CALLED FOR YOU," Casey said as soon as she stepped through the door.

"When?" She pulled her phone from her pocket and saw two missed calls, one voicemail. She'd been so distracted by the drama at the Hart Ranch she hadn't heard the buzzing.

"Said I should expect a call from my lawyer tomorrow, too."

"That could be promising."

"Or damning. He said it was about that evidence you wanted. Didn't know the sheriff is now taking directives from you, but stranger things have happened."

"So funny. I asked him to take a look at the Hart inheritance, in case there's someone there who would have good reasons to want Justin gone. I assumed he would have done that already but situations are changing. More than just you talking about pulling up stakes and getting out of Dodge."

"Seriously?"

"What?"

"Elizabeth, the man was trampled to death. By cows, not his long-lost cousins or something."

"I know that, you know that, but still, something is off. Why was Justin out there? Who let the animals out of their pen? You saw that gate. I really don't think a bear or something came and—"

"Elizabeth." He crossed to her and anchored a hand on each of her shoulders. "I know what you're trying to do. I get it. Believe me, I'm totally in awe of how much you're doing to clear my name. I know it must feel like I'm leaving you again, with going to Montana. I'm not. I promise. I want you both to come with me. You'd be even closer to Nick for visits, and—"

"Casey, did you tell anyone else?"

"Tell anyone else what?"

"About you and Justin?"

"Never. I wouldn't."

"Someone knows something."

"Who? How?"

"That's what I'm trying to find out."

"I'm hardly the center of excitement out here."

"Shut up, this is serious."

"I am serious. You aren't the one who has to live a life of lies. I know what is serious."

"You told Roz, didn't you?"

"I had to, Liz. She cornered me at the hospital when I went to visit Nick. Told me she'd seen the way Justin looked at me. Always wondered about our extended weekends after rodeos. Heard us whistling the same George Strait song. She'd put two and two together and said she couldn't forgive me and would tell Marg."

"When was this?"

"After the memorial. I didn't want to tell you and add to the problems."

"No wonder you were so ready to sell. It was like you flipped on a dime."

Casey hung his head, staring at the ground. "Once Marg had it confirmed, it was game over for me. She's friends with everyone in this county and the next few over."

"Damn them for letting money be everything, connections be everything. You're innocent, dammit."

"Trial by peers, media, or whatever you have it where it doesn't matter what happens in a courtroom, you're screwed."

"Ugggghhh!" Elizabeth let out a guttural yell in frustration, startling Rhett. His face crumpled at the sound, and she reached for him, but he pulled back, went for Casey, instead.

The chimes on her phone startled all of them from the intensity of the moment. Jo's voice was tinny through the phone, as if she spoke through a large, metal telephone.

"Hey, Liz, is that you at the school?"

"I'm at my brother's place, why?"

"The bank of lights are on, that's all."

Elizabeth smacked her forehead. "I left them on earlier when I went to collect Nick's things and must have spaced turning them off. I'll go over there and shut them off. I've got to get my laptop anyway."

"Launi called to tell me they're on. I'd go over myself but I have Yorkshire puddings in the oven, and you know how high risk those are at this altitude."

"I'll go take care of it. Thanks, Jo." Elizabeth hung up the phone and reached for her purse. "Casey, can I—"

"Take my truck?"

While they'd bickered, the bloated, dove-gray clouds had brought a snowstorm. The snow blew in, the sizable, flat flakes, like dinner plates settling toward the ground. The barometer dropped, promising upheaval. Elizabeth wanted to drive Nick's snug, luxury SUV in the winter weather but risked getting it dirty or scratched.

"Yes, please and thank you."

"How about I just go?"

"I'm going to grab some of my materials, in case this snow turns into something."

"They don't often have snow days here, you know."

"I know, but I want to be prepared, in case." She'd promised Benny a lesson on ants and needed to do some extra prepwork to be ready for the unit. All she knew of the die-hard workers was their dedication to scent along their pathway, trusting those that came before to guide them.

"All right, but when you get back, cacciatore will be on the table. We are celebrating tonight."

"Celebrating what?"

"I had a couple offers come in today."

"If you're excited, I'm excited." As she watched the words escape her mouth she wanted to reach out and pull them all back in. Elizabeth didn't want Casey to leave her, nor did she want to leave this place, their friends and neighbors.

"I'm going to go over the offers with Charlie tomorrow."

"I will look forward to the details."

Casey nodded, flipping through a catalogue that appeared to sell nothing but vases. "Hey, did you hear sirens earlier?"

"I did. I went to visit Marg, and—"

He looked up at her. "To give back the check? Foolish."

"Not exactly. Anyway, something happened to her, and they called for the ambulance."

"That old bird will be okay. She's still got a few tricks up her sleeve."

60

THE ROAD WAS COVERED in a thick layer of ice crystals mixed in with snow. It sparkled like a glitter-covered disco ball, a magical start. She could trace individual flakes for a painting idea in which she would choose two colors, only one of which could be primary.

Her son watched the landscape through the window, observant. Elizabeth would have to come to terms with her agreement with Nick; they would connect with a doctor if he still didn't use speech at two. This gave her a couple of months to find an acceptable doctor, a couple of months to think through her future options. Time would betray any of Nick's false promises for sincerity.

The school sat, stark and shadowed, on the hill, a single light in the front hall a beacon in the night. Buildings took on different personalities at night, intent filtering in among the shadows.

Elizabeth left her headlights on to light the pathway as the flood lamp over the schoolyard was out. The small porch light at the teacherage stretched only to its porch, most of the building shrouded in darkness. A horse nickered somewhere nearby, and Elizabeth turned her head toward the sound. Ranch land surrounded the buildings, and they'd seen cattle near the fence line several afternoons. The Ramirez twins offered carrots from their lunch to a heifer with the biggest pair of brown eyes Elizabeth had ever seen. Now, what she glimpsed of the wiry border was vacant. *Must be the wind.*

Flipping the key to the right in the lock, it met no resistance.

The school didn't have extensive technology, but there was enough that an enterprising thief could turn into a profit. Leaving the place unlocked only helped them along. She hadn't left it unlocked, had she? Her hand reached out to jiggle the handle twice, to be sure.

A short hallway in the entryway offered the coat rack and the entrance to the single bathroom. Elizabeth abandoned her purse on the small bench and led Rhett down the hallway, holding his hand. As she approached the classroom, a bobbing light traced the wall from within, and she followed it with her eyes.

On instinct, Elizabeth tucked Rhett behind her, pressing him back with her arm as she approached the entrance, before peering into the room. The desk was scattered with papers, the drawers hung open.

Ice ran through Elizabeth's veins as she snatched up Rhett and ran for the door and back to Casey's truck, taking the purse from the entrance as she heard the other door slam. She dove for the front seat, slid Rhett to her side, locked the doors and started the engine. As she backed out, her headlights caught the shadows of a rider, headed into the brush.

Elizabeth skidded into the Wolfs' driveway, parking next to the long patrol car flanking the house. She choked on the resulting dust as she pounded on the door.

Jo opened the door a moment later to Elizabeth breathing hard, looking over her shoulder. "Hey, are you okay?"

"Someone was just at the school when I was there. On a horse."

"A horse?"

"Yes." Elizabeth grew impatient as she waited for the story to sink in. To her, the urgency was apparent, immediate, like a fire escaping its ring. "I need to talk to Clint. Sheriff. Is he here?"

"I'll get him. Have a seat. I'll get tea or bourbon or both."

Elizabeth collapsed onto the couch to wait for her adrenaline to dissipate while Rhett ambled over to the toys. He brought a stuffed horse over to Elizabeth, climbing into her lap. She stroked his hair as he examined each strand of yarn that made the mane and tail, pointing at the glassy, button eyes.

Elizabeth's gaze roamed the room, taking in the classic barn painting, pale, flowered wallpaper, and couches with wooden legs. Matching lamps bookended the sofa on which she sat, a few magazines scattered on a table in front of her. Country comfort.

"Elizabeth." The sheriff wore a standard polo shirt and jeans, belted in brown, and dark brown house shoes. He held a remote in his hand, the picture of a man lounging on his day off.

She told him the story, her approach to the school, the horse whinny, the light in the schoolhouse, the desktop and drawers.

He listened, eyebrows raised. "You saw them leave?"

"I saw someone leave. I don't know if there was more than one person there."

"All right, I'll take a look."

"If by a miracle they didn't steal my laptop, would you mind grabbing that for me?"

One of his bushy eyebrows shot up. "I'll see what I can do."

After gathering a few items and donning a navy jacket, he scooped up his badge and gun belt from the hallway's table.

"I shouldn't be gone too long," he said.

"I will be waiting right here. Possibly forever." Fear from the almost encounter ate at her insides, worry gnawing on her confidence.

Jo brought spiked tea from the kitchen, and they waited, watching Rhett play on the floor in the Wolfs' living room.

After a few awkward conversation starts that fizzled into the insignificant, the rumble of the car in the driveway caught the attention of all people inside. A car door slam indicated proximity, opinions.

"You were right," the sheriff said, hanging his hat on a peg by the door and unpacking his paraphernalia back onto the hallway table. "Place is trashed. The school building. Living area looked fine, but I'll look again in the morning."

"What do you mean trashed?" Jo's brow furrowed at this news, apparently unsure how to reconcile his words with a picture in her mind.

"Papers everywhere. A broken mug, crayons snapped in two, books on the floor. Looks like a tornado went through, whipped everything up, and then slammed it back to the ground."

Elizabeth thought of the clean-up tomorrow morning. The overwhelming urge to run and stick her head in the sand pressed at her.

Jo whistled. "Geez. I don't get it. It's not like we keep money there."

"The back door was unlocked, the one you said you thought you'd heard closing as you left out the front. There are some shoe scuffles in the dirt but nothing discernable. I didn't see recent hoof prints, either."

"I know what I saw."

"I believe you."

"So, what are you going to do about it?"

He eyed her then, discerning the level of insult compared to the level of fear in her question. The scales tipped toward faith as he followed with his plan.

"Like you said, it could have been someone looking for an easy grab. Your laptop would have been the ticket. You keeping it with the coffee was smart. Deputy stationed there tomorrow during school hours. What time do you get there in the mornings?"

"Seven," she and Jo echoed.

"He'll be there at a quarter 'til. You are not to enter the building or get out of your car before he okays it. I'll need you to go over the place with a fine-toothed comb, look for anything they might have taken. My gut says it was nothing, just petty, but I don't want to be wrong."

"What about dusting for prints?"

"We don't have our own forensics lab out here or anything, but yes, Deputy Ryland will dust some key spaces. You've got to understand—spending hours analyzing all the prints that would be found in a school, even a small school, is not an effective use of our time."

"How can I help?

"Help us figure out what they were looking for. In the morning. Now I'm going to get you and the youngin' home. We could all use some sleep tonight."

Yes, we could.

"I'm going to follow you home, get you inside."

"Be careful," Jo called behind them. Elizabeth heard the bolt slide into place when they cleared the porch.

At the house, Casey waited at the door, receiving Rhett into his arms and nodding at the sheriff who waved from the car. Elizabeth sank onto the couch, grateful for the sound of her brother ushering his nephew off to dreamland.

She waited until Casey joined her, perching on the arm of the couch, before she spoke.

"I know you had nothing to do with Justin's death."

"I appreciate your sudden faith," he said, rolling his eyes.

"I know you didn't do it because I know who did."

61

DEPUTY RYLAND SMOKED. ELIZABETH APPROACHED the school with a wrinkled nose as the man puffed into the cold. The man was the rough side of lean, like a shepherd out of supplies before range season is over. A thick canvas coat topped jeans and a massive utility belt, the kind that not only held a weapon, flashlight, and cartridges, but also just about everything else. A metal box with a handle sat in the dirt near the wall, topped with a navy, nylon lunch bag.

"Bad habit," she said, watching the man field dress the butt of the cigarette, pocketing the filter.

"Which one?"

Elizabeth liked him.

She tossed the keys to Ryland who unlocked the door and preceded her into the room. Counting a beat before following, she left her bag on the bench and waited for the officer to explore the recesses of the room for additional occupants.

"All clear."

Ryland followed her around the room as she peeked in open drawers, tried to remember what all was on the shelves, and gave up trying to identify any missing items. At most, she had a half hour to finish her research before the students arrived.

When the students trickled in, Elizabeth was ready. Ryland
had helped her clean up and sort what had been scattered the
night before, and he smiled at the kids as they trooped into
the room and took their seats.

Elizabeth explained his presence to the students as a career
day exploration, promising a question and answer session
after lunch. Rachel and Mirabel dropped off their kids and
whispered furiously to each other, the smiling deputy waving
at them and high-fiving the kids. Only Polly had a pinched
expression, hurried in her drop-off.

Ryland refereed a few rounds of tetherball in the yard.
The rhythmic smacking of the ball and chain link clinking
against the pole rang out in the vast landscape. He'd been the
first person tall enough to attach the rope end to the top of
the pole, and the kids treated him with reverence. Elizabeth
watched from the window as they played, the approaching
clouds nipping at her calm.

Her temporary shadow, Ryland idled in the Wolfs' driveway when she went in to collect Jonah after school, having
promised to escort her home. He'd only left her side once, to
ensure the teacherage, too, was still empty and locked. Elizabeth had to admit, having another adult around during the
day provided comfort, a camaraderie she didn't get otherwise. Too bad an intruder was the impetus.

"How'd it go?" Jo waited for anything other than a mundane
answer.

"Fine. The kids loved Ryland, asked him all sorts of questions. How many times he'd had to use his gun, whether he'd
driven his cruiser like in the movies, his favorite flavor of ice
cream, the usual."

"What is it?"

"Hmm?"

"His favorite flavor."

"Moose tracks."

"Makes sense, a local thing. I was initially asking about you, though, how did things go for you?"

Elizabeth checked herself. In truth, she hadn't allowed panic in. Hadn't let herself freak out. She didn't know if her frayed semblance of mental control could take any admission of nerves.

"A little tough," she said. "I kept twisting the door handle to make sure it was locked. Kept looking out the windows."

Jo nodded. "That's normal, hon. I'd be more worried if you tried to tell me you felt nothing."

"Have you ever had someone break in here?"

"Oh no, but as a sheriff's wife, you see it all."

"I don't know how you couldn't."

"Wolf and Ryland are it, at least until the population goes up or we get the money to hire recruits. No, I'm just the shoulder for those who need one. A holding pen for the damaged while Clint goes out to find the guy who gave the black eye, pulls the kid out of the well, confirms that Grandma is gone. You hear so many people's stories you start adopting them as parts of your own self, see patterns and the like."

Curiosity roused Elizabeth like a shot of caffeine. "Do you ever try to figure out who did it, in mysteries?"

"You mean am I officially deputized? No. I am a dedicated wife of the good sheriff, though. I can't help but take an interest in my husband's line of work."

A jigsaw puzzle lay in an early stage of assembly, on the kitchen table. Elizabeth fought the urge to pick up a shape of bright blue, hold it next to the others.

"I think I'm the same. Brewing is like that a little bit, too. Once I get my hands on the ingredients and have hours to work magic, the rest of my mind starts sifting through my day job, sorting out problems. Figuring out what a student needs, what to do about pissed off parents, how to work with a crazy coworker."

"We need to get you up and brewing. A little stress relief. I know at least one bar that would buy a keg."

"I'm out of practice." Elizabeth's heart was torn between telling Jo now that she planned to leave, to join the ranks of the teachers before her. Explaining the impending loss of her newfound sense of belonging walloped her with emotion, like finding a picture of an old flame slipped behind a dresser, long forgotten. A kernel of hope kept her quiet. "Not tonight, though, I'm dead on my feet."

"Expect a call," Jo said. "He'll want to hear how things went with Ryland."

62

"TOP MARKS," ELIZABETH SAID when the sheriff called. "He can have a side gig as my classroom helper any day."

"Glad to hear it. Sounds like I'm saddled with that charmer. Guessing the county wants him for my replacement in a few years. Endless summer fishing and winters in Scottsdale are calling."

Ryland had followed her back to Casey's, making sure Elizabeth's brother was home.

"Is he coming tomorrow?"

"I think we can park him out there at least one more day. I'll send him with some paperwork, keep him occupied."

"Sheriff. Clint. I need to talk to you. I've been thinking about some things and I..."

"Before you give me evidence—because you know that's all I can use, is evidence, right?—I have some information I can share with you. We got the results on that rock back."

Elizabeth remembered the ravine, finding the smear extending into a crevice.

"Is it—"

"We're having it tested for a few ongoing cases we have. That's all I can say."

Chills snaked up Elizabeth's calves and across her back. She hadn't wanted to be right, not really.

"Now, do you have any evidence for me?"

"Yes. No. I will. Tomorrow."

Casey would run her to town right after school. She needed to pick up her car, maybe apologize to Kade, and get to the Records Office at the courthouse before they closed.

"I'll be waiting."

Tuesday morning, she again parked next to an official Sheriff's Department vehicle. While the students were dropped off without incident, Elizabeth suspected their mothers would be on the phone minutes after arriving home, or more likely, would pull off down the road, windows down, to gossip. She should have checked with Jo about another cover story. Too late now.

Ryland's walkthrough was brief. There were no signs anyone had been back. Doors locked, windows secured, everything in its place. He'd taken his stack of paperwork and a laptop to the teacherage, guessing the radio would disrupt lessons. He'd promised to come back for science—and lunch.

Elizabeth had planned a different science lesson for the day, capitalizing on their guest of honor.

Benny read the white board. "What's fore-en-sicks?"

"Forensics is the study of how people like Deputy Ryland use science to figure out what happened in a place."

"Oooh like in labs with tubes?" Ashton leaned in, eyes wide at the prospect of taking the part.

"Yes, like that. People like Deputy Ryland collect information from a location and then test it or sometimes take it to science labs where people there do the testing. The information they get helps them figure out what happened."

"Cool."

"Is this legal?"

Elizabeth laughed at Rachel's question. "One hundred percent. We will just be learning a couple of techniques that anyone can do, and just for fun. Deputy Ryland is going to help us."

The man had been all but ecstatic to have something to shake up his processing day. He'd grown up in Aurora, Colorado. She guessed that, for the most part, Sheridan County was sleepy in comparison.

"Yes!" chimed Ashton and Benny in unison.

"Clean up, first, then science." The chorus of groans made her smile. There was always something about the days you could tuck in a lesson so engaging that students clamored for more, begged to learn. Science gave her the opportunity to combine all the subjects together into one class, giving students skills they could apply in life to understand their world, figure things out.

Her own problem-solving skills were put to the test.

⋘

Chloe Ramirez asked for a second piece of tape and to borrow the stamp pad again. She wanted to take toe prints and compare them to her fingers. Elizabeth handed over the supplies with a conspiratorial grin, loving this inquiry.

The students glommed onto the forensics activities, using jeweler loupes she'd found in a rock collecting box to examine different fibers Elizabeth had snagged from around Casey's house, their task to find the odd one out.

"This one!" Benny had been the first to look up, still holding the loupe to his eye, and pointing to a single goat hair. The twins scrambled over to him to look with their own loupes.

Ryland took them on a nature walk to examine scat and guess which animal had passed through. Elizabeth didn't miss the pile of dried horse apples near a sage bush but said nothing. The kids identified rabbits, deer, and coyotes, and Ryland taught them basic tracking skills. Elizabeth wondered if this was a lesson all children from the area learned, the ability to stalk prey.

63

"YOU TOOK THE KIDS' fingerprints?" Wolf exploded, and Elizabeth slammed the office door shut for him.

"I didn't keep them or anything," she replied. "They took it all home. I just showed them how to get them with tape and to look at each other's cards. I'm not an idiot."

"And their parents were okay with this?"

"Are you kidding me? The kids loved it. They got to do something real, not more of the mindless worksheets sent by the district. Ryland was a huge help, and the parents just thought it was career week or something. He told kids stories from his training—it was great. He is welcome back anytime."

Wolf muttered under his breath, grumbling. "Fine. Just don't let it go to his head. I need him back in the office."

"You mean don't tell him he has a back-up career waiting in the wings?"

"Exactly."

Ryland had also offered her a ride to her car after school since Casey was headed north and wanted to make Billings before dark.

At Kade's garage, she hesitated outside the door. This could go a few different ways, most of them sour.

Kade was the only one there, putting tools away in a bay, and she waved. "Thanks again," she started, "for the tires and the parking spot."

"You paid for them." He shrugged. "In another few weeks, you might want to switch them out for snow tires. Things get dicey here in a blink, especially for those of you out in south county."

Elizabeth held back the comment that she might not be here long enough to need them. She hadn't cemented anything..

"Your ex is still in Sheridan General?" He watched her reaction out of the corner of his eye, pretending to busy himself with setting a few sockets back into place and lowering a red metal lid over the collection.

"Flew back this morning." She meant to tell Nick about the intruder but hadn't. She told herself it was to save him the stress while he was healing but knew it was a lack of trust in their truce. The letters from the lawyer would have to stop before she could treat Nick as a confidant again, let alone a co-parent.

"I see."

What was this interchange? She set out a lure of her own. "I'm relieved," she said, and it was true. "Nothing like having an ex hanging around to complicate things."

Kade's hair was stuffed in a trucker hat, the bill curved to frame his face. Casey had spent hours on his own hats, wrapping the bills with rubber bands to get the shape right. Kade's name was embroidered over a chest pocket, the garage design across the back. Carpenter jeans, black boots, and Elizabeth lost track of what she needed from him and let thoughts of what she wanted creep in.

"Indeed," he said, waiting.

Damn. Here I am, ruining another good thing.

"Kade?"

"Yeah?" He'd stepped closer. She could smell bay rum on his body, noted a scar under his jawline. She thought it was likely a shaving nick that healed wrong and fought the urge to run a finger across the tiny, pale line.

"How do you know Justin gambled?"

Moment, shot.

His jaw set, then shifted as he reassessed the situation. Took her in with a new light before raising a wall. She knew this would happen. This was the moment when she lost her chance with him, paying tenfold for the information, one way or the other. Elizabeth had to have the truth though, could not rest until it was in her hand, exposed.

Kade shook his head at her and looked away for a moment. When his gaze returned, it was icy green. "He borrowed money from me. To pay a bookie. That's how."

"What kind of bookie?"

"Didn't ask," he said, crossing to lower the door on the farthest bay door. The motors whirred and groaned as the heavy metal settled into place.

Elizabeth pressed on, knowing her audience time was fleeting. "What kind of gambling?"

"Horses. Said they weren't running like they should."

"But he had money. Why come to you? I mean, could he not pay his own debts? I thought the ranch was beyond profitable."

"Roz is my cousin." His expression darkened, the clouds a warning.

"Roz?"

"If you're asking me why a spoiled, washed-up roper would stoop to borrow cash from the likes of me to solve his marital problems, my guess is he knew I'd help Roz and didn't want Margery Hart to find out the situation."

"Why would his mother find out?"

"I don't care how rich you are, I'd like to think you'd notice when fifty Gs goes missing."

"Fifty grand?"

"My cousin was in an unhappy marriage. She picked a vice. Find me someone in the same situation who hasn't." He used the pneumatic controls to lower a bay door, the loud slide of metal against metal an end to their conversation.

"Kade."

Garage bays closed up for the night, he'd been about to enter the office. He paused, one hand on the door frame, his shoulders tight. With a sigh, he turned round to face Elizabeth.

"I owe you a drink. More than a drink."

His eyebrow raised.

"A drink and an apology. Maybe dinner, too. Can I call you?"

He looked through her, then, as if checking her motivation, assessing his own willingness to risk, and dipped a toe right into the water.

"Yeah," he said. "Do that."

64

ELIZABETH WOVE THROUGH SLOWER traffic, hands tightening on the steering wheel as she used every ounce of patience she had left not to honk at every driver who dared maintain a casual pace.

The courthouse loomed above the corner of Coffeen and Main, its architecture detailed, nuanced, and on full display, like a peacock in mating season. A few coins in the meter and Elizabeth bounded up the front steps, looking for signs to the Records room. Twenty minutes later, she had what she needed, copied and stapled, thanks to a pert counter person named Vanessa.

Getting back to the Sheriff's Department on her new tires was easy, but getting Wolf to get past her forensics lesson was challenging. He could be a bear when agitated, but so could she.

"Listen. The kids loved it. They're going home tonight and telling their families all about how they now want to be scientists and detectives. Is that not a win?"

Standing behind his desk, he looked the part of a taxidermy bear; stiff, intimidating. A bushy mustache added to the picture. Whether it was exhaustion from the last week, the hilarity of his stance, or the urgency of her errand, she laughed. This man, this office, these circumstances, this state. This absurdity.

"Ms. Blau," he began, "you are a woman with a lot on her plate, and I am a busy man. If we could get to the essence of this visit, rather than riling me to your apparent delight, I would appreciate it."

"Evidence," she said, slapping a copied packet on the burgundy desk blotter.

His mustache twitched as he reached for the papers, eyes lifting to hers when he read the names on the cover pages.

"I thought I warned you to be careful—"

"I did my research. I have something."

"These are probate papers, filed last week. Public record. How is this evidence of anything other than standard paperwork?"

"Once the grant of probate is issued, it becomes a public record, yes. Look at my highlights."

"...per the...oh."

"Yep."

The cogs moved to life behind his irises. "In a small town, you hear things and take them for gospel. I guess it's all on Marg then, to take care of things."

"She is—or has been. She even offered me a gift from the estate."

"Did you—never mind. Don't answer that."

"I think that whoever killed Justin—"

"Now wait a minute—"

"I'm guessing that rock had identifiable blood on it. I'm guessing that whoever killed Justin was after money."

"I noticed that your brother isn't mentioned anywhere in the will. This doesn't clear him."

"I know." The glaring vacancy where she'd thought to find her brother's name rubbed on her. Not even a saddle to remember his friend.

"When was the will signed?"

"2004."

Wolf flipped through the papers. "He would have been eighteen."

"Before he met Casey, or early on. Casey watches those old videos often enough that I know all their top events happened in 2007, at least his favorites, anyway." She now knew several of the events by heart. Casey, the header, out in a wild purple and hot pink shirt, white hat. Justin, racing behind as heeler, neatly looping the calves' back hooves. The duo was so fast, so confident, she felt sorry for the little animal, beleaguered by the process.

"Jo and I were a bit surprised when the will was read. Weren't many there, we heard, just Mrs. Hart and—"

"I've got to go. Look into the highlights," she called, running out the door.

Elizabeth sped down the highway, knowing one of the two county speed monitors was in his office, puzzled in her wake. In a county of twenty-five hundred square miles, statistics were on her side.

She scanned the roadsides, looking for the briefest flashes of brown and gray. Her errand was urgent, but colliding with a quadruped would throw a wrench in her plans—not to mention her car.

The new tires made a brief skid as she almost missed the driveway. The line shack on her left leaned against the fence, dark and abandoned. Whatever energy Justin gave the place, it had dissipated into the wind.

In front of the ranch house, she put her car in park, snagged her folder from the back seat, and crested the steps in two quick jumps, like an antelope. Randall answered the door at her second knock.

"Ms. Blau. I am not aware of your appointment with Mrs. Hart."

"I don't have one. I'm hoping she'll see me."

"She is busy at the moment. You could come—"

"Oh, but I can't. It's about the money. Will you please tell her I'm here?"

He stepped across the threshold to check for others, then ushered her in.

"Wait here, please. I'll see if she's up for a visit."

The man ignored her raised eyebrow, leaving her at the front door as he walked down a large dark hallway under a row of skylights at one end.

Her foot tapped a staccato rhythm, frantic on the hardwood floor. She willed herself to still all movement. Framed photos of Justin lined the hall in front of her. Those closest to her were from school picture days, his hair overly slicked back with product, shirt buttoned to his neck, a big goofy grin shared with the camera. The shape of his face changed as the pictures progressed, the lines of his jaw edging his profile as his hairstyle rotated through various lengths. The same brown eyes shone out from each snapshot of the past.

This would be a hard hallway to pace as a mother, one that showed your child's life from the beginning, flowing through time, then finding an abrupt end. An unexpected finality. Her life would be empty without Rhett. Her heart bruised at the thought of Margery Hart going through motions that she could not fathom weathering herself.

Elizabeth missed JRhett, wanted to see him, hold him, escape this museum of heartache. She sent Jo a message that she would be there after this last stop. Casey had left her a pan of mac and cheese, ready to meet the oven. They'd have a snug night in, she and Rhett, maybe to watch a goat documentary, if such a thing existed.

"I didn't think you'd be back." The voice preceded the woman shuffling behind.

"I'm hard to get rid of."

"So the sheriff told me. Said you'd be on your way over, he thought, and wanted to make it clear he had nothing to do with whatever hair-brained scenario you've cooked up."

"Now there's a man I often want to hug and kick at the same time."

"You and me, both," Marg said. "Now, is this business or pleasure? I don't see that adorable son of yours, and as my sands are running out, I don't spend much time on business these days."

"Is there somewhere we can talk?" Elizabeth watched Randall disappear into a room across the walkway.

"My office," Marg said and headed toward an impressive, hand-carved door that depicted scenes from a cattle drive, the action criss-crossing the panels. Marg opened the doors and stepped into the room, the centerpiece of which was a sprawling oak desk. "Used to be Bernard's. I took it over when he passed. Would have been too much trouble to move the books somewhere else."

Two walls filled this library, floor to vaulted ceiling. Leather bound volumes rested near worn paperbacks, Chaucer keeping company with L'Amour. Marg slid into a mammoth upholstered chair behind the desk, relief washing her face.

"Sit, sit," the woman said, gesturing at the opposite chair. "I'm having an off afternoon, and the doctor said to put my feet up. I pay him good money to tell me obvious things, seems like."

Elizabeth peered out the door before closing it. She stopped short of locking it but made sure it caught in the latch.

"I'll be frank—" she started.

"And I'll be Ernest. Enough with the drama. Out with it, girl."

"I read the will."

"Oh?" Interest tightened the wrinkled face, lines elongating, drawing back.

"I was surprised Justin hadn't updated it since he became an adult."

"Me, too," Marg said. "Then again, that's like Justin. He was not one to stay on top of things."

"I also know that a month before he died, he borrowed at least fifty-thousand dollars from an...acquaintance."

Marg reeled back as though she'd been slapped. Elizabeth marked the dark circles under her eyes, the softness in her jowls. The woman who'd anticipated Elizabeth's visit was now off her game and in the weeds.

"That's impossible."

"It isn't. He hadn't paid the lender back when he died."

"You lie. That is an outrageous sum. Even if he did need it—and I'm not saying he did, or would—we have the money."

"I don't think he wanted you to know it was for debt. A gambling debt."

Marg grunted, dismissing her. "Justin didn't gamble."

"It wasn't his debt. He—"

Marg Hart vomited behind the desk and would have fallen into the sick had Elizabeth not raced to her side to catch the woman and prop her up.

"Marg. Margery!" Elizabeth looked into the woman's eyes, felt her clammy forehead before the cattle baroness again retched onto the carpet at their feet.

"Randall! Hurry—Marg is sick!" Elizabeth yelled at the top of her lungs, then after assessing that Marg was still breathing, lowered her to the floor, put a throw pillow under her head, and ran to the door. She wrenched it open, prepared to renew the alarm, only to run into Randall.

He shoved a phone in her hands, telling Elizabeth to call for help, and ran to his employer. When the line connected, Elizabeth explained what had happened while Randall held Margery in his arms.

The ambulance from Sheridan arrived a few minutes later. Elizabeth listened as the responders asked whether Margery had had anything to eat or drink that day, requested her medications, and loaded her onto the stretcher. The woman moaned at the movement, a bejeweled hand going to her head before Randall collected it into his own and climbed into the vehicle behind the responders.

When the flashing lights faded from sight and headed toward town, Elizabeth realized it was Marg's staff who cared most for the old woman as she headed to the hospital for the second time in a week. She was a woman in a castle without a family.

65

THE SCHOOL ROSE INTO view as Elizabeth crested the hill. Twilight had yet to fall on the scrub brush, the deer establishing their evening grazing territory. Elizabeth had daylight to get inside, get out, and get back home.

As she brushed past the coat hooks, a broom, propped up against the wall, slid and with a clatter broke the silence. She paused to right it.

"Like a bull in a damn china shop," she muttered.

The fading light cast latent shadows through the classroom as Elizabeth approached her desk. The iron fittings and walnut pieces of the vintage behemoth made for an imposing piece of furniture. A century of markings in the vintage top were largely rubbed smooth with time. Elizabeth had discovered the key to the one locking drawer underneath the desktop, tucked into a small slit in the wood. She extracted it from her purse, inserted it in the keyhole, and gave a quarter turn before popping open the freed drawer and its contents.

Elizabeth rifled through the papers she'd stored inside, the few not scattered in the intruder's wake. Whoever it was hadn't had time to break into the drawer before she arrived. She'd extracted the old cigar box when her phone rang.

"Elizabeth." The sheriff's voice was assuring and disquieting all at once.

"You caught me at a busy moment. Can I call you back?"

"They think it might be poison."

"What?"

"Margery Hart. They say you found her."

The color drained from Elizabeth's face as the meaning of the words tiptoed up her neck, one vertebra at a time. "I did."

"I looked into those documents and got a hold of Hart's lawyer. He said she's been giving Justin's money away starting the day after he died."

"She was trying to get rid of it," Elizabeth whispered.

"There are details, lots of them, some I can share when you get to the house, but there's one I think you want to hear now."

"Yeah?"

"You were right about the prenup."

The phone went silent in her hand. Elizabeth placed it on the desktop.

She was right. She had to get the box, get it to Wolf, and they could end this drama.

"I'll take that."

The owner of the voice snatched the wooden box from Elizabeth's hands, a photo fluttering out through the cracked lid. Elizabeth spun around to find Roz Hart, her crossbow aimed at Elizabeth's chest. Kill zone.

"You can't do this. My son!"

"I know. It's something Marg reminds me of on the regular, how everyone but her has a grandson. Got a little old after years of hearing the same message."

"You don't have to do this."

"Oh, but I do. You see, I tried to keep it in the family, save my marriage or at least make it to motherhood before divorcing, but you threw a wrench into that plan. Major distraction."

"But why have a kid with a man you don't love?" Elizabeth tried to put herself in the shoes of this woman. Attractive, with plenty of years left for kids and who could have settled for a chunk of change in a divorce. Yet Roz was desperate. She smacked her forehead when it hit her. "The prenup?"

"So, you haven't read it? That makes one aspect of my life you managed to keep your nose out of today."

"A grandchild meant more money, didn't it?"

"For me and little junior. But without—I got the same pay-out as the rest of you random Justin fans. I was such an idiot to sign that thing. I didn't think I'd see it again, believed love would see us through until our rocking chair days. That's the kind of crap they sell you on TV anyway, and I was too stupid then to know that Prince Charming doesn't exist, but conniving mothers-in-law sure do."

"So, now you're after all of it."

"That I am. I didn't get what I deserved, what I earned for all those years of putting up with a cheating husband. Worse, one who cheated with anything and everything with two legs. Bet Casey knows how I feel. How's his business doing by the way?"

Elizabeth's eyes narrowed to slits. "What would you know about it?"

"A little bird told Margery that it wouldn't look so good if her friends and business partners were patrons of her son's murderer, so she made some calls."

"What did Casey do to you?"

"You mean besides seduce my husband? I'm not an idiot, Elizabeth. A wife knows things, can smell things." Roz was all predator now, eyes flashing down the shaft of an arrow that hadn't wavered from its aim. Elizabeth knew how this woman felt, knew the ache of betrayal, the sting of being leftover goods, discarded for the next new entertainment.

"Oh, speaking of people's husbands, how did yours like the flowers?"

"You are one sick woman."

"Watch your mouth, city girl. You don't know what you're saying. He was just part of my back up plan."

"Your what?"

"Him. Isaiah. Anyone who looks vaguely enough like Justin to where a pregnancy could be tied back to my dearly departed husband. Marg believes in me, but not enough to leave it all to me. She has a soft spot for anyone Justin loved."

Elizabeth recoiled from the woman, her desperation laid thick. "That is beyond messed up."

"Marg would get a grandson, and I would be supported forever. No one loses. It's not like I'd be relying on the real father for anything."

Elizabeth spotted her abandoned phone on the desk near where she'd set it. If she could keep Roz talking long enough to inch over and palm the device, its emergency dialing capabilities would be a matter of a single button press.

"I wasn't trying to get in your way, I just went on a couple dates with him. I swear that's all it was. He said he had an ex, that's all I knew."

"Maybe, maybe not. I saw the way you two were looking at each other that night. I remember when he looked that way at me. Hell, I remember him looking that way at your brother, sometimes. I could see the writing on the wall."

"You killed him." Elizabeth leaned back against the desk, giving the impression of a scared rabbit under a bobcat's claws as one hand snaked toward the phone behind her back.

"I removed a lying, cheating obstacle."

"After that obstacle borrowed stupid amounts of money to cover for you."

Roz shot her a look of surprise, then shrugged. "So I went a little bored-housewife on a bookie. What was I supposed to do with my time when Justin took off every night? Even if he wasn't keeping someone else's bed warm, he'd stay out in that stupid shack of his just to avoid me, avoid a future together."

As Roz talked, Elizabeth's fingertips touched the phone, and she attempted to gecko it closer, centimeter by centimeter.

"Why poison Margery? Sounds like she'd take any grandkid, Justin's or not."

"Why do you think she's selling? Easiest way to get rid of me, save face. 'Sides, I didn't poison her, no matter how much I would love to see her ride off a cliff."

Liz's fingers flattened over the screen, and she rotated the device, stretching to connect her thumb with the side button.

"I'll take that, Liz."

Behind Elizabeth, someone slipped the phone from underneath her white-knuckled hand.

66

"POLLY? WHAT ARE YOU DOING here?"

"Roz promised me my own place for me and Benny." The woman shrugged, guilty. She waved the phone about. "You know, a new life."

"A better life," Roz insisted. "One where we can write our own backstory, one in which we call the shots. I promised you your own diner, Poll, and it's going to happen. This is just a speed bump. She"—she traced a line in the air across Elizabeth with the tip of her arrow—"is just a speedbump."

Polly looked between the women, clutching the phone.

Elizabeth thought Polly looked lost, wavering. "Where's Benny?"

"With Kade. I've got a double shift."

"Shut up. You don't have to tell her anything."

"Oh, Polly." Elizabeth remembered the paramedics asking what Margery had eaten that day. Randall told them it was takeout. "Why?"

"Took time to find the right amount," Roz said.

"Roz!"

"Polly. You can confess now. Tell them what happened. Why you did it. You might still get to see Benny."

Polly's face crumpled, her body curved forward, sheltering vitals.

"Don't listen to her. She doesn't know us."

Polly's mouth worked itself into a determined line, her brow furrowed, summoning faith. "They won't take Benny away because we are getting out of here. Far away from this hell hole." The woman removed a water bottle from her bag and set it on the table.

"And taking me away from my son is okay in this plan somehow."

Polly winced and said nothing but paused, her hand on the black, plastic cap.

"We are wasting time. Let's go!"

"What if we didn't? Hurt her. You've got the money. Let's just go."

"What?" Roz, incredulous, let her bow arm dip to glare at her sister.

"We've got enough to start. Let's just get Benny and drive. We don't need more. We have a down payment."

"She's going to die, and we will get even more." Elizabeth didn't know if Roz was talking about her or Margery. "Think of what we can do with everything."

Roz's eyes pleaded with her sister, willing her to see the future, preview the life they must have planned out. Liz imagined a diner, booths with shiny metal stools, a pie safe, a cook singing from the kitchen. Their own place, away from the past. Far from the small town that served as a weight around their shoulders, a yoke that kept them tied to men and their mistakes. Two sisters somewhere new, starting over with a blank slate.

"You spent it." Polly's eyes narrowed to slits as she put her hands on the desk and leaned toward her sister.

"What are you talking about?"

"You did. You spent it already. Quit lying!" Polly's hands went to her temples, and she paced along the floorboards.

"We're getting more, I told you. So much more. When she dies, the rest of Justin's estate goes to me. That's a lot of money, Poll. More than we will ever need in Deadwood or anywhere else you want to go."

Elizabeth's eyes volleyed between the women; one burned and distrusting, the other urgent and pleading. Her attention flicked to the door through which Polly had entered and had left unlocked. She could run. Maybe.

"You lie. You always lie to me. You say it's for us, but you really mean this is for you. You keep everything from me until the last possible moment. As if I was the stupid one."

"Shut your mouth." Roz's voice seethed, a warning.

"Oh, get over it. The only reason Justin settled for you is because his mom thought you'd make beautiful babies. Even you weren't pretty enough to keep his attention."

"Watch. Your. Mouth."

"Or what? What will you do about it?"

The trigger popped, and an arrow shot straight into Polly's shoulder, the stunned woman tripping backward from the impact, then sinking to her knees before collapsing on the floor, dark red seeping into the blue Crow Bar polo.

"Polly!" Roz shrieked, dropping the cross bow to run to her sister who lay convulsing on the floor. Elizabeth didn't wait for her to look up again.

67

RUNNING SET FIRE BLAZING through Elizabeth's lungs until she thought they would burst from the effort. She heard the shot, saw the shock in Polly's eyes, and was out the door before the woman hit the floor.

Elizabeth pounded shale dust with her feet, ankles lighting up with pain. She begged her body to make the half mile disappear under her boots, willing the lights of the Wolf house to manifest before her eyes.

Elizabeth breathed in short gasps, straining to hear any sounds from the road behind. She reasoned that if Roz came after her, diving into the bushes and flattening herself among the prairie grasses was her only option. She'd watched the woman reach for Polly but hadn't stuck around for the animal wail, the sobs that followed.

A sharp pain shot up her heel when the sole of her right boot found a rock, and she stumbled, pausing to gulp in air. She listened beyond her own ragged intake of air and heaving heartbeat.

Nothing.

Risking a glance, she turned to face the school. The lights were on, that was all. Elizabeth remembered that her captor was armed and accurate and put all she had into closing the last of the distance between herself and safety.

The hip-high post with three reflective, red circles signaled the driveway to the Wolfs' house, and she sprinted for the door. Blazing porch lights lit the front walk revealing Jo's SUV and a barking dog in the window.

Jo answered, Rhett in her arms.

"What's happened? Are you okay? We were just about to head to the school, make sure you hadn't been taken out by a bear. I saw your car go by a half hour ago and figured you'd be by—"

Elizabeth doubled over, hands on her thighs as she struggled to catch her breath. When she could trust herself to talk, she lifted her head and said, "Polly. Has been shot. Roz—"

"Oh my God. I'll call 911." Jo released Rhett to his mother and ran into the depths of the house.

⋘

By the time the sirens came and went, including those of Sheriff Wolf himself, Jo had wrapped Elizabeth in a blanket and tucked her into her husband's favorite chair with tea and a book about the birds of Wyoming. Jo explained that under no circumstances was she to move and told the sheriff the two would be their guests for the evening. Ryland offered to feed Casey's livestock, and Elizabeth fell asleep where she sat.

The earliest bird woke her at four. She startled, gripping the arms of the lounger as she surfaced from a litany of nightmares. She found Rhett asleep in a pack-and-play tucked in a corner of the guest room, a clean towel and robe on the bed for Elizabeth. She stepped out on the front porch, blanket wrapped around her shoulders, blue morning light seeping through the crisp, clean air.

She could make out the two buildings on the hill, one larger, one newer. No lights from either. Each stood, abandoned, their histories rewritten into darker realities.

"She'll live," came the gruff voice behind her. "Polly."

Wolf stepped forward and offered a mug to Elizabeth. She inhaled, the smell of coffee filling her nostrils as warmth seeped into her hands.

"Thank you," she said.

"Thank Jo. She sets the timer on that machine every night. Knows I'll be up with the larks, no matter the season."

Elizabeth took a sip, delaying her questions, finding temporary peace in ignorance. Not yet.

"I called your brother last night. Told him you were fine."

"He'll be in his truck then, almost here."

"I tried to stop him, tell him to sleep first, but you know Casey."

"I do."

A month ago, Elizabeth would not have made such a claim. Things had changed, though. She and Casey had become a unit again. Sometimes shaky, but a collective, and with Rhett, a family.

"And Margery?"

"Still with us. They had to intubate her and who knows what else. Word is they are going to helicopter her out to Billings first real light." He looked at Elizabeth, her profile turned toward the rays of light inching over the eastern horizon. "Said if she'd had any more of the antifreeze, it would have been a quick end."

"Antifreeze?"

"We think it was in a water bottle we found at the school. The lab has that now. Sweet stuff, nasty. Between you, me, and the fence post, we are all but sure Roz drank the last of it."

"Roz?"

"Gone." Here, he leaned over the fence that fronted their home, the faint light shadowing his eyes, highlighting his mouth. "By choice, looks like."

That was why Roz hadn't followed her, why the archer hadn't hunted her down as she ran for help. She'd given up, given in.

"What will happen to Polly?"

"She's under guard at the hospital. Benny is with his uncle. What comes next depends on a lot of details we've been missing until now."

An hour later, they nibbled at eggs, quiet in the new dawn. Jo puttered around them. Refilled coffee, added a slice of toast. When they finished, the sheriff collected his gear, kissed his wife, and asked Elizabeth to come by his office to make an official statement.

Jo took the coffee pot off the burner and refilled Elizabeth's cup before pouring her own and sitting adjacent to her.

"When we see trauma, live through trauma, it shakes us. Sticks with us for a while." The woman took a sip from her mug before setting it on a placemat.

Elizabeth picked at the orange fringe of fabric under her own cup, twisting the threads before stroking them back into place. "It feels like trauma won't leave me alone, like it's a season in my life."

"Could be," Jo said. "Then again, to some, you are the lucky one."

68

Jo INSISTED ON DRIVING Elizabeth to Cloud Nine, rather than to collect her car. Her excuse rested on Wolf needing all in place for the investigation to follow the night's events yet Elizabeth wondered if it was more so Jo could rely on her neighbors staying home and out of trouble.

Casey barreled into the driveway as Elizabeth was carrying Rhett inside, the little boy clinging to sleep. She tucked him into bed before returning to the living room, her brother, and Jo.

The other two adults whispered on the couch, stopping when she entered the room.

"I was there. You don't have to hide things from me."

"Jo just gave me the rundown of what happened. Jesus, Liz. I'm so glad you aren't hurt, that you're here."

"Shaken, but here."

"Can you drive Elizabeth down to see the sheriff today? He still needs her statement, and he'll know when she can get her car."

"On it."

Jo stood, reaching for her keys. "And Casey?"

"Yeah?"

"You've got one hell of a little family here. Don't let lies chase you away from something good." Jo nodded at them both before snagging her jacket from the coat rack and taking her leave.

"How was Montana?"

"Big. Pretty. Far."

Elizabeth exhaled. "Yeah."

"When I was a kid, I wanted to get the hell away from Mom and Dad and that sad little house and our sad little life. When I came out here, I loved how much space there is, how you don't have to see anyone for days if you don't want to. Some days, I wanted to do that, run farther away, go so deep into the wilderness that I couldn't be found. But I figured something out."

"What's that?"

"That I'm not always my own best company."

"Sometimes we do what we do just to survive. There's no shame in that."

"There is if you let a good thing go."

Deputy Ryland took her statement, tanned cheeks taut over his cheekbones and long, thin fingers flying over the keyboard as she spoke. A day later and some details were fuzzy, questionable. What remained without doubt was the tension between the sisters, the bow aimed at Elizabeth, and the wet thwack of an arrow sinking into flesh.

She resisted letting Rhett out of her sight, but Casey had insisted she needed to be focused when she outlined the events of the prior day. He promised they would be there when she returned—largely as she borrowed his truck for the errand. The smell of marinara on the stovetop sent her out with a promising aroma.

When Elizabeth finished giving as detailed an account as she could, Ryland read her words back to her. Hearing it all again, she disbelieved the entirety of the terrifying ordeal, was happy to have it out of her mind.

"Justin?"

Elizabeth hadn't known how to ask but had to know. Knew Casey had to know.

"I think I'll let the boss fill you in on that one," Ryland said as Wolf entered. "Excuse me."

Sheriff Wolf looked beat, like a bear just out of hibernation. Intimidating yet suffering from a depletion of resources.

"Ms. Blau."

"Sheriff."

"Ryland get everything down all right?"

"I have no idea why he's still a deputy. That man is a gem."

"You have been seeing a lot of him lately..." An eyebrow shot up.

"The man is practically a baby!" The distraction was helping, Elizabeth owned.

"Got to keep him on his toes. This county doesn't monitor itself. Can't have him on the playground every day. What kind of mentor would I be then?

"Sheriff. Clint."

"Yeah?"

"Justin?"

"I'm just back from the hospital. Polly confessed. It will be on the news shortly, so you might as well know it all."

"Polly?"

"They did it together. She and Roz. Roz lured him out, asked him to meet her at their spot." Elizabeth remembered the rock in the ravine, the meeting place of lovers. "Polly started the stampede, then followed behind to pick up Roz. The cattle were the murder weapon."

Elizabeth thought of them. One in Casey's boots, the other on horseback. The two of them riding away from the gruesome scene.

"All for money."

"And freedom, of sorts."

"What will happen to Benny?"

"Kade has him, and I've already been there. He'll file to foster him; the courts will approve. They prefer family."

Elizabeth thought of the little boy and his mother's pride in his accomplishments.

"And Polly?"

"It will be up to the courts. She confessed. They may be lenient for honesty but only so much you can do."

Benny would lose his mother a handful of years after he'd lost his father. Would he grow up to follow in their footsteps or use his abilities to go somewhere new, to get away and thrive?

"As his teacher, for the present," Wolf started, "when you and he are feeling up to it, I know Kade would welcome some support, maybe tutoring? Not sure when he, or any of you, will feel up to returning to school."

Elizabeth's heart ached for the precocious little boy who'd begun to warm, like a flower trusting that winter is gone.

"What about you?"

His question was a rip in her stream of consciousness, a record scratch.

"What about me?"

"What will happen with you?"

"You mean now that Casey has been cleared of murder charges and ostensibly, I won't have people dropping by the school to scare and or kill me anymore?" Elizabeth crossed her legs and looked out the window, chin in the palm of one hand, elbow resting on the arm of the chair. Wolf waited for her, whether to make up her mind or to share it. He was patient. "I'd be lying if I told you I knew."

Wolf nodded. "I figured as much. For what it's worth, I hope you stay."

Elizabeth smiled at him, this gruff man who read Milton, didn't let anyone rush him, and gave a damn about his community.

"I do, too."

69

"YOU TAKE THE BRUSH and stroke them from head to tail. Like this." Casey held his nephew in his arms for the grooming lesson. The brush handle drawfed the little boy's hand as Casey used his own hand to help Rhett practice. "See, they like it when you are careful and soft. Give it a try."

They stood near the horse's stall. Casey hefted Rhett closer so he could reach his short arms to tap at the animal's long neck with the bristles. The horse only swished her tail, muzzle deep in a feed bag full of oats.

Elizabeth watched her son's eyes light up with proximity to an animal, the dark curls of his hair shining in shafts of light that filtered into the barn. Rhett wore new overalls and barn boots with frogs on the toes. She snapped a picture when one of the goats tolerated his attention in exchange for a carrot chunk. Dimples dotted Rhett's cheeks when he was this joyful. Her son was in his element with the animals, the barn a cherished place for him.

Rhett turned two next month, his birthday a weight Elizabeth carried around her neck like a lodestone. Today, Casey promised to take his nephew to visit the Wolf's pets while Elizabeth ran errands and made a few calls. Jo's donkey and goat duo were some of Rhett's favorite and Elizabeth baked a dozen ginger snaps to send with them. She told her brother it might be a couple hours before she returned home and he nodded over Rhett's head.

Home. A term she used in many ways yet that never seemed to apply to her, somehow. At least, not yet.

"I'll be off, then," she called to her little family. Casey lifted Rhett's hand in a wave, and she blew her son a kiss in return.

In the car, she cranked up Tanya Tucker, rolling down the window to soak up the ounce of sunlight reaching down from the skies. She passed snow-blanketed fields, a handful of deer nibbling on residual foliage.

Elizabeth rubbed her hubcap on the curb as she entered a parking lot in town, maneuvering into a space between a shiny, slate sedan and a sun-paled red truck, a few garden tools in its bed.

She removed the pine bough wreath from the back seat of her car. Hand-woven from branches collected on her first snowshoeing trip, Elizabeth thought of the recipient when she twisted in a few pinecones. She hiked up the hill to place the wreath against a massive headstone and stepped back to read the inscription.

How do you mourn someone you knew for such a short time? Justin had upended her life in so many ways, right before his own was cut short. He'd reminded her that life is fleeting, its timeline unknown. Living anything short of your own dreams is a waste of that trajectory.

"You are the only person I've seen here today. Besides the grounds crew."

"You invited me, so that's not exactly a surprise."

"I couldn't think of a better friend to come along."

Margery Hart wore a houndstooth coat with a thick scarf wound around her neck. She stepped forward to lay a bouquet in front of the marble marker and stepped back again. Elizabeth counted new lines on her face, like a tree showing its age.

"I'm glad to be here." Elizabeth reached out to take Marg's gloved hand in her own.

"Thank you for indulging an old lady. And for saving my life."

Marg's voice quavered as she spoke. Elizabeth squeezed her hand, a soft assurance.

"I would have done it for any rich old widow who cost my brother his business. It's just the kind of gal I am."

"The woman who is working to rebuild that business and hired him to do some work for her, too, as I hope you'll recall."

"It's better than a kick in the teeth, as my grandmother used to say." Elizabeth gave Marg a smile.

"You're a tough nut, Liz. I like that."

"Your son was a friend when I needed one. Putting up with you is the least I can do."

Marg snorted. "See the three of you for Thanksgiving dinner?"

"Count on it."

Elizabeth tucked Marg into a fierce hug, then left the grieving mother to her vigil.

Back in her car, Elizabeth turned up the heat and drove home to wrap her arms around her son.

Read the Series

The Sheridan County Mysteries
The Sheriff's Wife
The New Teacher
The Sled Dog (coming Fall 2022)

Reviews help readers find books they'll enjoy and authors find people who love their stories.
Please consider leaving a review on your favorite bookshop's website or with Goodreads.

Subscribe to Erin's newsletter, get a free copy of *The Sheriff's Wife*, and more at erinlark.com

Acknowledgements

As always, thank you to my parents who said I could do anything, and meant it.

Three cheers to Terrilani for multiple read-throughs from an ocean away. Gratitude to Sarah and Ted for the red ink and eagle eyes.

Much thanks Paula Lester, my editor, and the artists at Miblart for working so hard while a war rages in their homeland.

A grateful nod to all the readers of The Sheridan County Mysteries. Your messages, wonderings, and comments are gold to me, thank you for cheering on my art.

Lastly, yet mostly, all my love to Bryan and Ava for keeping me whole. You two are just the best.

About Erin

From the desert southwest, Erin fell in love with Sheridan County on the banks of Piney Creek. An award-winning science teacher, avid archer, and hack watercolorist, she lives for the outdoors. Erin and her family divide their time between Wyoming, Washington, and Arizona because life is too short to play favorites.

Made in the USA
Middletown, DE
05 September 2022

72305938R00196